The Long Escape

By

Jeff Noonan

DEDICATION

This book is dedicated to my wife, Meryl, who has awakened me from thousands of nightmares over the past three decades. Thank you, Sweetheart!

Additionally, the book is dedicated to all of the descendents of Bob and Mary (Betty) Noonan with sincere appreciation for their ongoing efforts to live life to its fullest while always helping the less fortunate.

Table of Contents

PROLOGUE

The scene before me was weird, but pleasant. I was standing just inside of the mouth of a cave, and a swarm of small children were playing in front of me, deeper in the cave. I could see big Dan, little Danny, Danielle, Michelle, Kacy, Nathan, Tim, Kelsie, and Madison. There were others behind them, further back in the cave. "That's odd" I thought in a strange, detached, way, "I didn't realize they were all the same age".

"Dad, look out behind you!" It was little Michelle, screaming to warn me.

I spun around and it was there again, this time in the mouth of the cave. This time it was a huge snake with the jaws of an alligator and a body that looked like black smoke.

I yelled, "Get out!" but it kept moving toward us. I kept yelling and went into the boxer's crouch that Dad had taught me eons ago. I flicked out a left jab that went right through the beast, startling me. I followed with a roundhouse right and this time I felt something, but it was a soft something.

The kids were all screaming and I could hear my voice screaming along with them. I came out of the roundhouse right with a backhanded slap at the creature's face and this time I connected. I could feel the pain coursing through the back of my hand. The snake's face was as hard as a board!

"Wake up! Jeff, Wake up! You hit me and you're screaming again! You're scaring me!" It's Meryl, shaking me awake as she had done countless times in the past thirty years.

1

I come awake slowly, feeling the pain from where I backhanded my nightstand. Still half-asleep, I mumble, "Sorry, Hon. Did I hurt you?"

She answers, "No, I'm okay."

I give her a hug, "I'm really sorry. It was another bad dream. I'm okay now."

But I know that I'm not. I'm sweating and shaking uncontrollably. It's the same old dream and I know that it will have the same old results. I won't get back to sleep for hours. It's been this way for over fifty years and it isn't going to change tonight.

The dream is pretty much the same every time. I'm in a hole in the ground, sometimes alone and sometimes with friends or family members surrounding me. The hole is often the size of a coffin, but it can get as large as a dry dock. There is always something trying to get into the hole, something deadly— something that is looking for me. It's usually a faceless giant, but it sometimes comes into the dream as weird noises or a smoky creature that I can see through, or, often, just a huge snake. But it's always evil. In every dream, there comes a point where it gets too close, and I wake up terrified and shaking. In the worst of the dreams, the thing almost catches me, and then the earth opens and I fall…and fall…and fall…until I wake up screaming. After the dreams, I always lie awake for hours with my mind invariably going back over the decades to my childhood.

Tonight is no different. My shaking slowly subsides as my mind is inexorably drawn back to the pleasant memories of my early childhood and then on to the later, more difficult, years.

* * *

My early childhood was probably no more eventful than that of any other child of the time. I was born in 1940 at the end of the Great Depression, just before the start of World War II. I was destined to be the oldest of eight children, and the first of them, my sister Kathy, was born about two years after me. Just over a year later, she was followed by another sister, Patty. Both girls were born while Dad served in the Marines during the war.

Patty was born disabled and never walked or talked. She never had any control over her body, not even her most basic functions, and she spent her entire life totally dependent on the family. But she was a beautiful child, who, like me, was born with a full head of bright red hair.

When the war finally came to an end, Dad was discharged, and we returned to his hometown in Montana, where he soon found work as the school janitor. With a job in hand, he was able to lease forty acres from the state, and we began building our home on the outskirts of the small community of St. Regis.

Building the home was a family project. Dad would cut the logs and do the heavy work. It fell to Mom and me to trim the bark off the logs and shape them to go up on the walls.

I was five years old when we started building the home. Mom was soon pregnant with my first brother, Tim. Even pregnant, Mom worked with Dad and me on the house while my grandmother took care of Kathy and Patty. Fall came and I started school, but we kept at it all that winter, working every evening and weekend. Somehow we pulled it off and managed, between us, to build a home. It was, at that time, one of the largest houses in town.

Dad used his GI Bill to order a LaSalle Correspondence Course in radio and television technology. He completed the course with honors, but never used the knowledge except to fix our equipment and that of our neighbors.

Before marrying my mother, Dad had been a both a professional boxer and a park ranger in Glacier National Park. He loved the Zane Gray westerns and Tarzan adventure novels of the era and saw himself as a kind of "Old West Hero" who could do no wrong. He was an incredibly intelligent individual, but his ego never let him admit to a mistake of any kind. Similarly, he couldn't seem to understand that he had to study or otherwise prepare himself before starting major projects. He seemed to think that his intellect was enough to overcome any obstacle, so he had no need for education or preparation.

Dad honestly tried to do exceptional things, but somehow, he never quite succeeded. For example, in 1947, with a herculean effort, he planted over twenty acres of our leasehold in potatoes—by hand. But he had not looked into any type of recorded history for this type of project and the entire planting froze that spring. During this period, Dad's reputation in the community grew, but he never recognized his successes and every small setback became monumental in his mind.

He kept trying, but things just never seemed to work out the way he planned them. He never complained and I never saw him cry, but slowly life seemed to be destroying him. With every setback, his drinking increased. This was particularly bad because he was a big man who was violent and abusive when he drank.

Mom had had a different upbringing from Dad, and she was able to smooth off some of the old boxer's rougher edges. She was a handsome woman who had been raised on the prairies of Saskatchewan. Her father was a Polish immigrant who had worked hard and done well. The family owned a large wheat farm as well as the first commercial electric power plant in that part of Canada. Mom was the eldest child and was raised in a relatively luxurious environment. She graduated from a teachers college in Saskatchewan and was licensed to teach in Canadian schools.

But in the manner of the old country, the family holdings were passed to the sons. The girls were expected to marry and develop their own lives. So after college, Mom found herself on her own, with no financial support from her family.

She had been making her living as a teacher in a one-room Alberta school for several years before she met my father. They were married in 1938 when Mom was twenty-six and Dad was twenty-nine years old. She was a gregarious person who got along well with everyone, but she had been raised to believe that the man was always the head of the household and was not to be defied. She lived this philosophy very happily for many years. She absolutely adored my father and, for a very long time, would not dream of contradicting him on anything.

The years passed, and Dad found work in one of the lumber mills that had sprung up to supply the post-World War II building boom. He became a lumber grader, a prestigious position in the sawmill community. In 1948, the family produced another brother, Lyle. With five kids, one of whom was disabled, the family pressures mounted and Dad didn't handle them well. He just could not reconcile his "Western Hero" self-image with the fact that he was a family man with a day job.

Dad had been an outspoken Democrat for years and, by 1952, he was the county's Democratic Committee chairman. Then, with absolutely no preparation, he made a life-changing decision, declared himself a candidate for Congress, and made a serious run for the office. I was eleven years old and remember the campaign well. He often took me with him when he made speeches or visited with the voters door to door. Somehow, even though I was so young, I was fascinated with this process. On the issues of the day, Dad was far ahead of his time, talking about the need to install fish ladders on the dams and stop clear-cutting the forests. Most of the people he visited with, even hardcore Democrats, didn't agree with this type of thinking. In that era, environmental preservation just wasn't a concern to most Montanans.

The run for Congress was an honorable effort, but Dad had no financial backing and he put everything he owned into the effort. He ran against a sitting member of the Montana Supreme Court, a Democrat with years of political experience. But that fact never entered his calculations. In a manner typical of him, he decided that he wanted to be a congressman and proceeded to run for election with absolute confidence that he would win.

He lost in the primary and soon had to declare bankruptcy. This was the beginning of the end for Dad. His drinking went from bad to uncontrollable. The violence and abuse got much worse and the Dad that I admired slowly disappeared.

Dad had once been a great father. He took me fishing, taught me to box, and was a real friend. When I was in grade school, and he was the school janitor, we had a regular after-school routine. I would help him with the after-school cleanup, and then we would walk home together. On the way, we would either stop to pick up groceries for Mom, or we would stop at the local bar for a drink (me Coke—him wine), then go on home. Sometimes he would carry me home on his shoulders.

Dad was a big, tough, man who, during the early years, prided himself in being fair with everyone. I will never forget one evening when we stopped at the local bar on the way home.

We walked into the bar and were faced with what appeared to be a huge brawl. It took me a moment to sort it out. When I did, it became obvious that some Oriental men had come into the bar and were being badly beaten by a group of local loggers.

The Orientals were screaming "We are Americans. We are Americans."

The loggers were calling them, among other things, "Fucking Japs" and "Gooks." The loggers were far bigger than the Orientals and were beating them mercilessly. I watched in horror as two loggers threw a man repeatedly into the air, kicking him as he came down. They were making drunken sport out of cold-blooded murder.

Dad never hesitated. As soon as he walked into the bar, he started swinging. When he finished, two of the loggers were on their way to the hospital and the others were still running. (I heard later that they hid from Dad for weeks following that night.) When he was done with the loggers, he helped patch up the Orientals, after which he bought them a drink and made sure they were all right. When everything was calmed down, he took my little hand in his big one and we went home.

As we made our way home that evening, he explained to me, in great detail, that all men are equal and that no man should ever be made to suffer because of things beyond his control. He talked about people he had known and respected (mostly boxers) who were Mexican and Negro. He told me about the Japanese-American soldiers who had fought on our side in

7

Europe. He told me about the people he had known in his youth, when he had lived on an Indian reservation. He made me promise that I would always treat all people cordially until they gave me a concrete reason to dislike them.

After explaining this bit of his philosophy, I never again heard him mention that night's battle to anyone. It was as if he thought it was just a normal thing that anyone would do if given the opportunity.

That was the father that I had known for the first twelve years of my life. He was a man I was terribly proud to call Dad. But all that gradually changed while I was still approaching my teen years.

Mom was always my confidant and counselor. I spent hours just talking to her and absorbing her thoughts on life. Although it seemed to me that she was usually pregnant, I was always amazed by the amount of work that she could get done in a day. The day-to-day burden of caring for Patty must have been immense, but I never heard Mom complain.

Even with her workload, whenever there was a social event in the area, Mom was usually in the middle of it. During the late 1940s and early 1950s, she and Dad often hosted evening get-togethers and barbeques at our home that brought together some of the best and brightest in the area. Dad would play his guitar, and another of the neighbors would play banjo. Everyone sang. The parties would go on until the wee hours of the night. Those were the happy days.

When Dad decided to run for Congress, Mom wholeheartedly supported the effort. She told all who would listen about Bob Noonan, the great man to whom she was married. (She really believed every word of what she said.) She hosted political get-togethers almost weekly. She became great friends with Senator Mike Mansfield and his wife as well as several other well-known political figures of the era. She even became friends with Dad's main opponent, Lee Metcalf, who went on to a distinguished career in the US Senate. She was still a Canadian citizen, but that never slowed her down. Even then, she could talk politics and policy with the best of them.

But her world changed after the election loss and the family's bankruptcy. Dad's drinking started to eat into any money that came in and times got very tough for Mom. His brutality when he drank began taking a real toll as well. But it must be said that she still adored her man. (In fact, many years later, when she was in her nineties, she still spoke of him as her one true love—and she meant it.)

Mom had a rough time feeding the family in the 1950s and early 1960s. She often had to change grocery stores because she couldn't keep the bills paid. Though they were our friends, the grocers couldn't afford to carry us past a certain point, and they would cut off our credit. Then Mom would try to pay the old grocery bill down while charging food at a different store. This way, with the old bill paid, Mom would be able to beg for credit at the last place when the new grocer had to cut us off. This cycle went on for years.

During most of the 1950s and the first part of the 1960s, Mom could have been the poster-child for a study of battered women. She had her nose broken twice, her ribs smashed several times, and was forever bruised and obviously beaten. She was trapped at home with a brood of children (including Patty, who was totally dependent on her), and she had no money. She was on her own with no way out that she could have foreseen in those dark days. These had to have been the bleakest, most hopeless, times of her life.

These experiences led me to vow that I would never raise a hand in anger against a woman. Nor would I ever have more children than I could afford. These vows I have kept. Dad did a good job of teaching me what not to do.

I also took it upon myself to be the family guardian when Dad's drunken tantrums threatened us. To this end, I dug three carefully hidden "bunkers"—modeled after pictures I had seen of World War I bunkers—in the woods behind our home. They served as hideouts for the family whenever Dad went on one of his drunken rampages. We spent many nights hunkered down in these holes while we heard Dad screaming threats at us in the nearby woods.

Hiding in the bunkers was our only defense from Dad's tantrums. We had no modern police force to fall back on. There was only one policeman, the sheriff, for the entire county; a county about one and a half times as big as the state of Rhode Island. The sheriff was just too busy to be worried about a father's "disciplinary methods." Family problems just weren't a priority in those days and law enforcement didn't interfere unless someone ended up dead. So we endured the beatings and tried to live as well as possible. We just didn't understand any other life.

In the meantime, the family continued to grow. Eleanor was born in 1953, Jim in 1956, and Dan in 1958. My siblings were a large and rowdy crowd. I loved them all dearly, but I have to admit that I never got to know all of them as well as most big brothers do. I left the family home to work on the railroad in 1956 and only returned home for short stays after that. Growing up, Kathy and I had been close and had shared many good times as well as some not-so-good times. Patty we all loved and tried to help, but she really couldn't take part in the events of daily life, so that was a different kind of relationship. When I left home, I was fifteen, Kathy was thirteen, Patty was twelve, Tim was nine, Lyle was eight, Eleanor was three, Jim was a baby, and Dan hadn't been born yet. I do remember feeling very bad about leaving them behind when I left home, but I had no choice.

The winter of 1955 was particularly bad. It was a long winter and, by this time, Dad was perpetually drunk. I practically lived in the bunkers until the snow got too deep, and then I bounced from one friend's home to another. I hated myself for not being able to stop Dad when he went on his rampages and beat the family, but I just couldn't do it.

I was always a bit of a dreamer. I read everything that I could get my hands on, particularly adventure tales set in exotic parts of the world. I would spend hours daydreaming about visiting the places in the novels. But my daydreams always had one common element; when the adventure was over, I would always come home to a little cottage with a white picket fence where my wonderful, loving family waited for me. There was never a harsh word in this dream family, never a threat or a hardship—and I was absolutely certain that I would never become a drunk or an abuser. This constant part of my daydreams was the most important part, a part that has always been a part of who I am.

* * *

As always, the memories have run their course. The fear and trembling have subsided and my eyelids have grown heavy. I will sleep well now…until another creature comes to invade whatever hole I find myself in.

This story begins on Thanksgiving Day, 1955. It is a story of how a man, and a family, came through hell and lived to tell about it. This is a story of survival.

CHAPTER ONE

Escape, Please Escape!

Tim, my eight-year-old brother, whispered, "Mom, I'm freezing!"

I looked over and saw that Lyle had rolled over, pulling the blanket away from his older brother. Mom saw it at the same time and made some adjustments so the blanket covered all four of them.

I heard Tim grunt a soft, "Thank you" before he went back to sleep. The boys were snuggled on either side of Mom, who was holding little Eleanor on her lap. The blanket, the only one in the bunker, was stretched tight, trying to cover all of them.

I was across the dirt floor from them, partially covered by an old coat someone had thrown away. I was holding a baseball bat and guarding the hole that served as a door. I'd heard Dad prowling around above us a little while ago and I was prepared to swing the bat if he found our hideout and tried to enter.

It was Thanksgiving night in the Year of Our Lord, 1955. The five of us were hiding in an underground bunker and all of us were cold. It was good that Kathy had escaped to a friend's home when the trouble started. The solitary blanket just wasn't big enough to cover anyone else. Sleepily, I decided that I would have to find more blankets somewhere.

I had started building these bunkers when I was thirteen, almost two years earlier. That was when Dad's decline into alcoholism and brutality became really serious. I now had three bunkers scattered around our forty acres. Hidden deep in the woods behind our home, each bunker had been dug about four feet deep, and then the holes had been covered with logs. Carefully placed sod, twigs, and old tree branches covered the logs. The only entrance to each bunker was a small hole on one end that was covered with a mesh of brush that was carefully woven to hide what lay beneath it. I had stocked the bunkers with water as well as some old blankets and coats that I had salvaged from the town dump. The bunkers were in place to give us shelter when Dad went on one of his drunken rampages, as he had done tonight.

Mom and I were now the only ones awake. I could hear the two boys and the baby, Eleanor, softly snoring. I whispered, "Mom, are you okay?"

She replied, "Of course, Jeff. But I'll probably have a shiner tomorrow." That was just like Mom; trying to make a joke out of a horrible situation.

I ignored her attempt at humor and said, "You know, we can't go on like this, Mom. One day, he's going to really hurt someone, maybe even kill one of us."

She started sobbing. I knew that this thought was one she dreaded and I hated to bring it up. But I felt like I had to.

She finally cleared her throat and said, "I know, but I just don't know what to do. I don't have any way to feed us unless Dad's there. I can't work and take care of Patty. I just hope that Dad comes to his senses!"

Mom and I had talked about all of this before and I knew that neither of us had a solution. She kept praying that Dad would somehow come out of it, but I had no such hope.

I said, "I know, Mom. Next summer I'm going to get a real job, and maybe then we can escape."

"Jeff, if you get a job, just get out of here! You didn't make this mess and I won't let you be dragged down by it." It was her standard answer. Usually she would go on and on about the future and how I could put all of this behind me by working hard. But tonight we just let the silence of our little cave wash over us.

After a long pause, Mom spoke one more time. "Jeff, as soon as you can do it, leave this place! Escape. Please, escape. You have to show the way so the other kids can have some hope. Please, please, escape as soon as you can."

I stayed silent and the words hung there for us to both think about.

Dad had just ruined another holiday celebration for the family. He just couldn't seem to get through a Christmas or Thanksgiving without destroying it for all of us. This year, he had drunkenly decided that the knife wasn't sharp enough when he started carving the turkey. He had thrown the turkey through the (closed) kitchen window, hit Mom in the face with the hand holding the knife handle, and then backhanded me out of my chair with his other hand. Kathy, who at twelve was my oldest sibling, had immediately run out the door towards a friend's home. Mom had grabbed little Eleanor and headed out the back door, with Tim and Lyle following her.

I'd decided to try delaying his pursuit so the others could get away. Flat on my back, I'd yelled, "Leave them alone, you coward!"

That had done it. He'd thrown the knife after the turkey and reached down to grab me. I'd scuttled across the floor, but too slowly. He'd picked me up by my shirt collar and slugged me a glancing blow to the cheek.

I'd struggled, and my shirt had torn, loosening his grip, so I jerked loose and made a frantic dash for the front door, getting through it before he could recover his balance and catch me.

He'd followed me outside, as usual. The rest of the family had all gone out the back way, so I'd led him away from them, and they'd escaped to the bunker.

Once I was through the front door, I was free. At fifteen, I was a lot faster runner than him, and I could run further, so he never had a chance of catching me. I knew which bunker the family had headed for, and eventually I circled around through the forest and joined them. My badly disabled sister, Patty, was still in the house, but I knew that Dad wouldn't bother her. At least he had that much decency left.

Now I sat there, with my back against the bunker wall and the bat in my hands, sleepily watching the others. My mind wandered and I thought about the younger kids and the life ahead of them. I had a pang of real sorrow as I realized that these kids would never know their father as anything other than the beast that had chased us here. I thought this was truly sad. I felt very fortunate that it had not always been like this for me. I had known Dad in another time, in what now seemed like a different life.

My mind drifted and finally I slept, still holding the bat in my hands, slumped against the cold dirt wall. Mom's words echoed in my mind: "Please escape."

CHAPTER TWO

The Teen Years

During the "Bunker Years," I became less and less of a student. A few years earlier, I had skipped a grade, so I went into high school at the age of twelve. But I stopped there. Every fall, I would start attending for a month or so to please my mother, but by the end of September, I would drift off to something else. School was incredibly boring. By the time I left home permanently, the only high school credits I'd received were in Physical Education, Driver's Education, and Woodworking Shop. I had just never showed up for any other classes.

Instead, I became one of the local "cool guys." I had a black leather jacket and my naturally bright-red hair was carefully shaped into a Duck's Ass hairdo kept in place by a generous layer of hair grease. At that point, I didn't drink or smoke, but I was the designated driver for those who did. Since we didn't have a bathtub or a shower, I must have been pretty ripe, especially in winter, when it was too cold to swim in the river. But most of us were in the same boat in those days, so no one seemed to notice or care. Similarly, I always seemed to be plagued by swollen jaws since most of my teeth were in very bad shape. (I learned how to brush my teeth years later, when I was in the Army.) But we were the coolest dudes to be found in our small logging town—or we thought we were.

When I wasn't in town being cool, I spent hours, days, and weeks in the nearby forest. I had an old single-shot .22 caliber rifle that I carried. With that and a hand-fishing line, I learned to subsist in the woods for long periods of time.

Once I "borrowed" a horse that was loose in our field and went into the mountains for over a month. Mom thought that I was staying with some friends a few miles from town, but I was many, many, miles from there, checking out the forest on the other side of the mountains in Idaho. I had the clothes I was wearing, a blanket, a fishing line, the old .22, and a box of shells, as well as a rope and an old bridle for the horse. I was as at home there as I have ever been anywhere.

I will never forget the reaction when I returned home from that trip. I was proud of myself and I did tell Mom and Dad about it. Mom was aghast and immediately grounded me. Dad was so proud that he bragged about it to all of his drinking buddies.

During the long winters of 1955 and 1956, I found Dad's old LaSalle Correspondence Course and got very interested in it. I went through the whole course, studying basic electricity, basic electronics, and Radio/Television theory. Somehow this dry studying kept my interest and I was never bored with it. I could study at my own pace and, for once, I was studying something that I could honestly see a purpose for. In this way, I developed a little bit of knowledge that paid off handsomely a few years later.

During my teenage years, I went through several old beat-up cars, all of which I made as cool as possible. The first of them, acquired when I was thirteen, was a 1929 Model-A Ford Sedan that I was given as payment for work I had done for a neighbor.

When I first saw it, it was setting in a field where the neighbor had parked it several years earlier. I borrowed a battery from one of Dad's old cars, primed the Model A's carburetor with gasoline, and the darned thing started right up! It ran, but the canvas roof and all of the upholstery had long since rotted away. So I gathered a bunch of cardboard boxes and drafted all of Kathy's girl friends to upholster the car in carefully colored cardboard. We were all convinced that it was the coolest car in town.

I still hear at school reunions about the day I was driving the old Model A down a hill, ferrying a carload of teenagers, when the left rear wheel came off and passed me by, going much faster than I had ever been able to get the rest of the car to go. We were all late for school and had to go visit the principal. (When we told him what happened, he couldn't keep a straight face and he sent us back to class. We could hear him roaring with laughter behind his closed door as we made our escape.) We fixed that problem, and ran the car for another few months before its old engine finally went to the Cool Car Resting Grounds. The Model A was followed by a multitude of Junkers. In those days, like today, it was hard to live in the vastness of Montana without wheels.

A very good friend of mine, Dave Bennett, lived about thirty miles west of me on a tree farm owned and operated by his father. I would often take the school bus home with Dave and stay overnight on the tree farm. The Bennett Family was Mormon and I would occasionally go to church with them when I was staying over for the weekend. I enjoyed the camaraderie of the church group and was very impressed with a couple of the girls who attended, so it was not long before I joined the church. I also became a regular at the Bennett home. They were a wonderful family who taught me a lot about how real families live.

As a youngster, I had seen the strain of the family finances working on Mom. In those days, all of our creditors, other than the electric utility, were local people and you saw them almost daily, so Mom was really mortified when she couldn't pay the bills on payday. I tried to help when I could. I started delivering newspapers when I was nine years old. At about the same time, I built a stand and set it up along the highway, beside Ida's grocery store. Then during the summers, I would dig worms and sell them from the stand to tourists and other fishermen. When I was twelve, I started helping local farmers during their haying season.

My first real job came in the summer of 1955, when I was fourteen. I was hired at the local sawmill as a water boy, carrying canvas one-gallon water bags to the sawmill workers twice a day. This lasted for most of the summer.

Then, one evening, Dad came home drunk and I didn't move fast enough to get away. Dad was chasing me when he picked up a heavy stick and threw it at me. The stick went over an inch into the side of my right knee and stuck there. I went down, bleeding badly. He gave me a few kicks and then went after the others, who, by then, were long gone.

The next morning, I poured iodine into the hole, put a makeshift bandage over it, and wrapped it up with an old Ace bandage that we had in the house. Then I tried to go to work. But, the mill owner saw me hobbling around, trying to carry the water bags and laid me off. I hadn't noticed, but there was a lot of blood coming through the Ace bandage, soaking the leg of my jeans.

The mill owner was kind, but firm, as he told me, "Jeff, I know that you're trying to get the job done. But if that leg is as bad as it looks, you could cripple yourself carrying those things around and I don't want that on my conscience. I'm sorry. Pick up your check at the office later today." With that, he took the water bags and my summer's work ended.

The following spring (1956), I really struck it rich. I talked myself into a job as a welder's helper for the Northern Pacific Railroad, making the princely sum of $1.78 per hour! To do this job, I had to be mobile, because we lived wherever the job took us. So I lived with the rest of the welding crew in converted boxcars known far and wide as "Gandy Dancer's Quarters." Each of these converted boxcars housed three to four workers and contained bunks in the rear, a small kitchen, and a bathroom—with a shower! The crew and the boxcars were mobile, moving from town to town while we worked our way down the railroad line, performing welding repairs on the never-ending rail system. I held this job for about nine months and was promoted to apprentice welder before I had to move on. I hated to give it up, but someone reported my age to the railroad, so they had to let me go. They were nice about it and invited me back "when you turn eighteen." But by then, my world had changed.

When I left the railroad job, winter was well underway. I went home and tried to work at whatever little jobs I could find, but they were mostly charity jobs given to me by people who worried about Mom and the kids. In the winter, no one in this little logging town had much money, so work was scarce. Dad worked until the mill shut down for winter, but most of his money was going to the bars and liquor stores by that time.

Without work or money, things were very tough. In desperation, I even tried to join the Navy. Although I was just sixteen years old, I talked Mom into signing a form that said I was old enough to join and went to Butte to take the oath. In January 1957, I shipped out with a group of recruits headed to San Diego by train.

The thing I remember most about that trip was the Train Conductor. I remember him as a kind man who leaned on the side of my seat and talked with me for hours.

The conversation started with him catching me looking at him. He came over and said, "Can I help you, Sir?"

I was flustered and replied, "No. I'm sorry if I was staring, but you're the first colored man that I've ever seen." I was blushing then and horribly embarrassed, and I went on, "I mean outside of the National Geographic."

He laughed easily and said, "Well, how do I stack up against the pictures?"

This disconcerted me even more. I didn't know what to say, so he took up the slack, still chuckling, with, "Don't worry, Son. You are at least the fifth person that's told me that. It isn't anything to get all in a tizzy about. But please don't call us Colored People. I'm very proud to be a Negro."

We exchanged a few pleasantries after that, with me telling him that I was on my way to join the Navy and him telling me about the time he had been in the Army during the last war.

Later on, after we had talked off and on for an hour or so, we got into a discussion that made a real impression on me. I asked him, "Is it true that Down South, Negroes have to use separate bathrooms from the rest of us?"

He looked serious for once and told me, "It isn't just Down South, Son. Look around you. There are no Negroes on this train except me, and if I want to go to the bathroom, I walk all the way back to the little bathroom in the caboose."

"Why?" I asked.

"Because some of the passengers on this train would throw a fit if I tried to use any other bathroom."

I thought about this for a moment and then I asked him, "How can you live this way, always having to worry about the next bigot that comes along?

It was his turn to think for a minute. Then he said something that I will never forget. He said, "This is America. It's a melting pot of people, most of whom are pretty damned good. I've read a lot, and been around a bit, and I'm convinced that, eventually, all of this will pass. Not during my time, and maybe not during my kid's time, but certainly by the time my grandchildren are my age. You see, this is America. The good guys always win in America and, one day, they'll win this battle too."

I don't remember what I said then, nor do I remember much of the conversations that we had after that. But I sure hope that man lived to witness the changes that came with the Civil Rights Movement just a few years later. He was right about America. He just thought that it would take longer than it did.

I got off the train in San Diego, ready for boot camp. But again, someone had called the authorities. I was met at the train station in San Diego by a Navy chief petty officer who gave me a return ticket and told me to come back when I was old enough. Frustrated, I went back home and worked odd jobs through the winter.

When the spring of 1957 rolled around, I went far and wide looking for work. A friend, Joe Thompson, and I drove across the state almost to South Dakota, looking for day jobs or any kind of work. It didn't happen. By the time we gave up and returned home, we had traded everything we owned for gasoline and we had lived for days on celery stolen from a farmer's field. I had never felt so beaten.

Finally, in May, a friend of a friend came through for me and hired me as a ranch hand in a small town about a hundred miles from St. Regis. I was given room and board and worked part time, as-needed, for the ranch. There was no pay, but at least it kept me eating and it didn't cost Mom anything. I took care of their goats and moved their cattle from pasture to pasture. During my down time, I managed to get a part-time job piling lumber in a local sawmill. It was a small mill, so I was able to juggle the jobs and keep both employers happy. The mill paid me by the board-foot as the lumber was stacked, so I had enough money for necessities and a little to send home.

Both jobs were work and I really appreciated having them, but God, how I hated those goats! It seemed like I couldn't get the smell of them off of me. I have to admit, I was not unhappy when winter set in and these jobs came to an end. When that happened, I went home again, restocked the bunkers, and started working odd jobs.

CHAPTER THREE

The Army

I came home from the ranch job just before my seventeenth birthday. I had long planned to join the military when I was old enough because, in my mind, this was the only way I would ever escape the life I was living. I had done some reading and learned about the benefits of a military life. I thought that the twenty-year retirement would give me a great start in life, after which I would have some independence to decide what I wanted to do for the rest of my life.

In my mind, any kind of college was simply unattainable. College was for the rich kids, and I just was not one of them. At that time, I had no concept that my high school record (or lack of one) would make any difference.

I was totally dedicated to the concept of a military career, but I hadn't decided on a branch of service. I had some friends in the Air Force, but airplanes just didn't interest me. The Marines were far too macho for me. Besides, Dad was a former Marine, so that was out. The Army and the Navy were my preferred services, but I was having trouble deciding between them.

Then the National Guard began advertising a program under which you could join the Guard and spend six months on active duty with the Army. They also guaranteed that enlistees would receive an Army school during the six months. This sounded good to me. It would give me a chance to evaluate the Army, and the school might start me on the road to some sort of career. So, a few days after my seventeenth birthday, I joined the

Montana National Guard and requested the six months' active duty.

It took the Guard a few months to arrange for my active duty billet. In the meantime, I hunkered down at home and worked odd jobs when I could find them. Mom was pregnant again (with my youngest brother, Danny), so I helped around the house a bit and tried to keep the bunkers in shape to provide refuge when we needed it.

In March 1958, I reported to Fort Ord, California, for Basic Training. About all that I remember about those first days was the total awe that I felt. Everything was simply overwhelming. I had expected the loud sergeants and the regimentation; I had read enough and seen enough movies to know that this was coming. What I didn't expect was the range of people that I was suddenly exposed to.

The six-month Reserve Forces Act (RFA) Program, coming when the draft was still a reality, had captured a totally diverse bunch of people. My fellow recruits ranged from people with serious social problems to people with advanced university degrees trying to slide past the draft. All races and religions were represented, which was a bit of a shocker for me. To make matters worse, most of them were from larger cities and talked about things I simply didn't comprehend. I was very small for my age (5'8", 115 lbs) and was naturally a bit bashful, so I tried to stay as unnoticed as possible.

I did everything that I was told and managed to get through the first couple of weeks almost unnoticed. Then, on a Saturday, my bad teeth betrayed me and I had to ask for help. My jaw had swollen to about twice its normal size and I was in serious pain. So I went to my assigned recruit platoon leader and asked to go to Sick Bay. The platoon leader was at least ten years older than me and was one of the more educated recruits. He immediately took pity on me. He asked and received permission to escort me to the Base Dental Clinic and we set off.

It turned out that, because it was the weekend, I was the only patient in the clinic when we got there. A young soldier who turned out to be a dental assistant looked me over and decided to call in an on-call dentist. All of this was new to me. I had never been to a dentist before, and it was a bit of an adventure. I had been ashamed of my teeth for years, but this was my first shot at getting work done on them. I was both scared and excited.

The dentist, when he finally showed up, was a tall, slightly overweight man with major's leaves on his uniform. He stank of booze, an odor that I knew only too well, but I was not about to do anything to antagonize him. I had never seen anyone with this much rank before, and he scared me silly.

The major took a cursory look in my mouth and started yelling. He called me every name in the book. Apparently, I was some type of "low-life, draft-dodging, motherfucking RFA bastard" who had absolutely ruined his Saturday afternoon.

The dental assistant tried to calm him down, but to no avail. The major got so loud that my platoon leader came in from the waiting room to see what was happening. The major called him some choice names and made him leave the room. Then he got busy on my mouth.

I was petrified by fear at this point. I did not know what the correct dental procedure was, so when he told me to open my mouth, that was exactly what I did. He inserted some type of brace that kept it open and began work, still cursing. Before he finished, he had pulled twelve of my teeth, six on each side. He had not bothered to use any Novocain or any other type of anesthetic. My face and my uniform shirt were covered with blood.

I will never forget what the major did then. He just looked at me as if I were an animal, spat in the sink, and walked out of the room. Luckily for me, he stopped in the waiting room and told my platoon leader, "Get that little cocksucker out of my clinic, and do it now!"

At this point, the platoon leader smelled the booze. He rushed in to where I was still in the chair. The dental assistant was getting ready to clean me up, but the platoon leader stopped him. Instead, he told me to sit still, and he called back to our barracks duty center. He told the duty sergeant (a real Army sergeant, not a recruit) what had happened. I learned later that the duty sergeant had then called the base's Military Police. I was still in the chair covered in blood when two MPs showed up in the door. I was very woozy, but as I remember it, they took pictures and statements. Then they took us to the Base Hospital where a doctor cleaned me up and gave me some painkillers. Then the MPs drove us back to our barracks.

I was placed on light duty for a few days, during which the platoon leader told everyone what had happened. In the meantime, the MPs had placed the major on report for a whole list of infractions, including being drunk on duty. The dental assistant, platoon leader, and I all had to provide testimony about the major's actions. It seemed like this went on for weeks.

My mouth healed rapidly and to tell the truth, I was glad the teeth were finally gone—but the Army was not so forgiving. I never found out what happened to the major, but I doubt seriously that he stayed with the Army after that episode.

Soon, I was back to the routine of Basic Training. A little later, I was singled out, along with about six other recruits, to interview for Officer Candidate School. Apparently, we had scored exceptionally high on the general-knowledge tests administered the first week of Basic. My platoon leader was also there and was selected to go to OCS after Basic. I was interviewed, but when they found out that I hadn't graduated from high school, they sent me back to the barracks.

I remember the weeks that I spent in Basic Training as mass confusion. I was learning the Army's basic information as they fed it to me. But, at the same time I was learning a whole new way of life. I was learning to talk to people as an adult and equal. I was learning about ways of life that were entirely alien to me. In this place, I was encountering cultural differences, racial differences, religious differences, and even language differences. With my background, even seemingly insignificant differences like personal hygiene and the use of hygienic products were of major interest to me. It seemed like everything, absolutely everything, differed radically from anything that I had experienced before! The social experience alone made Basic Training one of the most intense learning experiences of my life. I kept my mouth shut and watched, listened, and learned.

Finally Basic was over. I went home on my first military leave. Dad seemed to be actually a bit proud of the fact that I was a soldier. He never bothered any of us for that entire two weeks. My youngest brother, Dan, was born while I was home on leave.

While I was home this time, I saw another side of Dad that surprised me. As background, I should mention that Dad, before he started drinking seriously, had been a voracious reader who had actually studied the Bible extensively. But he never talked about religion, so I hadn't a clue as to his actual religious beliefs.

Dad was home one morning, still sober after eating breakfast, when two Protestant missionaries came to the door. Dad answered the door and invited them in. Soon the three of them were earnestly discussing religion. Dad listened politely as the missionaries talked about how Christ could save his soul, interrupting occasionally with questions that they eagerly answered. I was listening closely because I could not believe that Dad was really discussing religion.

Gradually, Dad steered the conversation onto biblical tales and then on to what had happened to the apostles after Jesus was crucified. He zeroed in on the Apostle John and the legend that John had been placed in a cauldron of boiling oil, but had survived. The missionaries were more than happy to discuss this, and started to go on about "God's miracles," but Dad interrupted them with, "You know, when you think about it, they really french-fried that bastard, didn't they?"

The missionaries were totally taken aback, staring slack-jawed at the man in front of them. Dad leaned back in his chair, cupped his hands behind his head, and said, "That's what should happen to any son of a bitch that tries to preach this superstitious crap to someone who isn't interested." The two missionaries beat a hasty retreat, never to return.

The rest of my leave was uneventful. When it was over, I reported to the Army's Field Communications Crewman School at Fort Ord. There I spent eight weeks learning to climb telephone poles, splice wires, operate field radios, and drive large trucks. The school was very easy and I breezed through it. The thing I remember most from the school was going to see

Elvis Presley in concert at the base theater. Elvis was awesome. School was boring.

I served the remainder of my six months working in an Army short-wave radio station and returned home about a month before my eighteenth birthday.

The Army intensified my desire to have a military career. I had the idea that I could go into the military, spend the required twenty years, and then work the rest of my life in some new field that I would find during the military time. In other words, the military was to be only the beginning of my escape.

But I still had not decided which service to join. I had tried the Army and was no longer excited by it, but the Air Force and the Navy recruiters were both promising me good schools. Then fate intervened and made the decision easy.

CHAPTER FOUR

Boot Camp

I had only been home from the Army a couple of weeks, and I was walking along the highway in St. Regis when my old friend, Joe Thompson, drove up. He leaned out of his car window, grinned, and said, "I'm going to Missoula to join the Navy. Want to come along?"

I didn't hesitate; "Sure, got nothing better to do."

With those six words, I sealed my fate and started on a track that took me into a world that lasted far beyond the next twenty Navy years.

We had to wait several weeks between our trip to Missoula and the day that we actually shipped out for San Diego. Somehow, I managed to run into a lot of excitement during this short period.

A good friend from the Mormon Church, a really nice girl named Sue, had made a mistake and was pregnant. The father was an older guy who had absolutely no intention of interrupting his life for a minor thing like a baby. So she was in trouble. A group of us found out about it—before anyone else did—one night while we were sitting together in the local truck stop café, just being teenagers. Sue was there and she broke down; telling us about her problem. She was very emotional and humiliated, and she hadn't told her parents yet, so she was scared. We put our teenage heads together and came up with a plan.

In all of our teen wisdom, we decided that Sue and I would claim that I was the father and then we would get married. Since

I was going to be in the Navy, she could get medical care during her pregnancy. Then, after the baby was born, we could make a decision as to whether we would stay married or not.

This plan made good sense to us at that time, so we put it in motion. First we told my parents. I have to admit that they took the news better than I thought they would. Dad even took a day off work and went with me to discuss the situation with Sue's parents. All four parents accepted our story as the truth, and both fathers insisted that we wait until after I completed Boot Camp before we actually got married. So that became the plan.

I was very excited by this development. There was nothing in the world that I wanted more than a real family like the one that I'd seen at the Bennett's home. My old daydreams of the family in the little cottage with the white picket fence came alive again. I had always known that, one day, I would have a real family—a good family—of my own. With Sue, this could become a reality much sooner than I had thought possible. I knew that we didn't love one another. But I was certain that love would come with time.

The days passed rapidly, and I prepared to leave for San Diego. Then, on the day before I was due to leave, I realized that Mom was low on food and I decided to go deer hunting one last time. Needless to say, it wasn't hunting season, but that'd never really been a big thing in the past if the family needed food. So I headed off and, before long, I'd killed a nice whitetail buck. I was about a half-mile off of an old dirt logging road when I shot it. I cleaned it and buried the unwanted parts, then hauled it out to where I had left the car. I was in the process of trying to load it into the trunk of my car when the county sheriff pulled up behind me.

I was in major trouble. I knew that I'd be arrested for poaching the deer and that would put the Navy beyond my reach. In those few seconds, I saw my future falling apart.

I knew the sheriff by reputation only. His name was Francis Tamietti, and he was legendary in that part of Montana. He was a slim man that always wore carefully-pressed brown and tan clothes topped by a white cowboy hat. He ran a tight county and no one disobeyed the law there without paying the price. When he pulled up, I just stood there. I knew I was on my way to jail.

He got out of his car and stood there, looking at me. "Jeff! What in the devil do you think you're doing?"

I almost fainted. *How does he know my name?* Somehow I pulled myself together enough to answer. The words flooded out in an embarrassed, scared, stream: "Hi, Sheriff. I'm leaving for the Navy tomorrow and the family needs food. I wanted to leave Mom with enough to eat while I'm gone." I was stammering.

He just stood there with his stare going through me. It seemed like forever before he finally spoke. "Well, let's get it loaded before someone comes by here and sees us."

I almost fainted again.

We loaded the buck into the trunk, tying down the lid so it couldn't be seen.

When we finished, he gave me that long, steady, look again and said, "Son, this never happened."

I agreed and shook his hand. Then I headed for home with the family's winter meat. I don't think I ever saw Sheriff Tamietti again, but I'll never forget him.

Early the next morning, Joe and I reported to the recruiting station in Missoula. Our recruiter was a little, skinny, guy (about my size) who had introduced himself as Gunners Mate First Class Hinkle. At that time, the title meant nothing to me, but he was older and had an arm full of red stripes, so I just assumed that he was a minor god and we got on with it. I had already taken the Navy battery of tests and had done well, so Recruiter Hinkle had promised me that I would get an electronics school after Boot Camp. I actually believed him!

From Missoula we went to Butte, where we were sworn in. From there, we caught a train to San Diego, where we were picked up and transported to the Recruit Training Center.

Boot Camp was not nearly as confusing as the Army's Basic Training had been. Many of the trainees in my company were from Montana and all were roughly my age, so the major education and experience differences that I had experienced at Fort Ord weren't there this time.

The first few weeks went very well. Joe and I were inseparable and, having a friend made the whole ordeal much easier. In addition, I was really looking forward to getting married when I got home. So I was enthused and I actually wrote letters and made plans. Life was hectic, but good.

Then Sue wrote me a letter that I never forgot. At the time, it was as if she had dropped a bomb on me. She wrote to tell me that she could not go through with it. She said that she had thought long and hard about it, and it just wasn't fair to me. She had confessed the truth to her parents and had even gone to visit with my mother about it. She went on to tell me not to try to find her because she had made arrangements to go live with relatives, and she was not telling anyone where she would be.

Needless to say, this news was a real shock. I could see the little house with the white picket fence fading off into the distant future, and that wasn't good news. I immediately wrote back and tried to change her mind. She replied right away, but stayed firm. She said that we could meet after the baby was born, whenever I was home, and go from there. But for now, her decision was final.

I almost went AWOL the night I got the second letter. I was convinced that I could change Sue's mind if I could just get home to see her. But luckily, my friend Joe was a lot calmer (and stronger) than me. He talked to me for hours and even, at one point, threatened to just knock me down and hold me there until I came to my senses. It was a long night, and I went through a lot of emotions, but he kept me together. By morning, I realized that he was right and so was Sue. We were not ready for marriage and family. Hell, we didn't even know each other except for church and an occasional group get-together.

Thank the Lord for Joe! If it hadn't been for him and his help, my Navy career would have ended that night.

Boot Camp became a routine for us and we sailed through it. Then, in the last week or so of Boot Camp, another shoe dropped. We received our orders telling us where we were going after we graduated. Although the recruiter had promised me an electronics school, the Navy refused to honor the promise. Their rationale was that, without a high school diploma, I couldn't be expected to pass any school that they sent me to, so they were not willing to waste the money.

My orders were to take me from Boot Camp directly to an older destroyer where I was to be assigned to the deck force. Joe, who had graduated from high school, was to be transferred to Tennessee to be trained as a jet engine mechanic. So we were to be split up after Boot Camp.

I did some research and found out that ship I was assigned to, *USS Cogswell* (DD-651), was built during World War II and had been in almost continuous service since then. I knew enough by this time to know that serving on the deck force of such an old destroyer would be rough duty. The deck force was the crew that worked as the ship's janitors and handymen. They cleaned and painted the ship, shined the bright work, handled the lines (ropes), and operated the small boats. The deck force was run by boatswain's mates, reputed to be the roughest, toughest, hardest-drinking, hardest-fighting people in the Navy.

If there was a bright side to this, it was the fact that the ship would be deploying, and I would be able to see some of the world. But that really didn't cheer me up.

I took a bus home after Boot Camp for two weeks' leave over Christmas. As had become normal in our family, Dad ruined the holiday by throwing Christmas dinner out into the snow. As usual on the holidays, he was drunk, and when he was drunk it always seemed like he could not stand to see us happy.

This time I stood up and tried to stop him. But, he weighed about a hundred pounds more than me at that point, so it only took about a half-dozen punches to leave me bleeding on the kitchen floor. I ended up pretty battered, but at least he stopped hitting Mom for the afternoon.

Shortly after my encounter with Dad, I had the first of the nightmares that have haunted me through life. This time it was a coffin-sized hole that was so tight my arms couldn't move. Something was stalking me. Then the earth opened and I fell… and fell…until I came awake, startled by the sound of my own incoherent screams.

Sue never came home while I was there and I wasn't able to find out where she was hiding. I had secretly hoped that she would be home when I arrived and that I would be able to change her mind. But, with that hope quashed, and Dad still being his old abusive self, I was actually happy to get on the bus and head back to San Diego.

CHAPTER FIVE

Destroyer Life

I reported aboard USS *Cogswell* (DD-651) at 11:00 p.m. on December 31, 1958. The ship was tied up at the foot of Broadway in San Diego, in a nest of four destroyers. The ships were decorated for the holidays, with Christmas lights from the forecastles (foc'sles) up and over the masts then down to the fantails.

I went aboard the first of the ships, stopping at the top of the gangplank to lower my seabag, come to attention and salute the Officer of the Deck (OOD). Then I picked up the seabag and moved on to the next ship where I repeated the routine. I crossed the second of the two inboard ships safely and correctly, thanking myself for having memorized these procedures while I was on the bus from Montana.

When I reached the quarterdeck on the third ship, a bright brass-on-wood sign announced that this was USS *Cogswell* (DD-651). I was there.

I saluted and requested permission to board, lowered my seabag, and handed the OOD my official orders. The OOD was a young ensign, who I later learned had only been out of college about six months, but he certainly looked old and official to me.

When I was all signed in at the quarterdeck, the OOD had his messenger-of-the-watch escort me down to one of the crew living quarters with instructions to find an empty bunk for me. I went through a maze of passages and stairs, surrounded by bunks and sleeping people, always trying to be as quiet as possible. The bunks around me were mostly three-high, with the top bunk slightly above my head. There were red night lights located strategically along the decks, so I could see. Everything was grey, and I can still remember the overwhelming maze of grey cables running everywhere through the overhead.

When I got to my destination, the messenger pointed me to a bunk in the middle tier and told me, "You can sleep here tonight 'cause Bos'n Cowell is on leave and no one will be using it tonight. Tomorrow they'll assign you your own bunk." He showed me where to find the nearest head (bathroom) and left me there. I crawled into the bunk he had indicated and was soon sound asleep.

I was very rudely awakened a few hours later. Someone had lifted me out of the bunk and dropped me on the floor! The perpetuator of this offense was not particularly quiet either. "Who in the fuck do you think you are, sleeping in *my* rack?" I was staring up at one of the biggest black men that I'd ever seen, and he was definitely not happy.

I must've mumbled something, but I have no idea what I said.

He apparently decided that I was just not worth worrying about, because he asked me my name and, after I replied, said, "Get the fuck out of here" and crawled over me and into the bunk that I had just vacated.

I took my seabag and moved to a small table in the corner and sat down. I stayed there until shortly after 6:00 a.m., cleaned myself up, and got dressed. So went my first night in my new home, the place where I would spend the next three years.

I later found out later that the messenger had thought it would be hilarious if he put the new Boot in the bunk of the toughest boatswain's mate aboard—a man who had a reputation for coming aboard in the wee hours after a hard night on the town. Luckily for me, Cowell was actually a pretty smart guy, had understood the situation immediately, and had taken mercy on me.

Even aboard ship, New Year's Day was a holiday and no one was stirring that morning. As I had been directed the night before, I reported to the OOD on the quarterdeck, and he assigned another young sailor to show me how to find the mess decks and get breakfast. After breakfast, I reported to the duty boatswain's mate, who assigned me a bunk and a locker just across the passageway (aisle) from where Cowell was still snoring. I received instructions as to where to go the next day and was given my freedom for the remainder of the holiday. I immediately began unloading my seabag and making my new "home" as comfortable as possible.

After my belongings were stowed, I put on my casual uniform and started walking around the ship, finding my way wherever I could go. I found that I was much more comfortable above decks, where I could see the world and breathe fresh air than I was below decks. I did go down into the boiler rooms and machinery rooms, but I didn't care for them. For the only time in my life, before or after, I felt claustrophobic down in those spaces. The heat and the narrow passages between massive rows of pipe were just too much for me.

Topside, though, I found things much more interesting. The ship's bridge fascinated me, with its windows looking out over the bay, its control center, big steering wheel, compasses, and radar screens. Even the big leather captain's chair spoke to me of adventures to come.

When I tore myself free of the bridge, I worked my way aft, stopping to admire the signalmen's deck with its array of signal flags poised for use. Then I came onto two big twin gun mounts that sat almost in the middle of the ship. I spent a good bit of time inspecting them and trying to figure out how they worked. Of course, I had seen them in a million old movies—filling the sky with tracers and huge bullets as they blasted away at Japanese kamikaze planes—but these guns, the real thing, looked far bigger and more impressive than the ones in the movies had ever looked.

The ship was virtually deserted since it was a holiday. The two-thirds of the crew who were not on duty were all gone ashore. The remaining third, the duty section, were aboard, as were a few stray sailors who, like me, had no place else to go. On this holiday it was a bit chilly, so even the duty section was below decks, and I was able to wander unchallenged until I reached the amidships torpedo tubes. I was on the narrow outboard walkway one level above the quarterdeck looking over at the huge torpedo tubes when I heard a friendly Southern drawl behind me, saying "Good Mornin', Red."

Startled, I spun around and almost fell off the walkway, but a strong hand grabbed my arm and steadied me. "Careful, Red. We don't wanna get blood on the quarterdeck."

I found myself facing a powerfully-built man about my height, with brown hair and a wide, friendly grin that somehow seemed to make the world right with itself. He was wearing dungarees and had a greasy rag in his hand, as if he was working on something. I immediately noticed that he was a third-class petty officer, so I grew more flustered, saying, "Sorry, Sir" and stammering something about not meaning to cause him any trouble.

He laughed loudly, "Calm down, Redhead. You're not doing anything wrong—except don't ever call me, 'Sir.' Only the officers are 'Sirs.' That's a mistake only a Boot would make, and it'll get you a world of problems if you do it where anyone else can hear you. Just call me Bob." He then introduced himself as Torpedoman Third Class Bob Lawler. He had been lying on his back under the torpedo tubes, apparently cleaning some miniscule part, when I had come by. He had come out to see the new guy who was wandering topside when everyone else, as he put it, had sense enough to stay below where it was warm.

His big grin won me over, and we started talking. Somehow we seemed to recognize kindred spirits and we ended up talking for hours, first on the torpedo deck and later on the mess decks. It turned out that he was a few years older than me and was also a high school dropout from "the swamps of Florida." Like me, he had been assigned to the deck force when he had first come aboard, but he had "worked his ass off" and had eventually been transferred to fill a vacancy in the torpedo crew. He had studied and passed the test for third-class petty officer and had recently been promoted.

Bob explained to me that the deck force was a dead end for many people. Usually the people who went from Boot Camp directly to a deck force had either tested badly on the Navy aptitude tests, had a very poor education, or both. Others came to the deck forces after flunking out of a Navy school. People who were on the deck force saw very few promotions above seaman (E-3). If they became petty officers, it was in the boatswain's mate rating where promotions were so slow that it was not unusual to see a third-class bos'n with sixteen to twenty years service.

Usually the people who were assigned to the deck force just stayed there until they were discharged. But the *Cogswell* had a policy that allowed the gunnery officer to let some of the more exceptional "deck apes" try working with other shipboard groups.

Bob told me stories about the people who had tried the program. A few, like Bob, had actually made it in their new jobs and had become petty officers in their new specialty. Others just became the cleaners and painters in their new work groups. Others had screwed up and gone back to the deck force to serve their time out.

He told me what to do and how to do it, and I listened and learned. His advice was fairly simple: "Work until you know that you can't do another thing, then work some more, but always work smart. Think about what you're doing, and do it right!"

My introduction to shipboard life was made much easier by the friendship that I developed with Bob. I didn't realize it then, but this was the beginning of a friendship that lasted for a lifetime.

The next morning brought the typical military check-in routine. I found my way to the ship's personnel office after breakfast and I spent the rest of the day meeting my chain of command and checking in. I had been assigned to the ship's Second Division, a group comprised of deck seamen, boatswain's mates, and gunner's mates. As luck would have it, Boatswain's Mate Third Class Cowell was to be my supervisor. But by the time the day was over, he had actually laughed with me about his finding me in his bunk. He'd decided that it had been a "pretty good joke" when he'd woken up and thought about it.

Later that day, I was assigned my new job on the ship. I was officially the "After Head Cleaner." The after head was, in reality, a huge bathroom on the main deck of the ship that serviced over a hundred sailors who were berthed in the vicinity.

It had about thirty sinks, eight showers, and several troughs with seats over them that served as toilets. It was my job to somehow make that space immaculate, working on it between the hours of 8:00 a.m. (0800) and 12:00 a.m. (1200). Then, each day at 1:00 p.m. (1300), I reported to Bos'n Cowell for my afternoon assignment. Since I was the junior man on the deck force, the afternoon assignment was seldom any more desirable or appetizing than the morning one had been. Then, late each afternoon, it was my job to go back and "spiff up" the head to take care of any problems that the afternoon had brought.

I think that I can honestly say, without fear of contradiction, that I started my Navy career in one of the worst job that the Navy had to offer!

I worked as I never had before. Bob's advice stayed with me and I knew that my only hope of escaping from this hellhole was to work my way out of it. I had to convince my superiors that I deserved a chance to do something else aboard *Cogswell*. The ship was small enough that a person would be noticed, one way or the other. I was determined to make sure that when I was noticed, it would be for the better. No ship's head ever shined better than mine did!

It didn't take very many days of this kind of life to convince me that perhaps I should've given high school more of a chance. I decided that, if I wanted to make anything of myself while I was in the Navy, I had to get a high school diploma as soon as possible. I'd been aboard ship less than a month before I ordered a GED Test which, as I was informed by the ship's personnel office, would be administered "as soon as we get enough applicants to make it worthwhile to hold a test." So I waited. It never occurred to me that I should probably study for the test.

In the meantime, I literally polished the After Head, volunteered for other jobs, kept my clothes immaculate and even shined my boondockers (work boots). I also ordered the correspondence courses that were required for me to advance from seaman apprentice to seaman. The courses came right away and I went to work on them in the evenings.

My evenings were not busy. I had taken out an allotment to my mother in an attempt to help her feed the family. With her allotment taken out, my "take-home" pay was $12 per payday or $24 per month. That took care of my necessities, but money for Liberty was nonexistent, so I stayed aboard and either read or studied. The ship had a small library and a movie was shown every night on the mess decks, so I had some entertainment.

The *Cogswell* had just returned from a six-month deployment to the Western Pacific (WestPac) a month before I came aboard, so it was a relatively slow period when I arrived. The ship was not scheduled to get underway for almost two months, after which we were heading for San Francisco where it would spend three months in a shipyard. This was perfect for me, since I could get a lot more personal work done while the ship was in port and most of the crew was focused on Liberty and time with their families. I had the opportunity and the time, so I worked and studied harder than I had ever done before.

When I reported aboard, I had been assigned a General Quarters Station in one of the ship's four 5"54 caliber gun mounts. We held regular training sessions aboard ship, during which the ship's gunner's mates would explain our roles and train us in the operation of the huge gun. I was an "Ammunition Handler," working in the ammo handling room immediately below the gun. My job was to take the projectiles from a rack and load them on a chain hoist that took them up to the gun where another sailor would load them into the gun's breech for firing. (The projectiles were heavy and the job was, as I was to find out, backbreaking. But the worst part of the job was the unbelievable noise in the tiny ammo handling room when the gun fired immediately above you.)

About two months after I reported aboard, I went to sea for the first time. We were enroute to Hunter's Point Naval Shipyard in San Francisco with a stop on the way to offload the ship's ammunition.

Going to sea started out as a real adventure as we pulled in the lines while the Skipper maneuvered the big ship away from the pier and out into the channel. We were, as was the norm in those days, all in our undress blue uniforms. We got the lines in, stowed them, and then fell into ranks along the ships rails where we stood at parade rest, watching the sights of San Diego Bay pass by us. To my young mind, this was truly exhilarating!

When we passed Point Loma, we went below and got into work uniforms. About then I realized that not everything about this new adventure was sweetness and light. The ship was tossing around a bit more than I liked and my young tummy wasn't caring for the sensation. To make a long story short, I was horribly seasick for the first two days at sea and nauseous for the remainder of the trip. I carried a bucket with me everywhere I went and I used it with gusto. The only thing I ate that entire trip was soda crackers, and even they ended up in the bucket. But I did my job and stood my assigned watches, bucket never far from my hand.

When underway, we stood watches in a four-hour-on and eight-hour-off rotation in addition to doing our assigned work functions. I was assigned to stand my watches as a lookout, stationed on the port wing of the bridge. In spite of the misery that was roiling my innards, I loved this assignment. I was issued a pair of binoculars and had to keep a lookout over the horizon in front of the ship and down the port side 180 degrees to the stern. It was my job to ensure that nothing approached the ship without the Officer of the Deck knowing about it. Since we were at sea far out beyond the range of small craft, there was a lot of time spent in this job with absolutely nothing to watch. But, from the bridge wing vantage point, the Lookouts could see everything that happened in the bridge. I was fascinated by the give and take between the members of the bridge team as they exercised absolute precision in the operation of the ship. I watched and tried to memorize the commands, actions, and responses that they so casually performed. I literally dreamed of the day when I could be a part of the team that drove the ship. I was thinking, *"This is where the action is and I want to be part of it"*, as I barfed in my bucket for the thousandth time.

The ship stopped for a few hours at an ammunition depot in Seal Beach, just south of Los Angeles, where we tied up to a pier and began unloading the ship's ammunition. Immediately after tying up, we formed long lines and started passing the heavy 3-inch and 5-inch shells from the ammunition lockers deep in the bowels of the ship up to the main deck and then across heavy gangplanks to pallets on the pier where the ammo was carefully stacked and tied down. There it was inventoried by civilian workers and carried off to huge warehouses by forklifts. The long lines worked continuously for over six hours as we passed the ammunition off to the Depot workers. I was a happy sailor when it was over and we got underway again.

The ship pulled into San Francisco in late February 1959. As soon as we passed the breakwater and entered San Francisco bay, my seasickness disappeared and my spirits lightened. Again we manned the rail, this time in our dress uniforms with our peacoats on. It was a typical blustery San Francisco winter day and it was fairly cold in the wind on the ship's fantail. But we stood at parade rest and watched as we passed by Alcatraz and under the Golden Gate Bridge. My shipmates stood there and groused about the cold, but I was enthralled. I was seeing things that I had only read about. I was mesmerized.

The ship tied up to a pier in Hunters Point Naval Shipyard and reality returned. We immediately changed our uniforms, putting on dungarees and then going to work in preparation for the influx of civilian shipyard workers that would start the next day.

My job never changed much when we entered the shipyard. I still cleaned the After Head in the mornings and then chipped, scraped, sanded and painted bulkheads in the afternoons. But it was different. The ship's crew had to live aboard the ship, so they had always been very careful about the cleanliness of their shipboard surroundings. The shipyard workers (we called them "Yardbirds") were not nearly as fastidious as the sailors were. It probably wasn't their faults, because the nature of their work, with all of its soot and welding debris, was just plain dirty. But, as a person that took great pride in the cleanliness of my ship and my work station, I really learned to hate the shipyard environment.

I took the High School GED Test in March. The tests were graded off the ship, so I never learned the results for a few days. In the meantime I completed the Seaman Course and the ship administered a test for promotion to seaman.

On the same day in mid-April, I learned that I had passed the GED and that I had been promoted to seaman. It was a major day for me, but there were no celebrations. I was on duty that day and stood a quarterdeck watch as the Messenger of the Watch. The OOD was a young ensign, and the Petty Officer of the Watch was my new friend, Bob Lawler.

We had a terrific time on that watch in the middle of the night. I was so proud that I was bursting and my fellow watch standers were both amused and paternal with me. I think that Bob must have kinda-sorta adopted me by that time. He made it very plain that he was very proud of me. He advised me to start looking for an open vacancy in another field so that I could eventually work my way off the deck force. Both he and the ensign advised me to look into moving to one of the electronic disciplines aboard the ship. I took their advice to heart and started looking into the areas that Bob and the ensign suggested.

I had just been aboard ship for about three months when I was promoted to seaman. The promotion jumped me ahead of several of my fellow Deck Apes who had been aboard ship longer than me, but who had not yet passed the test for promotion. Therefore, I was absolutely amazed when, raw recruit that I was, the Bos'n honored the promotion. I was taken off of the head-cleaning job and put to work on the real deck force.

Once I was out working with the regular deck people, I found that our primary job was to maintain the appearance of the hull, decks, and outside bulkheads of the ship. This involved a never-ending cycle of chipping off old paint with its associated rust, scraping the metal, sanding it, applying a primer coat called "Red Lead," then applying the new grey paint. It was not long before all of my boot-camp-issued dungarees were coated with red and grey paint. It was hard and thankless work, but at least it was out in the fresh air and I wasn't cleaning a huge, nasty-assed, bathroom!

With my promotion came a small pay raise. I could now afford to go ashore occasionally! Life was good!

I went ashore a few times in San Francisco, where I walked for miles. I saw all of the local sights that I could find and ate at both Fisherman's Wharf and Chinatown. By walking everywhere, and catching inexpensive busses, I could save enough money to see the sights, but there wasn't much left over.

It wasn't long before I was bored with walking around the town. So I concentrated on my work aboard ship and even took out a couple of Navy Correspondence Courses. I studied Military Leadership and similar things; subjects that would help me regardless of whatever job I was going to end up with while I was in the Navy.

CHAPTER SIX

My Aunt, The Innkeeper

I knew that I had an Aunt Ruth somewhere in San Francisco, but I didn't remember ever meeting her. She was Dad's sister and she had been in California most of her adult life. About all that I knew about her was from rumors I'd heard back home. I knew that she was a single businesswoman in her thirties, but I didn't know much else. Just out of curiosity, I wrote my mother and asked her to see if she could get Ruth's address for me. It took a while, but Mom was finally was able to get it, and she passed it on to me about six weeks or so before we were scheduled to leave the shipyard.

I immediately called Ruth and talked to her. It turned out that she was very happy to hear from me. We agreed that I would come over to see her for dinner the following Saturday. She gave me directions, including very specific directions on the correct way to approach her home. She told me that the address Mom had given me was correct for the large apartment house she lived in, but her apartment was on the rear of the building, so I should approach from the alley behind the building.

On Saturday, I set out to meet my Aunt Ruth. I had seen pictures of her and knew that, like me, she was a redhead (but if the pictures were true, she was far prettier than me). She and her sister, my Aunt Mary, both boasted the same flaming red hair that Patty and I had inherited. I also knew that Ruth and Mary had both graduated from college in Spokane, with Mary pursuing Nursing and Ruth taking up Business. Mary had joined the Army during World War II and had been an Army Nurse before marrying an Army officer and starting a family. Ruth I had never heard much about, so I had no idea what to expect.

Ruth turned out to be a gracious and lovely lady. She was very honestly excited to see me and greeted me effusively, even crying a bit. She told me that she remembered me from visiting us in Seattle during World War II. But I was the first family member to ever come to see her at her home, so I was treated as if I were royalty. She had prepared a spare bedroom for me, and I was made to understand that, whenever I could get off the ship, I was welcome to make my "home away from home" with her there. It was truly a welcome change from shipboard life.

Ruth explained to me that she worked during the day at a local business and she supplemented her income by running the apartment house as a boardinghouse for other working women. Of course, this perked my sailor's ears right up. But she explained to me that the ladies who rented apartments there were all much older than me and while they all worked in San Francisco, they all had families—in some cases husbands and children—outside of the city. So they were to be "off-limits" to me. My ardor dampened, I cheerfully went on with the business of getting to know my long-lost relative.

That evening, I met the lady boarders at dinner. As with any boardinghouse of the day, meals were served to all of the boarders at a single setting. When it came time for dinner, Aunt Ruth took me to the dining room and introduced me to everyone. The only other male present was the person who cooked and served the dinner. He was a large black man who never seemed very friendly. In fact, during the month that I visited there, I don't think that I ever heard him speak a full sentence. He just cooked and served and performed chores around the house as directed by Aunt Ruth. He lived elsewhere, but he was there in time to cook breakfast and he didn't leave until after dinner was served.

As the weeks wore on, I became a kind of a favorite pet of the lady boarders. They harassed me at mealtime, gave me friendly tips on the sights to see in the city, and even, on one occasion, bought me a set of civilian clothes so that I didn't "always look like a lost sailor." It was almost as if I had become their adopted kid brother. But Ruth was right. They were all older than me and they obviously had their own lives outside of the boardinghouse.

I did notice one thing that bothered me a lot. Aunt Ruth, like my father, drank too much. She didn't seem to have his temper, but she clearly had a drinking problem. She never made a big deal of it, so I chose to ignore it. But it did bother me. Ruth, like Dad, seemed to always have a drink in her hand, even when just relaxing at home. I thought a lot about this. If two members of my father's family were so dependent on alcohol, did that mean there was a danger for the rest of us? I didn't believe that this was just a coincidence. I firmly believed that such dependence could be inherited. It was about this time that I set a rule that I live with to this day: I never drink at home, or during the work week (unless it is a very special occasion), and I never, ever drink alone.

I stayed with Ruth for several weekends and a few weeknights. I always walked and took buses to get there, but I would take a cab back to the ship in the mornings because I couldn't walk the distance in time to get back without being late. When Ruth realized what I was doing, she introduced me to a local cabbie who was her friend. He agreed that he would bring me back to the ship in the mornings for half the price of the other cabs. That helped a lot.

I had another of my nightmares while I was staying there. It was another one where I was falling through the earth, screaming. I woke to find Aunt Ruth shaking me gently, with a couple of her boarders looking on. I was embarrassed, but they weren't overly concerned. "Just a bad dream," was the comment at breakfast the next morning, and soon it was forgotten.

Finally, I came to the end of my stay in San Francisco. The night before the ship was scheduled to leave San Francisco, I visited Aunt Ruth for a last time. In honor of my departure, the lady boarders put on a small celebration complete with cake and ice cream. I got a lot of hugs and good wishes. The next morning, Aunt Ruth cried all through breakfast and was still sobbing when I got in the cab.

I had a really nice conversation with the cabbie that morning. I asked him how he knew my aunt, and if he knew anything about her that I could pass on to the family back in Montana. I had asked the same thing to the boarder ladies, but it seemed that they didn't know much about her other than the fact that she was a good landlady and kept the apartment house in good shape.

When I asked the cabbie about Ruth, he started laughing. He made me swear that I would never repeat what he told me. Then he told me something that shocked me to the bottom of my unshockable soul. He said, "Son, that place you been staying, that is the best damned whorehouse in San Francisco! I've been hauling guys there for over five years and I have never heard a complaint." He went on, saying "I don't think you want the relatives to know, but that Ruth is one of the finest Madams this town has ever seen!"

When I didn't believe him, he made a detour to the front of the house, which somehow I had never seen before. Sure enough, there was a red light over the door! The cabbie then showed me the advertisements that he kept in his cab for "men who are looking." Sure enough, the advertisements were explicit and the address and phone number were right.

Later, I looked it up in the San Francisco phone book, which again confirmed the cabbie's story.

I never told anyone in the family, nor did I ever tell Aunt Ruth what I knew. Ruth and I exchanged letters off and on for a couple of years before we let it taper off. I never saw her again, and I understand that she passed away a few years later when she was just forty-four years old.

Thinking back on it, I really do appreciate the effort that she, and all of her girls, must have made in order to make her naive nephew innocently welcome in their lives.

CHAPTER SEVEN

Goodbye Deck Force!

It was a beautiful sunny morning as the ship navigated its way out of San Francisco harbor. We manned the rails and watched the city fade behind us. When we reached the breakwater, I was pleasantly surprised to find that I had no need for the bucket that had been my constant companion during the last underway period.

The transit down the coast was, for me, uneventful and pleasant. We stood our watches and did our day-jobs before being lulled to sleep by the steady pounding of the ship's screws. In the evening, I found that I truly loved watching the sunset as the ship's widening wake churned the ocean behind us. Even on watch, looking out over the bow as it sliced through the water, it was obvious that the ship was moving me toward new horizons, new experiences and new adventures! I was starting to really appreciate the Navy.

The *Cogswell* had a tight schedule for the next few months. We returned to San Diego and were only in port over the weekend before getting underway again. We spent the next two months in a training environment, getting underway on Mondays and returning on Fridays.

During the first week of training, we actually fired the ship's big five-inch guns. For the first time I experienced the shock of the massive gun's firing and heard the ear-numbing sound as it echoed in the confinement of the ammo handling room. The heat and noise in this confined space caused my seasickness to return and, as I performed my job, the bucket was solidly placed between my feet. If I ever experience hell, I am convinced that it will have nothing to offer that surpasses that experience.

During the next two months, we were drilled relentlessly on every aspect of making war from the deck of a destroyer. We had gunnery exercises where we fired our guns at targets pulled by airplanes. We had shore bombardment exercises where we fired the big guns at San Clemente Island. We had anti-submarine drills where we dropped depth charges and fired torpedoes. We had fire and casualty drills where we simulated disasters and trained in the ways to counteract them. It seemed like we had drills to teach us to have drills. But, by the time we were done, my seasickness was gone for good and the Navy instructors who rode the ship to train us decided that we were now able to fight the ship.

When the training period was complete, we stayed tied up pier-side for about a month. This was a pre-deployment period that allowed the married sailors to have some time at home. The rest of us had a relatively liberal leave and liberty period. We were scheduled to depart for a six-month cruise to the Western Pacific in August, so time at home was important.

I tried going ashore in San Diego during this period, but without a car, there wasn't much to do. I even went to the USO, but the emphasis there was on saving my soul. Since I felt that my soul was doing all right without their ministrations, I didn't stay long with the USO crowd. I must have walked a million miles that month, trying to find something to do. I even walked to the zoo, several miles from the ship, a few times. It was interesting, but I felt like a lost soul, wandering aimlessly from place to place, so I turned more and more to reading and studying aboard ship instead of going to town.

About halfway through the ship's stand-down period, I was called to meet with the Gunnery Officer, Lieutenant Dun, in the wardroom. I was a bit apprehensive as I made my way to the meeting. I'd heard of other sailors that had gone to such meetings and had come away very chastened. I couldn't think of anything that I had done wrong (unless they knew the address where I stayed in San Francisco). But the fact that I was going to the wardroom was, in my mind, significant enough that I still remember the entire meeting after all these years.

When I entered the wardroom, hat in hand, I looked around in amazement. The wardroom was small, but to me it was magnificent with its tablecloths and framed pictures on the wall. Compared to what I was used to, it was opulent.

I was greeted by Lieutenant Dun and an ensign named Grant, with whom I had stood several quarterdeck watches. There were also two chief petty officers there. One of them, the chief electrician on the ship had also been on watches with me. I knew that he and had been watching me work a bit. I didn't know the other chief nearly as well. I knew that he was the ship's chief fire control technician, but I wasn't really sure what that meant.

Lieutenant Dun got right to the point. He said "Noonan, we've been watching you for the past few months, and you've been doing an exceptional job." I am sure that my mouth must have gaped open, because he smiled and said "Relax, Noonan. We aren't going to bite you."

My knees were shaking, but I managed to smile and move from attention to parade rest.

He went on, "We think that you have the potential to move from the deck force to another job. Are you interested?"

In a flash, I remembered Bob Lawler telling me to take a deep breath and think first when an officer asked a question.

"Never reply too fast," he had told me, "because that's how you stick your foot in your mouth." So I took a long moment and then replied, "I think so, Sir. What do you have in mind?"

Apparently my measured response surprised the Lieutenant. He looked at me sharply and asked, "Does it really matter?" Again I thought for a minute and then replied, "Yes Sir, it does. I plan to make the Navy my career and I don't want to have a job that I hate for the next twenty or thirty years."

That set all of them back and there was an awkward pause while they all looked at one another. Finally, the Chief Electrician spoke up, "What would you think about becoming an electrician's mate, Son?"

I had actually thought about this possibility a bit after I had seen him watching me, so I knew my answer, "I'm sorry, Chief. I know that this is a real opportunity. But your people work on the generators and stuff down below decks. I'm too used to working up where the air is fresh. I'd go crazy down in those holes. I really appreciate your offer, but I just can't take it."

The Chief looked at me and, after a long moment, grinned. He said "Damn it! I wish you were wrong. But I've hated those holes for fourteen years now and I don't blame you." With that he excused himself to the Lieutenant, shook my hand, and left the wardroom.

Lieutenant Dun took control of the meeting again. He said, "Well Noonan, there's only one more opening right now on the ship. It's with Chief Evans and the fire control technicians." He turned to the remaining chief and asked "Chief, are you still interested?"

The chief, who was a small man with a weathered, but kindly, face didn't hesitate, "Yes Sir. I'm more interested now than I was when we came in here." He looked at me and said, "What do you think, Noonan? Want to give us a try?"

Again, I thought about it. I knew that the fire control technicians (FTs) had something to do with the firing of the guns and that they worked with electronics, but that was all that I could remember about them. So I replied, "Chief, I really don't know anything about your crew or their job. From the little that I remember, it sounds good. But I'm really not sure. Do you need an answer right now?"

This time, I think that I had stalled one time too many. The Lieutenant snapped at me "Make a decision, Noonan. This job is in my department, and I don't have time to waste on it. It's the only job still available and I plan to fill it today. If you don't take it, another sailor will."

I knew I had played my last card, so I grinned and said, "In that case, Sir, I guess I'm now a fresh-caught apprentice FT. Thank you for the opportunity." I got a big laugh on that. We shook hands all around and Lieutenant Dun left us.

Ensign Grant was going to be my new division officer, and Chief Evans was my new boss. They told me to relax and sit down. Then they talked to me for about an hour about the new job, my new Division, and all of the things that my new opportunity entailed.

I was about as confused as a young sailor could be, but I held it together and pretended that I understood everything they were telling me. The one thing that stood out for me was that I was going to be assigned to the ship's Fox Division, which was comprised of all of the ships fire control technicians, sonarmen, and torpedomen. I knew that this meant that I was going to be in the same Division with Bob Lawler, and I knew that he would help me understand the things that had me confused. So I nodded wisely and pretended that I knew what they were talking about. We then broke up and I left with the Chief to take care of the paperwork, meet my new coworkers, and move my things to my new living space.

I had one pleasant surprise while I was emptying my old locker. Bos'n Cowell found me and shook my hand. His comment was "Congratulations, Kid. You earned this. Keep working like you have been and you'll do great wherever you go."

That was the only compliment that I ever heard Cowell give anyone.

CHAPTER EIGHT

Opportunity and Responsibility

I moved my belongings over to my new sleeping area and, literally, began a new life. I already had one friend in Fox Division, Bob Lawler, and I soon made several others. One that stands out in my mind was a sonar technician named Fred Ross. He was an orphan from St. Louis that had joined the Navy as soon as he was old enough. I think that somehow my shipboard friends tended to be men who had seen rough times growing up, like Bob and Fred. Bob, Fred, and I became almost inseparable friends. There were others as well. I seemed to fit in better with this group than I ever had with the deck force.

My new work assignment came as a real shock. Chief Evans took me around to see all of the Fire Control work areas and gave me a cursory explanation of each of them. There were four Fire Control Systems aboard *Cogswell*. They were all older systems that had been developed to fight aircraft during the Second World War. The two larger systems each had a second class petty officer in charge of them, supported by a small staff of technicians. These systems controlled the four five-inch gun mounts and the after set of three inch guns. There were also two smaller systems that each controlled one of the amidships three-inch guns. Each system consisted of a radar set, a (mechanical) computer, an electro-mechanical director that physically tracked the targets, and the electronic and electro-mechanical equipment that drove the guns to their assigned aiming points.

I will never forget seeing my first Fire Control Computer that morning. It was a steel monster, about four feet high and three feet square with little hand-cranks and dials covering the top and part of the sides. It was known as the Mark 1-A Computer and it was entirely mechanical except for some electrical units that transmitted orders to the guns. It was part of the five-inch gunnery system that was used for shore bombardment. (It scared the heck out of me. Luckily, I never did have to work with it.)

The Chief spent the morning with me, showing me the two bigger systems first. Then he took me to the first of the smaller systems and introduced me to the technician who was in charge of it. He was just a seaman like me, but he had been through a thirty-two-week basics course for fire control technicians followed by another twelve weeks of school on this particular Fire Control System. He had just come aboard after going through the schools. His name was Rick, and he was working in the starboard radar room when the Chief introduced us. The Chief told him that I would be working on the port system. Rick and I both assumed that I would be working for Rick, since he had all the schooling. Rick made a comment along those lines, but the Chief floored Rick and scared the crap out of me by announcing; "No, Rick. I'm going to try a bit of competition here. Noonan's gonna be in charge of the port system. You'll be in charge of this system. You both report to me. It'll be up to the two of you to show me what you can do."

I had not even been in the rooms where my new system was located! I was suddenly terrified!

Chief Evans then took me to the port radar room and sat me down. He told me that he knew that he was asking a lot of me, but, as he put it, "If I put Rick in charge of you, he'll just have you cleaning and painting while he tinkers with the system. You won't learn a thing. So I'm throwing you into the frying pan. I expect you to read the technical manuals, learn the system, and maintain it. When you get stumped, just ask me for help. But don't give up. I didn't take you off the deck force so that you could be a cleaner and painter. I think you can do better, and I'm going to insist that you do. Now let's get started."

Then he got a mischievous look on his weathered face, smiled, leaned close to me and said, "Besides, I'm from Bigfork, Montana, Son."

The Chief spent the rest of the day and a few hours on subsequent days, getting me familiar with the system and the associated documentation. Then, as the days went on, he faded back more and more and I began working on my own. The technical manuals on the system took up an entire four-foot shelf in the radar room, and I set about memorizing them. I would study a part of the system while I had the equipment open and could touch its parts. I seemed to be able to grasp it better if I had the books and the equipment both in front of me.

Thanks to Dad's old radio and TV repair course that I had studied at home, I found that I could actually understand a lot of the electronic concepts. But, although I was getting the electronics, I ran into problems learning some of the electro-mechanical and mechanical elements of the systems. Things like synchros, servos, gyros, lead-computing gunsights, and mechanical computing gears were totally foreign to me. But, by the time that I encountered them, I had become friends with some of the other fire control technicians. One in particular, a third class petty officer from Georgia named Robbie, came through for me in a big way, holding a little class for me whenever I hit a snag. Robbie was a lifesaver. I could have asked the Chief for help, but I just didn't feel right bothering him. Rick, the guy in charge of the Starboard System, seemed to consider me to be his competition, so there was no help there.

Robbie was a friend when I needed it. My sonar friend, Fred, was also helpful whenever he could be.

So life went on. Once again, I was studying as if my life depended on it; and, in a way, it did. I ordered correspondence courses in electricity, electronics, and the required courses needed for advancement to petty officer. I never got ashore again before we deployed.

When I wasn't studying, I was working on my system. Rick must have really hated me, because my system was always spotless and freshly painted. I knew how to do that, so I did it to the max. Poor Rick had to keep up or he would have looked bad. Fortunately, I didn't run into any system problems that I couldn't fix, so things were going well.

The ship got underway for a six-month cruise to the Far East in August 1959. I was so wrapped up in my studies that I hardly noticed the change. Sure, the ship was moving and I had to stand watches, but my life was in my studies. I spent every possible waking moment in my radar room, studying. I'm not sure what drove me, but there is absolutely no doubt that this was a major step towards the escape that Mom and I had discussed so often.

About a week later, we pulled in to Pearl Harbor. We stood at attention, manning the rails, and saluted as we passed the Arizona Memorial. I have to admit, I was very excited. This was the most exotic place that I had ever been. The more experienced sailors were pretty harsh in their comments about Hawaii in general, but I was enthralled.

That afternoon a group of us went ashore. Since no enlisted people were allowed to have civilian clothes aboard ship in those days, we were all in our dress white uniforms. All of us were new to the Island, and we were all under Hawaii's legal drinking age of twenty. We caught a cab and headed for

Waikiki, not really knowing what to expect. Needless to say, we were very disappointed. Once we arrived at Waikiki, we walked for miles and saw the sights and bought some souvenirs. But basically, it was no more exciting than being in San Diego.

Fred and I devised a plan that we thought would help. We drifted off from the others and bought a small overnight bag. Then we each invested in a pair of khakis, a Hawaiian shirt, and a swim suit. We went into a hotel bathroom and changed into the swim suits, putting our uniforms in the overnight bag. We then went swimming on Waikiki. It was great, though both of us ended up with vicious sunburns.

When we had enough of the beach, we put the new "civvies" on and walked around some more. We had assumed that we would be able to strike up conversations if we were out of uniform. It didn't work. Finally, in the early evening, we gave up and changed back to our uniforms and caught a cab back to the ship. We snuck the civvies aboard in the overnight bag and hid them under the false floor in my radar room. They stayed there for months.

I gave up on Hawaii for the time being and went back to my work/study routine. Work and study, work and study, work and study! I was absolutely obsessed with my work and my studies. I had a single focus that shut out everything else in my life for a time.

I had worked on the railroad; I had worked in lumber mills; I had worked as a handyman; I had worked on ranches; I had been in the Army; and I had worked on the deck force. I knew that I didn't want to do any of these things again. In my mind, the opportunity to work on this little system was my chance at a new life. Yes, I was obsessed. I was eighteen years old and I was at one of the most important crossroads of my life—and I knew it!

CHAPTER NINE

Bob, Will You Make Me a Virgin?

After a few days in Pearl Harbor, we got underway again and began the long transit to the Western Pacific. Our first stop was Guam, where we only stayed long enough to refuel and take on supplies before departing enroute to the Philippines.

The underway periods were now more intense. We were headed into a part of the world that was volatile in the late 1950s. The Philippines were friendly, but they were just a stop on the way to Formosa, Southeast Asia, Korea, and many places where Communism was challenging the Free World, so we drilled pretty much all day, every day.

My new General Quarters (GQ) Station was in my radar room, operating my fire control system. This was a job that I very soon mastered and whenever the ship went to GQ, I could get in even more studying.

By the time we crossed the Pacific and arrived in the Philippines, I had successfully completed four correspondence courses and almost memorized the technical manuals for my system. It was a good thing that I had accomplished so much, because the Philippines proved very distracting to this young sailor.

All during the transit, we had been hearing "Sea Stories" from the older sailors about what we would find when we reached Subic Bay, in the Republic of the Philippines. The stories all involved girls, beer, and more girls. The sailors loved Subic Bay, but the Command was not so optimistic. Before we got there, we all had to go through indoctrination on every venereal disease known to the human race. We watched more training films on the dangers of sex than I knew existed.

By the time that the first islands showed on the horizon, we "newbies" were both enthralled and scared silly. But we were all young men, so naturally the enthralled part far outweighed the scared part.

Subic Bay proved to be everything that Honolulu had not been. As the ship made its way through the bay to the Naval Base, we passed by several small fishing boats. The men in the boats were all friendly and shouts of "Hey Joe" came regularly from them, accompanied by hearty and friendly waves. The Philippines had not yet forgotten the GIs from World War II. Many of these fishermen had fought alongside the Americans and watched our men die for their country. They still remembered.

In 1959, Subic Bay was every sailor's favorite port and we were very excited to finally be there. We tied the ship up in the afternoon and, as soon as the housekeeping chores were done, the ship granted Liberty. Everyone that could get off the ship did; heading for town on "Cinderella Liberty." (It was called this because we had to be back on the Naval Station by midnight and aboard ship before 12:30 a.m. This was standard in those days anywhere in the Orient. It was also mandatory that we wear our uniforms exclusively. Only officers were allowed to wear "civvies" overseas.)

I wanted to go ashore with someone who had been there before, so I made sure that I was with Bob Lawler. Fred Ross and a couple of other guys came along with us. We made a stop on the base to change our dollars for Philippine Pesos. Then we walked to the main gate of the Naval Base, passed through a checkpoint manned by Marines, and made our way into the small city of Olongapo. As soon as we passed through the gate, we found ourselves walking over a bridge that crossed a small river.

"Shit River," Bob exclaimed loudly. "I don't believe it, but even this smells good to me!"

Believe me, Bob was the only one with this sentiment. The river was obviously an open sewer, and it smelled like it.

Now, I don't want to give anyone the idea that this shocked me—it didn't. In those days, the idea of using a river as a substitute for a sewer wasn't unusual. In fact, the biggest river in my hometown, the Clark Fork River, wasn't much better than "Shit River." If a St. Regis resident was lucky enough to live close to the river, they simply ran their sewer lines directly from the toilets into the river. I still remember joking about the toilet paper and "Brown Trout" that floated by when we were fishing there.

Seeing the thick, tan, stinking water flowing down Olongapo's Shit River didn't shock me. But what did was the fact that there were children swimming in it! They were on small boats and rafts, yelling up to the Americans crossing the bridge:

"Pesos, Joe?"

"Centavos, Joe?"

When someone would throw them some change, they would dive for it, often fighting one another for the coins.

In every gathering, there are some louts who enjoy seeing desperate people degraded. This was true here. I was absolutely appalled, and it showed.

Fred Ross, who had been raised in an orphanage, turned away from the sight, saying, "I think I'm going to be sick."

Bob saw the look on our faces and smiled, "Guys, I feel the same way. But I found out that we can't fix everything that's wrong with this world. I try not to look when I cross this fucking bridge. If I do look, I want to cry." This from one of the roughest, toughest, men I've ever known. I decided that there were a lot of reasons to like both him and Fred.

We got over the bridge and kept walking. Olongapo, in 1959, was a mere shadow of the huge place that it became a few years later during the Viet Nam period. In 1959, the town only had two major streets. Magsaysay Boulevard crossed the town from the Base to where the road took off for Manila. Then, a few blocks from the base, Gordon Road came into Magsaysay from the left to form a "Y." Both roads were lined with bars, cafes and shops, with a ratio of at least two or three bars to every other business.

Bob had a favorite bar, the U & I Club, a mile or so from the Naval Station on Gordon Street, so we headed there.

The roads were jammed with strange-looking little vehicles. Bob explained that they were called "Jeepneys" and were vehicles that had grown from the thousands of World War II Jeeps that the GIs had left behind. They looked like Jeeps except that the rear seat area had been modified to look like a small, covered, pickup bed with seats. They were decorated with the most outlandish colors and designs that I'd ever seen. Some of them were acting as taxis and others were obviously private vehicles. It sounded like Jeepney drivers couldn't drive without one hand on their horn. Interestingly, the horns had been enhanced to play everything from the beeping of a standard horn to a noisy rendition of "The Battle Hymn of the Republic." The din was deafening at times, but somehow it just added to the exotic allure of this place.

The sights and sounds of Olongapo inundated us as we walked. There was loud music coming from every building. In front of most bars were groups of local men, and occasionally women, trying to get us to detour into their bar as we passed them. We were tempted a few times, but Bob kept us walking.

Bob explained that he thought the high Olongapo VD rate was primarily from the "amateurs" who went into the bigger bars that were nearest to the main gate of the Naval Base. He said that he had seen some really bad-looking women in some of them and knew a few guys that had been mugged in them, so he stuck to the smaller, more out-of-the-way bars where, according to him, the people were "more real."

We passed shops that had Philippine products for sale. There were lots of leather goods and wood carvings. There were also vendors with carts on the street selling both soft drinks and roast pork skewers; things that looked like shish-ka-bob and smelled delicious. Bob called this "Monkey Meat on a Stick," but I have to confess that I learned to like it and it really did taste like pork barbeque to me.

Finally we reached the U & I Club, and we went in. It may have been a "small out-of-the-way bar," but it looked very big to me. When you walked in, you were in a huge room, decorated much like a stateside night club, with a bar along one side and a dance floor on the opposite wall. In between there were a lot of four-person square tables with an occasional sailor seated at them. But what was astounding was the fact that, even though it was only about four in the afternoon, there were at least thirty women in the bar, just sitting around, chatting.

As soon as we walked in, I heard a scream, "Bobbie, Bobbie," and the night was started.

I soon found that Bob Lawler had many friends. He had made a point, when he was here the last time, to befriend the older lady that ran the bar; the "Mama-San," as we came to know her. There were at least four or five women there that knew "Bobbie" and remembered him well. The fact that we were with him made us special people, and we soon found ourselves at a group of semi-private tables at the back of the hall surrounded by young ladies. The drink of choice there was San Miguel Beer, a concoction that tasted like a very green version of stateside beer. (In fact, I don't think that I saw any other alcoholic drink there. Whenever we were in any local bar, we were always asked, "Buy me drink, Joe?" by the bar-girls who were served in mixed drink glasses. But I soon learned that these "drinks" were either tea or soft drinks. The sailors were all drinking San Miguel.)

I didn't have any idea how to act in this situation, so I watched Bob and took my cues from him. He was very conversational and talkative and was joking with all of them. But he didn't seem to have any favorites and he treated all of them as if they were the finest of ladies. He was their friend; a quite respectful friend. As the evening wore on, I noticed that most of my buddies were pairing off with individual ladies and were quietly disappearing from the bar. I had plenty of opportunities to do the same, but I kept my cool and watched the action.

Then, out of the corner of my eye, I saw Bob whisper something to Mama-San. She looked at me with what I can only describe as a beatific smile on her face. She said something in Tagalog (the Philippine language) to the somewhat older and rather chubby woman who had taken up residence on my lap. She got up and left immediately. I have to admit, I was a bit disappointed. She had managed to warm me up a bit.

Then Mama-San excused herself, and I lost track of her. Bob and I gossiped for a minute and sipped at our beers. Then someone sat down next to me and said "Hi Joe," in a soft voice.

I looked at her and must have gasped or something, because Bob chuckled at me, and I saw Mama-San take her seat beside him again. But none of that mattered at all to me. I was staring at the one of the most beautiful woman, of any race, that I had ever seen.

She looked at me and said, "Let's go somewhere, Joe." I managed to gasp out, "My name is Jeff" and continued to stare, totally immobilized.

She took my hand and said, "Okay, Jeff. I'm Mary, and I'm glad to meet you. Now let's go."

My willpower became non-existent and all of those Navy medical films were suddenly the furthest thing from my mind. I heard Bob yell out "Don't forget to get back on time!" as I went out the door with this vision pulling gently at my hand.

The details of that encounter will always remain confidential to Mary and me, but I'll readily admit that it was one hell of an evening. I made it back to the base with about two minutes to spare, thanks to Mary, who had put us both in a Jeepney and had escorted me to the base to make sure I got there on time.

When I walked through the gate, Bob and Fred were standing there waiting for me. Both of them were laughing. I immediately asked Bob, "What in hell happened back there?"

He was in stitches and couldn't talk for a few moments. Then he gasped out "Mama-San asked me why you weren't getting friendly with any of her girls, so I told her that you were a Cherry-Boy. So she decided to make sure that your first time was memorable!"

I was stunned. I said, "But I'm not!"

Bob replied, "Don't make me a liar, Redhead. You've got a good thing going."

I started laughing, and Fred chimed in with, "Hey Bob, when we get to Japan, will you make me a virgin there?"

We laughed until our sides hurt. Life was good.

CHAPTER TEN

The Orient

The next day, I stood watch as the messenger on the quarterdeck from midnight until four in the morning. This was known as the "Midwatch" and it was both long and boring. At first, we watched the sailors come back aboard after their Cinderella Liberty. But by 1:00 a.m., there was absolutely nothing to do except shoot the breeze and watch the clock tick off the hours. I was on watch with Chief Evans and an older second class signalman named Cruz, a Philippine citizen that had joined the US Navy a few years earlier. As the long night wore on, we did a lot of talking about the Philippines, Subic Bay, and the life I had seen the night before.

The Chief had been in the Navy since the middle of World War II and he had spent most of his time on the West Coast. By now, he was a long-married family man, so he didn't go off the base in the Orient as a rule, but he had watched Olongapo evolve from a small fishing village in 1945 to the bustling, hedonistic city I had visited the night before. He and Cruz had a tremendous insight into the world that I was visiting for the first time and I was an eager listener.

I soon learned that, for the average Filipino in 1959, the Americans were still the best of friends. The "Ugly American" had not yet raised his head in that part of the world. The glowing stories that the GIs—and later the sailors and airmen stationed there—had told about their home country had made the USA seem like Utopia to the Filipino natives. The Hollywood movies of that era only enhanced this image.

As a result, many young Filipinos endeavored to get to the United States by whatever means possible. Cruz was one of the lucky ones, very envied by his local friends and family. His parents had been business people and were fairly wealthy by local standards. He was a graduate of a Philippine university, so he had managed to pass all of the required tests and, as he very frankly stated, his family had been able to pay off the right people to enable him to enlist in the Navy. He was well on his way toward a twenty-year Navy career. This career would allow him to stay in the USA when he retired, or he could come back to his home country with a Navy retirement that would allow him to live lavishly.

We talked a lot that night about the downtown bar scene. As the Chief told me, and Cruz confirmed, there were basically three "classes" of women working in Olongapo. First there were the "Cherry Girls," women whose ages ran from about fifteen to twenty-one, who had come to Olongapo with stars in their eyes, looking for an American who would sweep them off their feet and take them back to the utopia that was America.

Then there were the confirmed prostitutes, who came to make a fortune in a short time and go home. Some of the prostitutes were also former Cherry Girls who had succumbed to the lure of the fast dollar.

Finally, there were the women who ran the bars and all the little support businesses that depended on them. Called the "Mama-Sans," they had usually been there for years and had learned the business end of the scene, often through a combination of college-level night courses and the school of hard knocks.

I did learn that both the Chief and Cruz thought Bob had been right to take us back off the beaten path in Olongapo. They had no good things to say about the bigger and noisier clubs that I had walked by the night before. They said that these were the bars where the confirmed prostitutes worked and VD was rampant. They also told me stories of pickpockets and muggings that occurred in the vicinity of these places. They told me that, if I was careful, the people that I met in the smaller, quieter, bars could be good people that I could have as good friends whenever I was in the area.

Cruz told me, "They'll watch your back and take care of you if you are fair and honest with them."

The next night, I went back to the U & I with Bob and Fred. We stayed there for a while, but Mama-San wasn't there and Mary was being entertained by some big spenders, so we decided to check out a few other bars. We ended up drinking a bunch of San Miguel and buying a lot of "Bar-Drinks" for various girls, but none of us had any special escapades and we ended up back on the ship by 11:00 p.m.

Later that week, the three of us went to town again. It was my nineteenth birthday and we celebrated. Mama-San was there and gave us a lot of trouble because we hadn't waited for her to show up the last time we were in town. But since it was my birthday and Bob was an old friend, she soon forgave us. But one of the young helpers in the bar, a girl that fit the description that the Chief had given me of a "Cherry Girl" gave me an unmerciful bad time; "You, Joe. First you a Cherry Boy and then next day you a Butterfly going from girl to girl to girl. Why you no make up your mind? Can't be Cherry Boy and Butterfly both." She stayed on my case throughout the evening. She was an obviously outgoing kid that was a bit of a pet in the bar and was looked out after by the other girls. They called her "Skinny

Mini" and she fit the name. She was a tiny girl with a personality that made her a hit with all the customers. But she never sat with them or went out of the bar with them. She made it very plain "to all you dirty old men" that she was just a drink server and bar helper. But she had a major mouth on her and I caught the brunt of it that night.

We had a good time there and left in time to get in the gate before midnight. By now, Mama-San had kind of "adopted" Fred and I, so we knew we would be back. With her in our corner, there was no pressure to buy the Bar Girls drinks and that fit our pocketbooks just fine. We could go to town, have a few beers, joke with everyone and come back with only five or six dollars spent for the entire evening. So we returned whenever we could.

It soon became apparent to all of us that "Skinny Mini" had taken a liking to me. Whenever we came into the U & I, she would go out of her way to give me a hard time. She would occasionally set with us, but usually she was busy with her serving chores, as befitted a Cherry Girl in that society. She was very quick-witted and could easily match us in quips and comments. We became friends.

After being there for over a week, we were underway again. This time we were actually going somewhere that needed us, so we were hyped for the mission. We were headed for the Formosa Straights to do patrol duty between Formosa (later called Taiwan) and mainland China. Our job was to patrol back and forth between the two land masses so that China understood that the United States was firmly on the side of Formosa in their battle over who did or did not own the little island country.

We relieved another Destroyer in the Straights and began patrolling. We would slowly go from one end of the narrow waterway to the other and then we would turn around and go back over our wake to the other end. This went on for days, then weeks. We were manning the ship on "Condition Three" which was on an alert status just below General Quarters. For some unknown reason, my Condition Three Station was in the Sonar Control Room. So I put in my time learning how to operate the ship's sonar system. It was interesting, but after the "new" wore off, I disliked it intensely. It was a cramped little room and the lights were always off so that we could see the sonar screen better. Noise was held to a minimum because we were wearing headphones and listening to the Sonar's never-ending pinging. It was no fun. Whenever I could, I would escape to the Bridge, which was just forward of the sonar room, and get fresh air.

After a few weeks on the Formosa Patrol, we were relieved by another Destroyer and we headed south to Hong Kong for a week of Rest & Relaxation (R&R) in Hong Kong.

Hong Kong was the most exotic place I'd ever seen. As soon as we neared the port, we started seeing junks and sampans. The harbor was filled with them to the point that navigation was almost impossible. The Captain, guided by a harbor pilot, just slowed as far as he could, pointed the ship at our anchorage, and plowed forward.

Luckily all the little boats were used to this and they scattered before our bow could hit them. The whole scene was overwhelming. The water was alive with big ships and little boats. The mountains that rose directly from the shoreline had thousands of buildings of all sizes and shapes clinging to their sides. Even the smell of the port was somehow different, with the odors of exotic spices and oriental civilization mingling creatively into a blend that washed over us as we approached, somehow enhancing the experience.

We anchored about a half-mile from the city and soon took aboard several delegations of local businessmen and women. The one that stands out most in my mind was the famous "Mary Soo Side Cleaners," who agreed to clean and paint our ship's entire hull and superstructure. Mary Soo agreed to scrape the old paint, sand, and repaint it. She furnished the painters and the little boats that the painters worked from. Our deck force provided the paint, brushes and rollers they needed. She took her payment, literally, in garbage. She had a group of coolie ladies who took our treys after we ate, separated the leftover food and took it ashore. (I later learned that they then sold it to the local people at the little sidewalk stores that were everywhere on the mountainside above the city. When I last heard of Mary Soo, she was one of the richest people in Hong Kong with a net worth in the millions of dollars.)

Other entrepreneurs also came aboard when we arrived. Some were from local tailors and others were selling jade jewelry and similar items. They were not allowed to sell aboard ship, but they were allowed to stand on the ship's fantail and pass out their business cards. I made a special effort to get all the business cards that I could. I didn't have much money, but I figured that it would be interesting to go see the shops even if I didn't buy much.

In the meantime, the ship was surrounded by small boats selling anything from jewelry and clothing to food items. The ship posted extra watches to make sure no one came aboard from these boats and the ship's crew was told not to trade with the "Bum Boats," but of course they did at every opportunity.

We were also visited by a British Naval Officer and two Hong Kong Policemen who came aboard to let us know where we should not go when ashore. Before we were allowed to leave the ship, we were assembled on the fantail where the visiting policemen gave us a fairly detailed talk on the dangers of Hong Kong and what areas were "Off Limits." We were told that we were not allowed to visit either the rooftops or the nearby city of Kowloon.

The rooftops were off limits because some sailors from other ships had been hurt there. Apparently refugees from Communist China had built small cities on the roofs of the tall buildings that lined the waterfront. According to the police, a person could buy anything up there, but there were thugs that would lure you to the rooftops and rob you. Kowloon was off limits because it was actually located in Communist China and the authorities could not protect us there.

Soon we were turned loose to visit Hong Kong. Of course, about half the ship's crew immediately departed for either the rooftops or Kowloon, but Fred and I had decided that we wanted to see some sights and do some shopping. Bob had been there before, and he knew of another of his small bars; this one in the Wanchai District. We agreed to meet there later in the day and then we headed to town.

I had planned for this shopping trip. I needed a new dress-blue uniform because I'd actually grown about two inches since boot camp and my old uniform was now very short even though I'd lengthened the pants legs once already. (I guess the fact that I was now eating three meals every day must have triggered a late growing spurt.) In Hong Kong, I could have a uniform tailored to fit for about half of the cost of an off-the-rack uniform stateside.

I also wanted to buy a pair of the boots that Hong Kong was famous for. They were tailor-made by the "Hong Kong No-Squeak Shoe Company" and were almost a badge of honor among West Coast Sailors. They were slip-on boots that looks something like engineers' boots, but their toes and heels were smooth and looked identical to regulation Navy-issue shoes. Sailors who had been to Hong Kong wore them with their work uniforms and the Navy looked the other way about them.

Hong Kong proved to be a real experience. To say that I was enchanted with this city would be an understatement. The place was so incredibly different from anything I had experienced that it was absolutely fascinating. Fred felt the same, and we wandered for miles that day. We went to a good many of the small businesses that had given us business cards. I remember ordering some monogrammed and tailored civilian shirts as well as the necessary dress blue uniform, tailored to fit, of course. Then we both had boots tailored by the Hong Kong No-Squeak Shoe Company, and I bought a bunch of presents for Mom and the kids at home. Mom got a carved wooden jewelry box and some little jade jewelry items. The kids all got either toys or clothes appropriate for their ages.

We were mesmerized by the sights, sounds, and smells of Hong Kong. At that time, Hong Kong was basically a huge refugee camp. People lived everywhere and many just slept in lean-tos propped against the buildings. It seemed as if every square foot of space was occupied by a person and usually these people were abysmally poor. We walked up narrow alleyways that were crowded on both sides by people selling everything from food (most of which was absolutely stomach-turning) to hardware and clothes of all types. It was all so poor, yet so orderly, that it was amazing to see.

It was very obvious to us that the British, who then governed Hong Kong, were firm in their governance. We saw no sign of disorderly or criminal behavior, just abject poverty everywhere and proud people trying to deal with it.

Both Fred and I bought some things from the street vendors, although we had been told to avoid them by the police who had briefed us aboard ship. We both knew that we were paying far more for the little products that we bought than a native would have paid, but it was just the right thing to do. I remember that we both bought little toys from vendors, then gave them to the children we saw playing in the streets. We could not help ourselves. We had tears in our eyes more times than I could count that day.

We had agreed to pick up the clothes and boots later in the week, so we were not too loaded down when we met up with Bob for dinner and an evening at the bar of his choosing.

When we did finally rendezvous with Bob, we were not particularly fond of the bar scene. Like Olongapo, the bar was filled with women who wanted us to buy drinks for them and buy them out of the bar. But the similarities stopped there. The Hong Kong bars were more orderly and were air-conditioned. But the drinks were far more expensive than they had been in the Philippines and the bar-girls made no secret of their profession.

In Olongapo, a person could "buy a girl out" of the bar for a couple of dollars "to compensate the bar for the loss of her time." After you got the girl out of the bar, you could go wherever you wanted. Many of the Olongapo girls just went to movies or dinner with the guys who bought them out. After that, it depended on the individual girl, and the guy, what they did. There were prostitutes, of course, who had only the money in mind, but in Olongapo, there were some girls who never took the men home and others who had steady boyfriends that they never cheated on. In Hong Kong, there was only one objective in mind, and it was financial.

The Hong Kong bar-girls also had no say in the financial arrangements. Everything was negotiated with the Mama-San. There was continuous pressure on the customers to spend, spend, and then spend some more.

Although the Hong Kong girls were uniformly gorgeous, it was just too commercialized for Fred and me. We soon decided that the Wanchai District just wasn't in our budgets, and we headed back to the ship.

The *Cogswell* was scheduled for a change-of-command ceremony, and it took place in Hong Kong during this visit. We held the ceremony topside on the ship while bumboats maneuvered around our hull, trying vainly to get our attention. The crew stood in ranks, dressed in our best dress-blue uniforms, pretending that we could hear the speeches from the departing and arriving Captains as well as some other visiting dignitaries. The new Captain, Commander James Moore, turned out to be a very cool, calm, person who we all learned to like and respect. My life and his intersected several times in the next few years, both aboard *Cogswell* and later when we had both moved on in life. He was a very good man.

My funds were very low after the first trip into Hong Kong. I was still sending most of my money home to Mom, so there wasn't a lot to play with. The new shirts, boots, and uniform had about wiped out my miniscule savings, so I stayed aboard ship studying until it was time to pick up our new clothing. Then Fred and I went ashore again and spent another day wandering the city.

Hong Kong proved to be just as fascinating as it had been the previous visit. Before we left the ship this time we had done some research and located the city's tourist attractions. So when we went ashore, we first went to the Tiger Balm Gardens. This was an eight acre place of peace and serenity in the midst of the Hong Kong chaos. It was a fabulous garden area, set on the side of a mountain, filled with Chinese sculptures and mazes of exotic foliage.

An absolutely beautiful seven-story pagoda was the central attraction. The garden adjoined a mansion built by a Chinese entrepreneur who had developed and sold a famous healing ointment, Tiger Balm, all over the Orient. The Gardens were his way of giving back to Hong Kong—and they were wonderful.

When we finished at the gardens, we went to the China Fleet Club for lunch. This was a huge barroom and restaurant, about the size of a basketball court, maintained by the British for their military people. Americans were also welcome and the restaurant could make a good hamburger, so we enjoyed it.

After lunch, we headed out to pick up our new clothes. The clothes were a pleasant surprise; well-done and beautifully tailored. By the time they were paid for, I was out of money, so I headed back to the ship.

The week flew by and soon we were underway again. This time we headed for Yokosuka, Japan. We were to have some minor work done at the Yokosuka shipyard and load some supplies. Then we were scheduled for another few weeks on Formosa Patrol.

We were only in "Yoko" for a few days and I was still broke from Hong Kong, so I decided to stay aboard ship. I took the duty for other sailors and stood their quarterdeck watches so they could go ashore. (I made $20 per day doing this, which was really good money for me in those days.) I was really anxious to see some of Japan, but I was broke and we were scheduled to return several times before we were to go back to the States, so I waited.

CHAPTER ELEVEN

Typhoon!

A few days after leaving Yokosuka, we were again slowly steaming back and forth between Formosa and mainland China. It was monotonous duty until one afternoon when we noticed that the sky had turned dark and ominous.

The Officer of the deck passed the word on the ship's speaker system that we should "Batten down all hatches and secure all loose equipment." There was some very bad weather on the horizon. We had seen storms before, of course, and we knew what to do. Each of us had certain areas to go to and make sure that everything loose was either put away or tied securely to something solid. We lowered all the hatches and made sure that all the doors were tightly closed. Then we went about our normal business, comfortable in the knowledge that we were living in an invincible environment.

I had the watch in the sonar shack that night from 4:00 p.m. until 8:00 p.m. Since the old sonar was useless in a storm like this, I spent a good part of the time on the bridge watching the storm come in. It was a typhoon and it seemed huge to my inexperienced eyes. Lightning flashed and thunder boomed continuously. The wind was pushing the rain so hard that it moved horizontally, driving at a speed that made it hurt when it hit your skin.

Soon the waves were far higher than the ship as we drove into and over them. From the bridge, it was awesome to see the huge waves ahead of us and the ship's bow raising, raising, and then raising some more, to finally go over the waves and dive into the liquid valleys behind them. Often the ship didn't recover fast enough and we drove straight into the next wave's body. When that happened, green water from the wave broke over the top of the bridge and we found ourselves looking into a maelstrom through the bridge windows. I was amazed every time that the windows held and the ship surfaced again.

The ship was almost 400 feet long, but at times, it seemed as if it were standing on end as it ran down the far side of these immense waves. Then it would surface and ride the crest of the next huge wave like some sort of massive surfboard before the wave would come crashing over us. Words can't describe the awe that sights like this inspire. It makes one realize that man is really a puny creature in the physical world. In this storm, even a huge steel beast like *Cogswell* seemed tiny and helpless.

But the ship drove on through the gloom as if it couldn't be bothered by Mother Nature—as if it were impervious to all of this.

We were about halfway through our routine north to south cruise between China and Formosa. As I stood behind the bridge, I overheard the Captain tell the OOD to head directly south so we could get out of the straits between the two land masses as rapidly as possible. Out in the open sea, it would be easier for the ship to handle the storm, he said.

I got off watch and, very carefully, made my way back to my berthing compartment. This was a delicate process, because there was no way to go from the bridge to the after living compartments, except going topside. So I carefully went aft, holding onto lifelines and any available solid objects as if my life depended on them, while water drenched me through and through. I was a happy young sailor when I finally was able to get inside the ship.

After I arrived in our living compartment, we sat around for a while gabbing; then at 10:00 p.m., as usual, the lights went out and we went to sleep. I was in a top bunk and, like most of us; I had tied myself off loosely to one of the stanchions that the bunks were mounted to so that I wouldn't fall out if the ship took a bad roll. It rolled plenty and I was very happy that I was tied in. But finally I fell asleep.

Then all hell broke loose.

I found out later that the ship had hit a large wave and the bridge had lost control of the rudder. With the rudder loose, the ship had turned broadside to one of those huge waves and had literally rolled over onto its port side!

I woke with the breath knocked out of me, having been thrown into the stanchion beside me. I was hanging there with the stanchion across my middle and the bunk on my right, staring down at the stack of bunks that had been across the passage to the left of me.

Slowly—oh so slowly—the ship righted itself, then it slammed over the other way and I was hanging from the strap that I had tied myself with. Then again, the ship stabilized before slamming us in the other direction. This continued, slamming us back and forth, for what seemed hours, but must have been just minutes. The din was deafening. All kinds of alarms were going off. Sailors were yelling. The ship's speaker came on, warning us to stay below decks and keep all doors and hatches closed.

Somehow I got out of my bunk and down to the deck. I saw Bob trying to get the lights on, but there was no power, just the emergency red lights. For the first time in my life, I wondered, *Am I going to die here?*

Then slowly, very slowly, a kind of calmness came over us. The ship had righted itself and after a few more heavy, slamming, rolls, it seemed to have stabilized. (I found out afterward that the Bos'n on Watch in the after-steering, immediately above the rudder, had taken control of the rudder and was steering us on a course that was being directed over headphones from the bridge.)

We milled around, all a bit confused, and no one knowing quite what to do, or expect, next.

Then the bridge passed the word over the speakers for "All hands muster in your living quarters. Division Leading Petty Officers, report any missing people to the bridge immediately!"

We did that and soon were able to report that "Fox Division is all present and accounted for, Sir," to the bridge.

But we were the lucky ones. Soon we heard the awful announcement, "Man overboard! Man overboard!" That was followed by a long pause, then: "Leading petty officers, if you have people who can get topside safely, send them to assigned stations with binoculars, battle lanterns, and sound-powered phones. Make sure they can tie themselves to the superstructure. We think that there are at least three men in the water and we're searching for them. When people are on station, report to the Bos'n of the Watch on the phones. Be very careful."

We made plans rapidly. I got my gear and, dressed as if for a Montana blizzard went up to my director and lashed myself to it before I reported in to the bos'n. Rick was adjacent me, lashing himself to his director. I could see Bob, a bit aft of me and one deck lower, tied to his torpedo tubes. He was already scanning the water with his light and binoculars moving synchronously across the blackness. I followed suit and we could see several others doing the same. This went on for hours.

The seas didn't lessen. Tied to our equipment, we were regularly inundated by the ocean as the ship drove through the storm. I had to move the rope that tied me off several times, because it was bruising my ribs and tearing at my skin. Bob, being lower, had it even worse than me. But we all stayed on station, searching the water for our shipmates.

Before it became light, we heard an announcement that one of the missing people had been found aboard ship and was safe. He had been in a secluded supply material bin and had been knocked unconscious by flying material, but he was going to be fine.

Then, in what I firmly believed was a miracle, just after first light we spotted another person still swimming on the side of a huge wave. We all aimed the light from our Battle Lanterns at him and the Captain carefully maneuvered the ship as close as possible. This went on for what seemed like hours while the man desperately swam, just managing to stay afloat, but not making headway against the waves.

The deck force tried to get a boat into the water to go out after him, but before they could get it launched, the Captain got close enough, and one of the gunner's mates was able to shoot a line close enough that the man in the water was able to grab it. The deck crew began carefully pulling him toward the ship as the rest of us played our lights over him and the fierce water between us. Somehow, we got that guy aboard, to huge cheers from everyone watching.

That left one missing man. We never found him.

Sometime after dawn, the seas seemed to subside as the typhoon moved off. The clouds broke and eventually, the sun came through. With the light came the realization that our ship was badly damaged. From where I was, I could look down the port side and see bent and broken grey steel everywhere. Some of the lifeboat racks and one of the ship's small boats were missing. One of the three-inch gun mounts was dislodged from its foundation and was tilted wildly to the side, being held in place by electrical cables. Bulkheads were bent as if they had been punched in by a giant hand. The ship was moving through the water, but it was obviously not in any condition to do much.

Still we kept steaming in circles, steering from the after-steering station, looking for the lost sailor.

Eventually, other ships, including an aircraft carrier with search planes, came to our assistance and took over the search. We had seen no sign of the sailor. He was someone that I had not known well. He had been working in the ship's laundry, apparently with the door open to dissipate the laundry's heat, when the ship rolled over. The laundry was on the port side, and the water must have filled the space immediately, sucking him out with it when the ship righted. I sincerely believe that he could not have survived that hell, that tremendous force of water in that small space, for more than a few seconds—at least that is what I have always hoped. We never found any sign of him, nor did any of the other ships that searched for him over the next weeks.

The ship was badly crippled. We had no choice but to proceed very slowly to a shipyard. So we made our way to Sasebo, Japan, steering from after-steering and steaming very slowly. When we finally reached Sasebo, it was a relieved and very humbled crew that tied that ship to the pier. Somehow we were not the same people that had just left Japan a couple of weeks before. Death and near-death have a way of chastening even the most incorrigible among us.

This inport period was like no other that I have seen, either before or after. We were all working almost around the clock, trying to repair what we could. We on the fire-control crew had a major job before us: the storm had caused major misalignments of all elements of the ship's defense systems, from radars to directors to gun mounts to torpedo tubes, and it was our job to realign everything. This was a huge undertaking that had to be accomplished at night when the ship was cool and still. It was slow and painstaking work, done in a complicated process that not many sailors understood fully. Chief Evans took it on himself to work with me on this since I had no experience or training in it.

Liberty was non-existent for our crew during that inport period. My time was spent working, sleeping, and eating in a never-ending cycle. My director had a circular metal shield around it that had been badly bent in the storm. The shipyard cut the bent metal away and replaced it. After that, it was my job to get it cleaned, sanded, and painted. There were also some minor problems with my radar, caused by the physical shock of the storm. Luckily, the water had not reached any of the electronics, so I spent the days fixing the damage and the nights working with the Chief on the battery alignment.

But we got it all done. Like humans have done since time began, the men of the *Cogswell* rose to the emergency and did the job. We had a day of rest on Thanksgiving that year, but we were all so exhausted that we just ate turkey and slept.

By the middle of December, the ship was again ready for sea. We left Sasebo and steamed north to Yokosuka, where we were to have more repair work done and take on supplies. We would be inport over the Christmas and New Year Holidays for some much-needed rest and relaxation.

CHAPTER TWELVE

Christmas in Japan

Yokosuka was a true "sailor's port" in those days. The only real industries there were the shipyard and the sailor support network. The townspeople all catered to the sailors and we appreciated their efforts. Of course, Bob had been there before and had already staked a claim on a small, out-of-the-way bar, the Club Sakura, where we proceeded to set up housekeeping and made preparations for Christmas.

My first night on the town in Yokosuka was an adventure. A group of us from Fox Division decided to go ashore together and, of course, Bob volunteered to lead us. Except for me, all of them had been ashore there before, so I was the "newbie."

We were anchored out in the stream, so we caught a water-taxi ashore. It was just an oversized rowboat with a canopy and an outboard motor that delivered us to Fleet Landing after the querulous but valiant little motor putt-putted us past a throng of Navy and civilian ships. On arrival we immediately got into the local taxis that were lined up waiting for us. They were all little cars, about the size of Volkswagens, but were shaped more like American cars—just reduced in size. They sported names that I had never before heard of; names like Cedric, Datsun, and Toyota. It was a bit of an adventure just riding in these new and exotic cars.

The sights and sounds of Japan dazzled me as we rode through town. There were modern buildings interspersed between wooden structures that looked as if they had been built centuries before. Neon was everywhere, blazing the names and slogans of everything from rice to automobiles. It seemed like every building had its share of neon signs, some in English, but most in Japanese. The unrelenting din was astounding. It seemed like every car on the street (and there were a lot of them) was running at full speed and was depending on its horn to get through traffic. The scents were even more astounding, seeming to vary with every breath. First you would notice a sweet, but tangy scent that I soon came to associate with everything Japanese. (I never did figure out its source.) Then you would ride over a "Binjo Ditch," and the odor of raw sewage would overwhelm you.

In Japan before the late 1960s, raw sewage was dumped to a network of ditches, some lined with concrete, which routed the sewage from its source to distribution centers where it was sent on directly to farms for fertilizer. These ditches were called "Binjo Ditches," and when you were in their vicinity, you knew it. I always had trouble in my mind trying to understand how the always fastidious Japanese people could reconcile the ditches with their otherwise immaculate lifestyles.

It was mid-December, and Yokosuka was cold by any standards. Even though we were bundled in our Dress Blue uniforms and Peacoats, the cold bit through us. We were really glad to see the car pull up to a little bar, where Bob (who had been riding shotgun) announced, "This is your new home away from home, "Club of the Roses." When we didn't understand, he explained that this was what "Club Sakura" meant in the Japanese language.

The "Club of the Roses" was nowhere near as elegant as the name implied. It was a small building with only four stools at the bar and about ten booths along the wall. It had a very small dance floor with a juke box in the rear of the room. It was warmly heated by a gas-fueled heater that blew constantly and seemed to have one setting: *Hot.* But it seemed warm and cozy to us and the effusive welcome from the elderly Mama-San made us all feel at home.

When we arrived, only the Mama-San and one lady bartender were in the room, but soon other girls began to show up. After about an hour, somehow, miraculously, each of us was sitting with a young Japanese lady. All were old friends, and some knew Bob from previous visits, so we were soon drinking Kirin Beer and Sake, singing and dancing.

A comely youngster sat beside me and introduced herself with a simple "I am Kimi-San." I replied, "I'm Jeff," and the conversation began. I wanted to know everything about Japan and the local culture, so conversation was easy.

As the evening wore on, we decided to get food. Unlike the bar scene in the Philippines, we found that we didn't have to go out of the bar to eat. We just mentioned to Mama-San that we were hungry and soon we were eating pork fried rice that appeared from nowhere and was absolutely delicious. This was another adventure for me, since the only rice that I had seen in Montana was pure white and was sweetened by the sugar that we liberally applied to it. After a couple of hours of Sake and a full meal of fried rice, I was ready to stay in Club Sakura for the remainder of my existence. But that wasn't in the cards.

About 8:00 or 9:00 p.m., Kimi decided that we should go "to the Baths." Having read about Japan's Geisha girls, I was more than ready and needed no prodding. We bundled up and went down the street to another building, where I paid for a room and bath, and we went in.

The experience was not as structured or formal as what the documentaries describe for Japanese Geisha encounters, but I don't imagine that I was with a fully trained Geisha either. First, we went into an elaborately tiled room, where a huge bathtub was the centerpiece. Kimi-San handed me a large fluffy bathrobe and told me to go into the adjoining cubbyhole of a room, strip, and put it on.

I did that and came back out, not knowing what to expect. Kimi was standing there in a robe much like mine, except smaller, of course. She told me to take the robe off and get in the tub.

I turned crimson and protested that I was naked underneath. She giggled at me and told me, "You get it off and get in there, or I call Mama-San, and we'll take off for you!" I knew when I was beaten, so I did what she told me to do.

Then she took off her robe, and I was even more mortified—she was wearing what looked like a black two-piece swimming suit! I accused her of unfairness, and she just giggled some more. "You lean forward, Jeff-San. I wash back." So I did as I was told, and she scrubbed my back—hard! Soon the skin started to feel raw. After a while, I exclaimed "Ouch" after a particularly hard stroke.

She stopped and looked very hurt. "I sorry, but I cannot get the spots off your back!" She pointed at the freckles on my arm, "These things stuck on you very bad."

I went into hysterics, laughing until my sides hurt. She had never seen freckles, and she was absolutely mortified that she couldn't get them off my back. After a while, I recovered enough to explain freckles to her, and she started laughing along with me. It became a standing joke in my group of friends that we didn't want "the spots scrubbed off."

When we overcame the spot obstacle, things started working more smoothly. She moved to other parts of my body, from my head to my toes, giggling all the while. After a while, I started to sense that she was not just giggling for the fun of it and I asked her, "What are you laughing at?"

I was expecting a comment on the size of my man-parts or something like that, so her reply crushed me. "Jeff-San, you are nice man, but you have funny colors. You have little spots all over, and your hair is everywhere the same silly color."

After a while, we got past my red hair and freckles and I was finally clean enough for her. She then finally removed her clothes and joined me in the tub. Even then, she was totally in charge, telling me what to do and when to do it. I bathed her as thoroughly as she had bathed me, lingering on the good spots (much as she had also done—but I didn't giggle). When I had finished, she told me to stand while she dried me off. I did that and then dried her. Then we went into another room that had a big fluffy bed with huge down pillows and quilts.

An hour or so later, I was thoroughly enjoying myself when there came a loud banging on the door and I heard Mama-San's voice, "Time to go to ship, Jeff-San. See you tomorrow." I realized then that I had less than a half-hour to get to Fleet Landing, so I dressed hurriedly and said my goodbyes. I found a cab waiting outside the door and got into it.

I made it to Fleet Landing with about five minutes to spare. There were literally hundreds of sailors waiting there, so I checked in with the Shore Patrol from my ship and waited for one of the ship's boats to show up. It was after 2:00 a.m. when I crawled into my rack, but I couldn't sleep. This had been an adventure and I didn't want to sleep without savoring it.

The next morning, we all met over breakfast and traded stories of the night before. The stories were amazingly similar, so I decided that I wasn't unique, but I did get a huge laugh when I told them about my giggling Geisha and the freckle scrub. We decided that we would all go back to the Club Sakura again that night.

In standing the sonar watches when we were at sea, I had been often paired with a third class sonarman named Willie Barnes. Willie was one of the nicest, most considerate sailors that I ever met. He was also tall, well-educated, and black. Somewhere during those long, boring watches, we had become good friends. So, when we were getting ready to go back to the Club Sakura that second night, I saw Willie getting ready to go ashore. Thinking nothing of it, I invited him to go with us. He was very hesitant and started to make an excuse when both Bob and Fred joined in with me and we basically insisted that he join us. We all liked and respected Willie, and this was his first Liberty in Yoko, so we thought we would show him the same good time that we had enjoyed the night before. He finally joined us and we headed out.

We reached the club, and, like the night before, only Mama-San and the bartender were there. We went in as boisterously as before, took our seats and ordered drinks. Me, Fred, Bob, and Willie all crowded into a booth and gave Mama-San some coins for the jukebox.

We were ready for another night of fun, but there was a curious stiffness about Mama-San and the bartender. Neither were their old, friendly, welcoming selves.

We stayed and joked our way through some drinks, but nothing changed. Unlike the night before, no girls came into the bar. We started to notice and comment on the difference. Bob grilled all of us on our conduct from the night before, as we assumed that one of us must have done "something that pissed off Mama-San." But we couldn't come up with anything. So finally we decided that Bob should take Mama-San aside and ask her. Bob was just getting up when Willie stopped him. "It's me, guys," he said, "People on the ship told me that while I was in Japan, I should only go to the Negro Bars, but I didn't believe them. I don't want to screw up your night, so I'll leave." I absolutely exploded with a hearty "Bullshit!" Bob was right behind me, "Sit down, Willie. You ain't going anywhere."

We discussed this for a minute and decided that we shouldn't let Mama-San lose face. Bob volunteered, as her best friend, to go talk to her. So he asked her to go in the back room with him for a minute. As he told me later, this is what happened.

They went in the storeroom and Mama-San immediately started on Bob. "Whatsa matta you, Bob? You bring nigger to my bar; you insult me and everyone here. Sakura not a nigger bar!" She went on, "They have bars of their own. They have whores that put up with them. They tear up the bars and give drugs to the whores. I don't care. But they not belong here!"

Bob fought the good fight, but Mama-San was adamant. Finally, he brought her out to where we were sitting and told her to tell us to our faces.

She wasn't bashful and she didn't mince words. She repeated herself to us. Willie started to get up, but we sat him back down.

I then began talking and I told Mama-San, very calmly, that Willie was our friend, and we didn't see black and white, just a friend. Just as when we came into her bar, we didn't see Japanese and Americans; we saw friends and equals. I told her that I was really looking forward to spending my Christmas there, but if my friend couldn't enjoy it with us, all of us were leaving and not coming back. I reminded her that we were her best customers (as she had said repeatedly the night before) and we were not "bad sailors." I told her that she should learn for herself whether Willie was a good person, not just listen to stupid people who knew nothing about people. I absolutely surprised myself. I had never been so eloquent in my life, but I was mad. In my adult life, I had never, in any form, been confronted with blatant racial prejudice and it really got me going.

When I finished my tirade, I looked at Willie and saw that he had tears running down his cheek. I was floored, and so was Mama-San. Those little tears apparently made her realize, finally, that she was dealing with a human being. I think that they got through to her basic good nature. She looked at us and started to walk away. Then she stopped, spun around, and said, in her best official voice, "Okay! He stays as long as he with you! But, until I know him, he not comes here alone or with other people like him."

It wasn't a capitulation, but she had bent and we took advantage of it. Willie still felt uncomfortable and wanted to leave, but we talked him into staying with us.

Slowly, the girls began coming into the bar, and before long we were all having a good time. We started helping Mama-San decorate the bar for Christmas. It turned out that Willie was really good, almost artistic, at the decorating process and soon he had everyone working with him. It was not long before he became accepted as one of us. Interestingly enough, none of us went "to the baths" with the girls that night. We were too dedicated to making sure that Willie had a good time and that Mama-San saw the error of her ways.

Unlike Subic, where we had wandered from bar to bar, we stayed very close to our home bar in Yokosuka. For one thing, it was just too cold to want to wander anywhere. For another, Mama-San made sure that we felt "at home" there and we really did. She even put on a big Christmas dinner for us in the bar on Christmas day and we all exchanged Christmas presents, mainly because we knew we would have to endure the wrath of Mama-San if we didn't. It was a pleasant stay, and after the typhoon and all of our ship-repair efforts in Sasebo, we really appreciated it.

Over that Christmas period in 1959, Mama-San came to learn that all men are, indeed, created equal. After I got to know her better, I told her the story about my dad, the loggers, and the Japanese railroad workers.

She had a hard time at first, trying to understand how anyone could be prejudiced against a Japanese person. This was a concept that she had obviously never considered possible. But she finally got it and realized the similarities with Willie's situation. I don't know that Willie ever became one of her favorite people, but she really did try after that to not show any favoritism. The night before we went back to the ship for the last time before our next underway period, she said her goodbyes, hugging and kissing us all equally—with absolutely no one left out.

To this day, I believe that Club Sakura was the first integrated bar in Yokosuka, if not in all of Japan.

CHAPTER THIRTEEN

My Name is Edith!

Right after the holidays, we got underway again, this time to rendezvous with an aircraft carrier in the South China Sea. We steamed south past Okinawa, Formosa, and the Philippines and met up with *USS Hancock* as it patrolled off the coast of Laos. There had been a great deal of political unrest in Laos and we were there, "just in case."

The *Hancock* did quite a few aircraft launches during this time and it was our job to follow in the big ship's wake and watch for any planes that missed the flight deck. This "Plane Guard" mission was not as boring as the Formosa Patrol had been. The carrier would turn into the wind and run at top speed when it was launching aircraft, and we had to stay immediately behind them, so we would be idling along at eight or ten knots one minute and turning and ramping up to thirty-plus knots a moment later. Occasionally we would come close enough to see tropical jungle and beaches ashore, but we never saw any of the inhabitants on that trip.

We never encountered anything of interest, other than the launch of *Hancock's* planes, while we were in the South China Sea. We stayed at Condition Three, in modified battle stations, but, for the life of us, we couldn't figure out why. Like sailors everywhere, we bitched about the unnecessary watches and extra precautions that Condition Three entailed. After all, why should we worry about anything here, in this little lost corner of the world? Hell, we had never heard of Laos, or that other miniature trouble spot, Viet Nam, before this trip. We all knew that they couldn't possibly have enough of a military to cause us any problems! These rinky little backwater countries were not a worry, so why were the fleet commanders making us stand extra watches? We were really a bit pissed about this, but we did as told, watched the planes fly around in a show of force, and did our jobs. I got a lot of studying done.

In late January, we were detached from *Hancock* and steamed directly to Subic Bay. It was to be our last stop in the Orient before heading home to San Diego.

We arrived in Subic and my friends and I immediately headed for Olongapo. It was almost like coming home again. We were learning to make our home wherever we were, I guess, but even the process of crossing Shit River didn't seem too bad after walking beside the Binjo Ditches up north. (I still couldn't believe that the kids were swimming in it, though.)

Our little group got a hero's welcome when we walked into the U & I. Apparently we were well-liked there. I couldn't believe what a big deal they made of us. When they found out that we had brought presents for some of them, the whole place came down around us. We could do no wrong from then on.

Bob had made sure that we had all bought some little trinkets for the U & I ladies when we visited Hong Kong and Yokosuka. He had a nice blouse for Mama-San and other things for a girl that he liked. Since I didn't have any special girl in Olongapo, I had picked up an oriental-embroidered kimono for Skinny-Mini. It had only cost me about three dollars, but a person would have thought that it was pure gold from the reaction she had when I gave it to her. I later learned that it was the first present that she had ever received from an American—and it was a huge deal. I couldn't shake her that evening, and

Mama-San let her sit with us for once. We had a fun night and left the bar in time to get back to the base on time.

We were scheduled to be in Subic for almost a month before heading back. There wasn't a lot to do aboard ship, so we had a lot of free time on our hands. I knew that I couldn't afford to spend every night in the Olongapo bars, so the next day I explored the base. I found a beautiful beach, a hobby shop that looked interesting, and the Enlisted Men's Club.

That evening, I went to the EM Club with some friends and was bored to death. Some sailors enjoy just going to "The Club" with buddies and drinking beer; I just couldn't handle it. The conversations were the same ones that I heard all day, every day, except the conversations made even less sense when the participants were drunk. The objective of the "Clubbers" in these excursions seemed to be to see if they could get drunker than the next guy and still walk back to the ship. It was just not my thing. I was back on the ship by eight o'clock.

The next night, I had duty and stayed aboard ship. So, by the next night, I was more than ready to join my friends as they headed for the U & I. But I was not prepared for the reception I got when I arrived.

As usual, we walked in, sat down at our accustomed seats, and ordered our San Miguel beers. Then, out of the corner of my eye, I saw Skinny Mini walking toward me. I was talking and I didn't pay attention until I got hit on the shoulder as hard as I've ever been hit. She almost knocked me out of the chair! For a tiny person, she packed one hell of a wallop!

"You Somanabeetch! I thought you my friend and then you not show up! Whatsa matter, you got other girlfriend? You butterfly on me? I like you, and you do this to me?"

107

The words were coming faster than I could decipher them, and she was so mad that her English was breaking up. I was so stunned that I couldn't even reply. The guys jumped in and tried to explain that I had been on the ship, but she wasn't buying it. She was as pissed as anyone that I have ever seen. She just kept hollering and I couldn't get a word in edgewise.

Finally Mama-San came in from an errand and jumped into the fray. She planted herself in front of the irate girl and, very quietly, said "Shut Up!"

Skinny-Mini froze. No one argued with Mama-San.

Then Mama-San started refereeing the situation. First she asked Skinny-Mini what the problem was. Then she turned to me and said, "Okay Joe, what's the story? Are you a butterfly?"

She knew me well. For months, I had been "Jeff" to her, but the message was clear: if I was playing games with one of her "Cherry Girls," I was just another Joe to her and I'd better either have some answers or I'd be leaving this bar.

I was collected enough by now to explain where I had been for the past two days, and Bob chimed in with "Mama, this guy sends most of his money home to his family, so he just can't afford to be here every night." (I was surprised. I didn't know that Bob knew this about me.)

This caught Mama's attention and her next question was to me, "Why you send money home?"

I really didn't know what to say and I was so startled by the way this was turning that I just told the truth, "I have seven little brothers and sisters and the money helps to feed them."

She looked at me with a gaze that could have penetrated steel, "This is the truth?" "Yes."

She turned to Skinny-Mini, who was still looking pissed, and said, "He good man. You apologize!"

Skinny-Mini was still not convinced. She heard Mama-San and was obviously nervous about not doing as told, but she was still a feisty teenager. She turned to me and said, "All Americans are rich. Why you need to help family?"

At that, all of my friends broke up. None of us was anywhere near rich, and this did the trick. They couldn't help laughing. I kept my cool, though, and explained to her, "We probably do have more than the people here, but we aren't rich. All of our families"—I waved my hands to indicate the group of us—"struggle every day to make enough money to live. Our families work hard, but sometimes don't have enough. So we help when we can. We owe that to our parents." I went on, "I haven't been a butterfly. I've been on the ship, and I didn't know that you felt this way or I would have explained before. I'm really sorry if I've hurt you somehow."

That did it. She threw her arms around my neck and kissed me. She was actually crying!

I could not believe it. The last thing that I had ever expected was that I would have someone in this tropical hellhole that actually cared about me. I'm afraid that I didn't do a very good job of returning the kiss. I was too surprised to even react.

Mama-San came to the rescue, "I buy everybody beer. Let's all sit down and talk." So we did.

We all gabbed for about an hour there, mostly just explaining our lives "Stateside" to Skinny-Mini and the other girls. Their ideas about American life were all taken from the movies, and we were astounded about the things that they did not know about us. Since I was from Montana, their picture of my life was somewhere between a John Wayne Western and a Yellowstone Park travel brochure, with a Hollywood mansion of a home thrown in there somehow.

This topic gradually wore itself down, and the conversation turned to other things. I turned to Skinny-Mini and said "Look, I've had enough beer, and I'd like to do something else. If I pay Mama to get you out of here, would you like to get something to eat and go to a movie?"

She looked at me and said, "Two things you have to understand first: One, I don't go to bed with anyone, not even you. Two, my name is Edith, not ever again Skinny-Mini." I grinned and agreed.

Mama-San had overheard and said, "You two get out of here. First time, no charge." It took us about a microsecond to make it out the door.

I had a great evening with my new friend. We ate some kind of local food that was very good and then we went off to a movie. I was surprised to find out that the movie, although it was in English, was entirely made in the Philippines by a local production company with local actors. It was a gangster movie that could have been made in America except for the actors' appearances and accents. After the movie, we walked and talked. She told me about her life before Olongapo and I told her more about myself. It was such an enjoyable, innocent, evening that I have never forgotten it.

I walked her to her home, which it turned out was a boardinghouse on the outskirts of town. I kissed her goodnight and walked back to the base. It was a magic evening. Even the kiss was chaste, almost bashful. It was the nicest evening I could remember.

By the next day, I could hardly move my arm, and I had a huge purple bruise on my shoulder. I decided that I really didn't want to piss off Edith again.

The next few weeks flew by in a haze. Edith and I went everywhere together. We spent the weekends on the beach, or as much of them as I could stand. I was permanently sunburned during this time. Edith couldn't believe how red my poor body would get after just a little sun. In the evenings, I learned to make a beer or two last all night as we talked the evenings away. Mama-San was unbelievably supportive, even when her waitress was obviously ignoring her job to gab with me. We really did like each other. Looking back on it, I guess we were two lost teenagers that had found companionship, and a little bit of happiness, in that strange place. But at the time, all I knew was that I was happy, really happy, for the first time that I could remember.

Once again, my old dreams of the cottage with the white picket fence became active. I could really see myself and Edith in the place, watching over the happy little children that we would take such good care of. Life was really good for me right then.

I caught a real raft of trouble from my friends about Edith. They were mostly of the opinion that Filipino women, particularly in Olongapo, were just not worth the time and trouble that I was putting into this relationship. The fact that we were not sleeping together made it even harder for them to understand.

Only Fred Ross supported me. As an orphan boy, I guess he had seen enough loneliness in his life, and he was wholeheartedly behind us. He even got in some people's faces when their comments went too far.

I just cheerfully ignored it all. I was happy.

But all good things come to an end. Our stay in Subic Bay was over and we prepared to return to San Diego. In mid-

February 1960, Edith and I said our tearful goodbyes and promised to write faithfully until we saw each other on the ship's next cruise.

CHAPTER FOURTEEN

Stateside Studying

We steamed back to San Diego via Guam and Pearl Harbor. The married crew members were in a hurry to get home, so we didn't linger in either place. We stayed in Guam just long enough to refuel, and we overnighted in Hawaii. It was late February when we pulled into San Diego Harbor, tying the ship up to the accompaniment of a Navy band and yelling, madly waving, family members. My first cruise to the Western Pacific was over.

About this time, the Navy-wide promotion tests were administered. I just barely had enough time in the service to qualify to take the third class petty officer (Pay Grade E-4) exam. I had no formal training and was just a few months off of the deck force, so I was a very long shot for promotion, but the Chief had recommended me and given me a chance at the test, so I'd studied madly during the transit back to the States. I knew I couldn't match the knowledge that my peers/competitors had, since they had almost a year of school before they came aboard ship, but I decided to take the test anyway so that I would be better prepared when the next testing cycle came around in six months.

At that point in my life, one of my major goals was to be promoted to third class petty officer as soon as possible. It was especially important to me because my transfer off of the deck force was only a temporary action by a ship's officer. If I made a mistake or got in trouble, no matter how minor, I could be summarily sent back to the deck force and end up cleaning heads for the remainder of my service. But if I was promoted to petty officer, my transfer off of the deck force would be permanent.

The examination for fire control technician third class was divided into two parts. The first part was on military matters and leadership principles. I figured that I had a good chance of passing this part. But the second part was completely dedicated to technical factors. In my case this included electronics, electro-mechanical systems, mechanical computers, and Navy Fire Control Systems. This was where my contemporaries who had been to school had a major advantage over me. I had studied this stuff on my own for almost a year, but I knew that I still had a tremendous amount to learn.

Rick and I took the test for fire control technician third class on the ship's mess deck. Fred and Bob were both there, taking the test for second class petty officer. Of the four of us, I figured Fred and Rick were the ones most likely to pass. They had been to school before coming to the *Cogswell* and were known to be good technicians. Bob had a chance, since he had been working as a torpedoman for over four years now and had studied hard. Since I had come off the deck force recently and had absolutely no formal training, I knew that I was a very long shot for promotion.

When we finished with the tests, the answer sheets left the ship and went off to some far-away naval base for grading, and I went to my radar room and promptly made notes on what I had seen on the test. Then I started using the notes to begin studying for the next test.

The ship was in stand-down status, tied up to a pier, for a month after returning from WestPac. This gave the married crewmembers time with their families. A lot of the other sailors took leave during this period, but I decided to postpone going home for a few months so that I could save up a bit of money for the visit. I figured that I would go home just before the next cruise, which was scheduled to start in September. So I stayed aboard ship, taking the duty for people who wanted to go ashore and saving my money.

Then something happened that upset all of my plans. The test results came back and I had passed! I was going to be promoted to third class petty officer in June! This not only shocked me, but it absolutely astounded the Chief and my contemporaries. To come from the deck force and become a petty officer in less than a year was an unheard-of accomplishment. No one, including myself, could believe it. But it was happening!

To make things even better, Rick had also been promoted to third class, and both Bob and Fred were to be promoted to second class petty officers.

When they found out that I had somehow passed the test, Chief Evans and Ensign Grant went to Captain Moore and made an impassioned plea on my behalf; requesting that they find a way to send me to a Navy school. The Captain made some telephone calls, and I soon received official orders to go to Fire Control Technician "A" School.

Within a couple of weeks, I was on temporary duty at the San Diego Training Center, starting school. The only limitation on my school was that I would have to cut it short in order to be back aboard *Cogswell* in time for the next deployment. I would be getting the first eleven weeks of a thirty-two week school. I didn't care if it was short—it was a start.

The "escape" that Mom and I had whispered about in that bunker so long ago was not here yet, but it was getting closer.

The only downside was that I wouldn't be going home later in the year as planned. The school was going to keep me busy right up to deployment date, so taking leave was out of the question. By the time I could get back to Montana, I would have been gone almost two and a half years! That was a long time, but I had no choice.

I had been writing Mom regularly, so she had a good idea of how my life was going. I didn't realize it, but she was really counting the days until I came home in the fall. When I got word about the school and the fact that I wouldn't be making it home for at least another year, I called to tell her. She really broke down and cried when I told her what my schedule looked like. She was very encouraging and told me to give the school my best try, but she was obviously upset. That was tough.

I reported to school in early June, just a week or so before I was promoted. As a petty officer, I was fairly unique on the Navy Training Center where the school was located. Most of the sailors attending the schools were sent there directly from Boot Camp. So I was continually returning salutes from the kids that didn't know any better than to salute me. But it was good. I was in a school finally, getting the training that the recruiter had promised me a year and a half ago.

I was a little concerned about my last conversation with Mom, so, as soon as I was settled on the base, I gave her another call. We had a long, very good, conversation, talking about everything from my life to happenings in St. Regis. In a part of the conversation, I told her that I'd been trying to save money, but that it just wasn't working. Even if I had been able to go home, I didn't have enough money to do it—saving just didn't seem to be my thing.

So we came up with a plan. We agreed that I would increase the amount of money that I was sending her by the amount that my promotion was bringing in for me. In turn, she was to put the increase in a bank account for me so that I would have money to come home with when I got back from my next cruise. That sounded like a good idea, so I changed the allotment, and she opened a bank account in both of our names.

The school proved tougher than I had anticipated. With all of my past study and shipboard experience, the electrical and electronics part was easy. But there was a large theoretical component to the school that required heavy mathematics. This part was pure hell for me. The last math, of any kind, that I had studied was general mathematics in the eighth grade, almost eight years earlier. I tried, but most of the time I was just guessing at my answers to the math questions.

My old St. Regis/Boot Camp buddy, Joe Thompson, came to visit me while I was in school. It seemed like he had not changed even a little bit since we left Boot Camp. He had graduated from the Navy Jet Mechanic School in Tennessee and then been transferred to a Naval Air Station in Southern California. I was glad to see him. He had recently been back to St. Regis, so we spent a weekend gabbing about home and our friends.

About a month after Joe's visit, I had another visit from another St. Regis hometown boy, a younger guy named Tom. He'd recently graduated from Boot Camp and had just returned from his first leave, so he had news about home and the people there. Between him and Joe, I was very homesick.

Tom was interesting, though, from another perspective. He really wanted to learn about the Navy from me. He was eager to do well in the Navy and he looked to me for advice. I had never seen myself as particularly experienced, but with Tom, I was suddenly an old salt. I did my best by him, but I think that I was probably more impressed with my suddenly salty status than he was.

I had several nightmares while I was going to school and sleeping in the barracks. The same old scenarios came back; I was always in some kind of a hole in the ground, with evil seeking me out.

It struck me as very odd that I never had a dream like these when I was aboard ship—not even when we had lost a man to a typhoon. Somehow, I never had nightmares when I slept in the ship, in spite of all the machinery noise and the constant bustle of shipboard life. But here, in the quiet of the barracks, they came often. Maybe I felt safer on the ship, I didn't know. I thought a lot about it, but never really figured it out. In all of my time in the Navy, I never had a nightmare when I was aboard a ship.

The summer flew by, and soon I was ready to leave and rejoin my *Cogswell* shipmates. I had made it through the eleven weeks of school and, when I was finished, my class standing was third out of thirteen. That was as good as I could do with the math problem that I had.

I rejoined *Cogswell* during the first week in September 1960. A few days later, we got underway for a six-month cruise to the Western Pacific. I was truly excited. I had a friend over there!

CHAPTER FIFTEEN

Love Lost Forever

We pulled in to Pearl Harbor on the 23rd of September, 1960. The next day was my twentieth birthday, and, coincidentally, twenty was the legal drinking age in Hawaii. So we decided to really celebrate my birthday and the next afternoon a whole group of us headed for downtown Honolulu. There were several taxis full of celebrants, including many of my Fox Division friends, deck force friends, and other people who had become friends over the past year and a half. We were going to celebrate my promotion as well as my birthday. It was a rowdy crowd.

I have absolutely no idea where we ended up in Honolulu. I think that this part of town must have gone away over the years, since I can't find it today, but it was rough, to say the least. I drank way too much, which was abnormal for me, and I'm really hazy on the specifics of the evening. I do remember getting a massage—a legitimate massage by a legitimate masseuse—that didn't impress me at all. But someone decided that it would be a good birthday present, so I tried it.

I also remember the crowd getting in a huge fight in a dance hall that was on the second floor of a bar. I remember the stairs leading up to the dance hall very clearly, because I flew over all of them, without touching a single one, after I tried to stand on the bar and fight with a huge Hawaiian bouncer.

How any of us got back to the ship without being arrested, I will never know, but apparently we did, because the next thing that I remember, after looking down at the stairs, was waking up in my bunk with my dress uniform still on my bruised and battered body.

We were there for a week. I stayed aboard ship for a few days, and then Fred, Willie, Robbie, and I decided to try to really see Oahu. We went ashore and rented a car, then spent a very long day driving from one sight to another. We climbed Diamond Head and hiked through some beautiful tropical forests to see a famous waterfall. We tried swimming on the famous North Shore, and we even got into grass skirts and tried our hand at some of the local dances at one point. Robbie took a picture of me in a grass skirt that ended up in the ship's Cruise Book, preserved for posterity. As I look at it today, it proves, beyond any shadow of a doubt, just how ludicrous an American sailor can get if given his freedom and a couple of beers in a tropical paradise.

A few days later, we left for the Western Pacific. Our first stop was to be Guam for refueling and supply replenishment. Then we were headed for somewhere in Southeast Asia. The crisis in Laos had taken center stage in the international news recently and all of the Seventh Fleet was on a high state of alert waiting for something to happen there. The military advances being made by the Pathet Lao, with the assistance of North Vietnamese advisors, were making news worldwide. They were taking over the country rapidly, and tales of their inhumanity were generating a great deal of political concern. So we knew we would head in that direction, but none of us had any idea what our mission would be.

We worked our way across the Pacific, performing every type of practice drill that our leaders could think of. When we reached Guam, we met up with an aircraft carrier, and then spent the remainder of the trip conducting flight operations and plane-guard drills.

Then, in the first week of October, we finally arrived in Subic Bay.

I had been waiting for this day. Edith and I had been writing to each other during the long months that we had been separated. I couldn't wait to see her again. I had bought her some presents, mostly little makeup things that she couldn't get in the Philippines.

It seemed like it took hours to tie up the ship, get dressed, and get off the ship that day.

As we walked through the main gate, I remembered Bob's comment that I had thought so strange last year, about even Shit River smelling good. I finally understood. I was so happy to be here that nothing could, or would quench my spirits today. It was like coming home again! He was right. Even Shit River smelled good today.

I had just crossed the bridge and was talking with my head turned to the side when I was almost knocked over by a flying body. It was Edith! She had heard that the ship was arriving today and she had been waiting at the bridge for hours. She was hugging me as if I were the most precious thing in the world. I had never felt so loved, so warm, so wonderful. It was a moment to remember forever.

She was crying and trying to talk all at the same time. I wasn't much better. My friends all discreetly kept walking ahead, then gathered in a group to talk and wait for us.

Edith had taken the day off, so we found a little café where we could talk, and the guys went on to the U & I without us. Then we walked to her boardinghouse, and she dropped off the presents that I had brought. When we got there, I tried to get frisky, but she stopped me with, "Remember, Jeff. One, I don't go to bed with anyone. Two, my name is Edith."

That brought a laugh from me, and we talked some more. Then we went over to the U & I and had a beer with Mama-San and my friends.

The next afternoon, we went to a movie, then out to dinner. It was as if I had never left. I was a very happy man again. We laughed, we joked, and we had fun. Life was good.

The third day in Subic, I had duty and stayed aboard ship. It was a quiet day and nothing much happened. I stood my watch, did some maintenance work on my equipment, and spent some time reading a paperback.

The next morning, I was in my radar room working when the door opened and Fred and Bob came in. "Jeff, we have to talk to you."

I was startled. They looked so serious that, at first, I thought someone had died. But the news wasn't that good. They came in and sat down and then Bob opened with "Jeff, we were in town last night and we did some bar-hopping. When we got back to the U & I at about 10:00 p.m., Edith was just leaving—with a sailor."

I was startled, but I said, "Heck, it's probably nothing. She probably just had someone take her across the street for food or something like that."

At that Fred opened up, "No, my friend, it wasn't so simple." He paused and then went on, "We thought that it looked strange, and she didn't see us, so we decided to follow them. They went straight to a hotel and, through the window, we saw them register and go upstairs."

I must have had an unusual look on my face then, because Bob chimed in, "Jeff, don't shoot the messengers. We really didn't want to tell you this, but someone had to." He went on, "After we followed them, we went back to the bar and I collared Mama-San. She confirmed it. Skinny-Mini has been taking the sailors on regularly for months now. She is a bar-girl now and doesn't even work as a Cherry-Girl waitress anymore. Mama-San didn't think that it was a big deal, but we thought you should know."

I don't remember the rest of the conversation. I know that we talked for a while, and then I just sat in the radar room and thought about it for the rest of the work day. I couldn't wrap my brain around this news. I knew that my friends were telling me the truth as they saw it, but I was sure that there was another explanation. The girl that had been so happy to see me at the bridge two days ago just couldn't be a whore! It was impossible. So I decided to go to town and find out for myself.

I showered and changed into my dress uniform before the end of the work day for once. As soon as we could leave the ship, I was on my way. I asked my friends to let me go alone this time and I headed for the U & I. When I walked in, I was a couple of hours earlier than usual. Edith was sitting at a table talking to a sailor who I recognized as one of the sailors that was stationed on the base and hung out at the U & I. I just went back to our usual table and waited.

After a while, she noticed me and came over, just as bubbly and happy as ever. She bent over and gave me a hello kiss as if all was normal—as I so desperately wanted it to be. I asked her to sit down and I guess she saw the seriousness on my face because she immediately came out with, "What's wrong?"

I said, "I've been hearing that you're a full Bar Girl now." She smiled and proudly said, "Yeah, I've been promoted while you were gone."

I then asked, "Edith, does that mean you're sleeping with sailors now?" She became indignant and denied it, but I went on, "My friends tell me that they followed you to the hotel last night and saw you go upstairs with a sailor." Her face fell, and I could see the truth in her eyes. She looked away, and there was a long pause before she answered, "Jeff you don't understand this life. I do what I have to do to eat. I have one life with you, but I have to have another life that keeps me alive so that I can have my life with you. Please, please, don't judge me." I could not handle this. I could feel the tears burning in the back of my eyes. I stood up and turned toward the door.

She grabbed me in a desperate bear-hug and pleaded with me to stop and listen to her. She was crying hysterically, but I couldn't stop. I managed to stammer something through the huge lump in my throat, and I gently peeled her off of me and left the bar.

I walked for about a mile while the tears flowed freely. I must have been quite a sight, if anyone bothered to look at me. Finally I dried my face and stopped in a quiet little restaurant-bar, took a seat in a dark corner and nursed a beer. I was absolutely devastated and I couldn't think logically. My mind just wouldn't focus; it kept slipping away from the reality in front of it. It just wanted everything to be as it had been two days earlier and it didn't want to see what it had been made to see.

People write about how adversity makes a person stronger and how a person "grows up" from emotional experiences. Love and broken hearts are standard grist for the romance novelists. I can only assume that those who write so glibly about it have never been there. It is a horrible, horrible feeling and I don't ever again want to go through it again. I was twenty years old and I knew that life would never be the same for me again. In my mind, the woman that I loved had betrayed me in the worst possible way.

I stayed aboard ship for well over a week that time. We were going to be in Subic almost indefinitely because the world was watching the Laos situation, and we were standing by in case we were needed there. So, even though I wanted to put distance between myself and the source of my pain, that wasn't an option.

I racked my brain for things to do that would keep my mind occupied and keep me away from the U & I. I read a lot and went to the beach on the base a few times. I even tried going to the EM Club again, but that was still no fun.

Several of my friends had bought eyeglasses from a Filipino optometrist out in town and had received great results for very little money. I had been wearing the grey plastic Army/Navy frames for the past couple of years, so I decided to go buy civilian glasses while I was there. I went to town, was tested, and picked out some modern, and reasonably fashionable, frames. They were a reddish-brown color in front, with silver temple-pieces. As soon as I ordered them, I went back to the ship. I didn't want to take a chance on running into Edith or anyone else that knew us.

The glasses came in, and I was really proud of them. But I will never forget Bob's reaction. He took one look and said, "Jesus, JJ, you look like a little red choo-choo train with too much fucking chrome on the sides!"

Even I had to laugh at that.

Cogswell stayed in port for a few more days, and I stayed aboard ship. Then we got underway with an aircraft carrier, USS

Hancock, headed for South China Sea, the Gulf of Tonkin, and the Laotian coastline. We spent the better part of a month patrolling the coast and practicing the launch and recovery of aircraft. As before, it was slow, boring duty. As always, I passed the time studying and standing sonar watches.

The sonar watches were something of a joke to us on that particular mission. When we were in close to shore, we didn't see or hear anything except the shoreline. Usually the water was too shallow for submarines, but we still stood sonar watches. Then, when we worked with the aircraft carrier in plane guard roles, we were going so fast chasing the carrier that the sonar was just a noisy blur. The noise of the propellers and the sound of the ships beating their ways through the water at thirty-plus knots just made our old sonar useless. But we still stood our sonar watches.

During this time at sea, Fred and I talked a lot about our futures. We both planned to make a career out of the Navy. Fred was an orphan and had no home to go back to, so the ship had become a kind of a home to him. I had no desire to return to Montana and work in the lumber mills, so we were both very interested in a new program that the Navy had opened in order to retain technicians.

It was called the Star Program. It had some pretty stringent pre-qualifications, but if you applied for it, and the Navy approved your application, you could go to one of the Navy's Class "B" Schools, which were intense six-to-eight-month technical schools, followed by a specialty school. If you passed the Class "B" School with a high enough average, you could get an automatic promotion. This was very interesting to both Fred and me, so we applied for the program.

After a long, boring time at sea, we finally returned to Subic Bay.

Finally, I agreed to go ashore with the gang again, on the condition that we wouldn't go near the U & I Club. So we went to a little bar that was about a mile away from the U & I on Magsaysay Boulevard—the California Bar We had stopped there a couple of times and thought that it could become a good substitute for our old haunt. The guys all knew what had happened between me and Edith and they were all willing to support me by this relocation, so we drank beer and shot the breeze and got to know our new home away from home.

But Olongapo was a small town in those days; there were no secrets. I guess Edith had put out word on the local grapevine, because about an hour after we arrived, she walked into the bar. She came straight to the table where we were sitting. Of course, as was the way in Olongapo, there were three or four girls setting with us at the table.

Edith said something to them in Tagalog, and the girls moved away from us. Then she turned to me and said, "We need to talk. Will you come with me, or should I sit down here?"

I looked around and spotted a table in a quiet corner and pointed at it. "Over there. You have five minutes." We sat down and she started by telling me, again, that I didn't understand.

I interrupted her and told her, "It isn't me that doesn't understand; it's you." I went on, "I gave you more of myself, my feelings, and my caring, than I have ever given any woman before. I respected your body and your wish to stay a Cherry Girl by stopping like a gentleman, even when it caused me a lot of physical pain. You know that's true. I've been devoted to you, and only you, since we started going out together, but you repaid me by sleeping with any sailor that could afford to pay you. No Edith, I don't think it is me that owes an apology or understanding of anything!"

She looked at me for a long time and then said, "You want to sleep with me? Is that what you want?"

I misunderstood her, thinking she was still talking about the past. I replied, "Of course, I've always wanted to sleep with you. But I didn't because I respected you too much."

She held up her hand to stop me and said, "No Jeff. I mean now. Do you want to sleep with me now?"

My reaction was just plain mean-spirited. I was so mad at her that my only thought was that I would just do it and then walk out on her. That would teach her a lesson! So I said, "Hell yes, let's go!"

We left the bar in silence and caught a Jeepney to her boardinghouse. We traveled in complete silence, each lost in our own thoughts and both afraid to say the wrong thing. We went to her room, and I sat down on a chair and began taking my shoes off. I was starting to come down from being mad, so I was a bit shy and hesitant.

She went to the sink and got a glass of water and stood there, looking out into space. I watched her for a minute and then said, "What's wrong, Edith?"

She looked at me and then looked away. I could see that she was crying.

"Nothing," she said. But she kept standing there. Finally, she turned and looked at me, and said, "Jeff, I can't do this. I know you don't understand, but if I do this, I will be a whore—just another whore. I can't do this. I can't!" and she broke down into sobs, still leaning on the sink, bent almost double with the power of her emotions.

This was just too much to process for me. I could not, for the life of me, understand how she could indiscriminately go to bed with other people, but draw the line at the one person that cared for her. At that moment, I just thought that she had been playing me. I am sure now that I was wrong, but I was a twenty-year-old who was hurting badly. I just wanted to lash out—but I couldn't. I still cared too much.

I didn't say anything. I just got up and walked out. I looked back at her as I closed the door, and she was standing there, staring at me, still slightly bent over, with a stricken look on her face.

I never saw her again—but I will never forget that look. After a half of a century, it still haunts me.

Was I wrong to do what I did? I don't know. I will never know. But it does haunt me.

CHAPTER SIXTEEN

The Great Baguio Adventure

In mid-November, we got underway and transited to Buckner Bay, Okinawa, where we met up with another aircraft carrier, USS *Bennington*. We were only in Buckner Bay overnight, and I had the duty, so I never got ashore in this port. The ship's crew did love it, judging from the sea stories they told the next day.

We were underway early the next morning, heading again for the South China Sea to maintain a vigil over the Laotian insurgency. Again we cruised in circles for days, after which we returned to Subic Bay.

On the way back to Subic, the ship's executive officer announced that the ship would be inport on stand-down status over the Christmas and New Year's holiday periods. We were obviously not allowed to return home, but we were offered several Philippine tour packages if we wanted to get away over the holidays. Most of them were either to Manila or to Baguio, the summer capital of the islands. None of us were particularly interested at first.

The first night inport, we went back to the California Bar and had a few drinks. As we were imbibing, the subject of the tours came up. We decided that it was really unfair that "the pussies" who were going on the tours were allowed to stay off the ship for twenty-four hours a day, five to seven days at a time, yet those of us who wanted to stay closer to the ship, in the Olongapo area, had to be back aboard ship at midnight every night. It was just plain unfair!

Of course, after enough San Miguel beer, we came up with a plan designed to correct this obvious unfairness. We decided that we would sign up for a tour. Then, since the tours were self-guided, we would just stay in Olongapo and have our tour hours there. We talked to the California Club Mama-San, and she told us where to get a group of rooms that were off the beaten path where we wouldn't get caught. The plan was coming together!

The next morning, we went to sign up for a tour, only to find that the only one left was a seven-day tour to Baguio,scheduled to leave on December 30. We signed up.

The day came and we followed the plan. With leave papers in hand, we stopped at the Base Exchange and each bought two bottles of hard liquor (which was the most that we were allowed to take through the gate). We also bought some non-descript civilian clothes so that we wouldn't have to wear our white uniforms. Then we went to town and rented the rooms that Mama-San had reserved for us, changed clothes, and descended on the California Bar to commence a seven-day party. With the "civvies" on, we figured that we looked like sailors stationed on the base, or some of the Air Force people that we saw around town regularly, and we would just blend in with them.

It worked beautifully! The first night, we stayed in town, making the rounds of Olongapo's Magsaysay Boulevard bars and just having a good time. At midnight, we retired to our rooms with an assortment of "friends" and partied on until daybreak. Then we slept until noon, got up, and started over.

However, fate was not kind to us. On the second day, we had been drinking all day and were well "into our cups" at about 9:00 p.m. when the doors on the bar suddenly burst open and a

Shore Patrol team came in, blowing their whistles for attention. One of them shouted out, "Listen Up! Everyone is to get back to your ships. All ships are getting underway at midnight! I repeat: everyone up and out. The ships are leaving at midnight!"

This hit us like a wet blanket. We were having the times of our lives, and we had to quit and go back? I knew one of the Shore Patrol guys, so I approached him and asked, "What's going on?"

He said, "Probably nothing, but all ships have been directed to leave for the South China Sea for maneuvers. It has something to do with the Laos thing. Apparently the Brass wants to show the flag, so we all have to go."

I said, "Thanks," and went back to the troops.

We discussed this development as rationally as any bunch of drunks can discuss anything. The Shore Patrol had gone to alert other bars about the situation, so there was no pressure to leave right away. We were not happy. We still had leave papers in our pockets that didn't expire for another five and a half days, but we were supposed to be in Baguio, not Olongapo, and the leave papers wouldn't save us as long as we were there.

We decided to go to our rooms and get changed so we could go aboard ship. We finished our beers and, walking together, we headed for the hotel.

But, on the way, I had a thought: "Hey guys, if we were in Baguio, we wouldn't have to go back to the ship, would we?"

"No!"

Then we all lit up as the thought caught on. "Let's get our clothes and head for Baguio!"

"Where the hell is Baguio anyway?"

"I don't know, but I know where we can rent a big Jeepney to take us there."

"Let's do it!"

We were stopped by Shore Patrol twice on our way to the hotel. We told them that we were going for our uniforms, and they let us pass, but it was very obvious that we would have to be really careful when we got our clothes and headed for the Jeepney station.

We picked up our clothes and got back-alley directions to the Jeepney station from the desk clerk. We had a problem, however, because we had not planned to carry our uniforms anywhere, and we just didn't have any room in our bags. It came down to either we had to leave our uniforms or we had to leave our booze. So, with our impeccable logic intact, we made arrangements with the desk clerk to leave the less-valuable items—our uniforms—with him. We reasoned that we could easily pick them up on our return trip.

We started out carefully walking down the back street, making as little noise as six drunken sailors could make. We had agreed that, if we were stopped, we would split up and meet at the Jeepney station.

We had gone a couple of blocks when it happened: "Hey You guys! Stop! Where do you think you're going?"

I broke to the left at top speed, and the other guys took off in all different directions. The Shore Patrol broke into a run behind us, and darned if they didn't decide to chase me!

"Stop you!" they screamed.

Why in hell did they pick me to chase? I thought as I sped up.

I looked behind me, and I could see them. They were typical Shore Patrol, both first class petty officers and both a little paunchy. I hoped that meant that they were slower than me, and I redoubled my efforts. Then to my right, I saw a huge pig pen in back of a little Filipino home. It must have covered at least an acre, and the fence was attached to the house. It would take at least ten minutes to go around it.

The ooze looked impassible at first glance, but my experience on Montana ranches paid off. I knew that most of the pigpen would be rather shallow, with the deep parts being obvious because of the standing water on them. I could see dry spots here and there in the muck of this pigpen, so I took a chance. I vaulted the fence and dashed toward the other side, keeping to the more solid areas as much as possible. I had a fleeting regret for my beloved Hong Kong No-Squeak Boots as I plowed through the muck, but it paid off, big time.

I heard one of the Shore Patrol behind me say, "Fuck this. They don't pay me enough to go in there."

I was free!

I jogged the rest of the way to the Jeepney station, carrying my little overnight bag stuffed with shaving gear, a spare shirt, spare socks and underwear, and two almost-full bottles of precious Canadian Club Whiskey.

When I got to the Jeepney station, one of the guys was already there and was arranging for the Jeepney. The Filipino behind the counter wasn't going to lose the fare, so he hid us in a back room while we waited for the others. They showed up while I was out back, hosing off my No-Squeaks. Our only casualty was a young sailor named Tony, who had been bitten by a dog while he was running through someone's back yard. We cleaned him up and poured a goodly amount of whiskey over the wound. Then we all took a liberal internal dose just to make sure that we hadn't picked up any germs, and we were off!

The trip to Baguio was amazing. We went from the deep jungle around Olongapo to some of the most beautiful mountain country I had seen since I'd left Montana. The road through the mountains reminded me of Glacier Park's Going to the Sun Road except that it was narrower and not as well-maintained. We drank our way there. I have absolutely no idea how far it was or how long it took us, but we were all (including our Filipino driver) drunk and singing before we arrived.

The military had a beautiful recreation base in Baguio, with modern cottages, a nice restaurant, a club with nightly entertainment, and a golf course. This was where the Navy had envisioned that sailors would stay when they were on leave in the area. It was even fenced to keep out the riff-raff.

But my friends and I enjoyed the riff-raff more than we would ever enjoy the people that hid in this pseudo-American environment when they were in a tropical paradise. Plus, we figured we would be less easy to find in a civilian hotel. So we had our driver take us to a non-descript hotel on the other end of town. By then, the driver was our buddy, so we offered to rent him a room if he would stay and take us back. He declined the room, saying that he had relatives in town if he needed them, but he agreed to stay with us for the duration. When we stopped at the hotel, he promptly crawled in the back of his vehicle and went to sleep. We checked into the hotel and decided to sleep until noon and then meet up for breakfast.

We met up at noon, all a bit worse for the wear. But by the time we had breakfast and a couple of Screwdrivers, we were good to go again. We decided that we were easily the smartest bunch of sailors on the planet, but we tempered that with a bit of caution. We had no desire to be caught and sent to the ship before our leave was officially over, so we decided to keep our presence as low key as possible.

We walked out of the hotel and our Jeepney driver was there waiting for us. We climbed in and told him to take us to "the most remote bar in Baguio." Once there, we proceeded to carry on the party that had been so rudely interrupted the night before. It turned out that Baguio wasn't nearly as equipped for partying sailors as Olongapo had been, but by the time we'd been in the bar for a while, local girls started showing up. Before long, we were right back at it, dancing, singing, and having a ball.

I was particularly taken by a woman who would have been absolutely gorgeous except that she wore an eye-patch over her left eye and had a long scar across her forehead. She explained to me that she had lost her eye as a child when she was wounded by a Japanese bayonet. That made her a war hero to my sodden mind, and we stayed together for the duration. It didn't hurt our relationship that she had two other amazing attributes that were prominently displayed in her tight sweater.

Soon the group gained confidence and began to forget that we were semi-fugitives. The news of the deployed ships hadn't reached Baguio yet and no one appeared to care whether we were there or not. We ran into several Americans, mostly Air Force people who were there on leave. We figured that we had beaten the odds and the Shore Patrol, so we relaxed. We went out to a restaurant for dinner and then barhopped around town. We picked up other partiers as we went and soon had a crowd of about twenty Americans and at least as many Filipinas, plus our Jeepney driver, going bar to bar having a jovial and rowdy time of it.

This went on until the wee hours of the morning. Then, one by one, we faded out and went back to our hotel rooms. It had been a glorious party!

I had another nightmare that night in the quiet of the hotel room. This time, it was a faceless man and I was in a bunker;

trying to protect Mom and a bunch of kids. I was swinging a stick at him and yelling when my War Hero woke me.

I stammered, "I'm so sorry."

But somehow, she seemed to know what to do more than I did as she held me close and calmed my nerves. Her words really made an impression on me: "Jeff, be quiet. You don't be ashamed. Lots of us dream bad dreams. It comes from the war. I always dream of the rat face that stabbed my eye. I know that he's dead, but when I dream, he's still there. It's the war that's still there, inside us, when we dream."

I didn't want to tell her that I hadn't been in the war she was talking about, but her soothing voice and the memory of the dream, the faceless man, and Mom in the bunker, made me think; *Maybe I was in a war...just not the same one.*

But I was ignoring the War Hero, and that wasn't a good thing. Her large, soft, breasts were resting against my chest while she talked. They were a very calming influence on me—or maybe calming isn't quite the right word, but they certainly did distract me from all types of thought. I pulled her close, and soon I was able to get back to sleep, all thoughts of dreams and war far, far, behind me.

I was awakened by a horrendous noise at my door. I rolled over in protest and looked at my watch. It was 8:00 a.m.! I yelled at the door people to go away, and rolled over again, but they persisted and started hollering back, "Up and out, Trooper. Everyone has to go back to their bases. We are in a National Emergency Condition, and all leaves are cancelled!"

"Shit!" I mumbled under my breath, before yelling, "Okay. Give me a minute." I noticed out of the corner of my eye that my Filipina War Hero had slept in her eye patch. Probably just as well because I wasn't feeling too well anyway and that could have been a real shock to my system.

I got up, went to the door, and opened it. There was a Navy lieutenant—a pilot from the look of the Navy wings on his chest—and a second class boatswain's mate outside.

I said, "Give me a few minutes. I need to get cleaned up, and then I'll be with you."

"Okay. We'll roll out the rest of the rooms and wait in the lobby."

I closed the door and started for the bathroom.

Just then, the War Hero rolled over, with those magnificent mammary mountains flashing, and I decided that the pilot could wait a bit. I drained the rest of my Canadian Club in one long swallow. Then I took a few extra minutes to say good morning in an appropriate manner. Only after that did I begin getting cleaned up and ready for whatever awaited me downstairs.

I finally opened my door and started off for the lobby. But one of my friends, Tony, was in the hall. He had a half bottle of vodka with him and was slugging at it. He looked at me and said, "I paid good money for this. At least we can enjoy the trip down the mountain."

I agreed and proceeded to help him with his chores. When it was gone, we went downstairs and discovered that we were the last of the crowd to show up. But even though we had tried valiantly, we were far from being the drunkest people present.

There were about thirty of us in the lobby; people stationed at military bases all over the Philippines. The Lieutenant split us into two groups—one that was stationed in the vicinity of Subic Bay and another group that was stationed elsewhere in the Philippines. He then put the bos'n mate in charge of the "others," and he took control of the Subic Bay contingent.

After the bos'n left with his bedraggled crew, the Lieutenant explained to us that an airplane was waiting for us at Baguio Airport. He was going to walk us to the airport, which he said was "a couple of miles away." The waiting plane was to fly us to Cubi Point Naval Air Station, which was located near the Subic Bay Naval Base. Then we would be split up to return to our various commands.

The Lieutenant then told us to all put on our uniforms immediately. He was very adamant about it and almost totally lost his cool when he was informed that the six of us didn't have any uniforms with us. Since we didn't have uniforms, we offered to stay behind and catch up later, but he wasn't buying that. Finally, he decided that he would take us along, civvies and all.

While he was explaining the plan and resolving the uniform situation, the crew he was addressing was doing its best to do away with the booze that was left over from the night before. We had decided that, if we were going to go, we would make a party of it. By the time we left the hotel, virtually every one of us was legally intoxicated, to say the least.

That poor lieutenant! He was young and very earnest, but as a Navy pilot, he had no experience with managing the troops, particularly a bunch as rowdy as this one. He tried, but his job was worse than herding cats. Whenever we walked a while, one of us would sit down on the sidewalk and claim to need rest. In the meantime, others were sneaking into local establishments to get more booze. The two-mile walk took us over four hours. When we finally arrived at the airport, we were all totaled.

When I saw the plane, the magnitude of the situation suddenly hit me. I had never been in an airplane before! Now I was not only drunk, but I was also scared silly!

There were a group of Filipino policemen at the airport. The Lieutenant enlisted their help and between them, they took away all of our booze, got us lined up, and filed us into the airplane. It was a Navy plane, but I had no idea what kind because I had never even looked at a plane closely before. But it was big enough and soon we were all strapped down in its bowels, for better or worse.

I was in a window seat and had a nice view. I could see down the runway to its end. There were mountaintops and trees on both sides of the runway. I remember thinking that it was rather pretty there. I also remember thinking that the runway must be on a bit of a hill, because I couldn't see anything except blue sky beyond the end of the runway.

Soon the big engines were thundering and whining as they came up to speed. At the same time, my stomach was churning from too much booze and too little food. In addition, the fear of the unknown, flying in an airplane, was starting up deep inside me. Then the plane started moving and I calmed down. It was no worse than one of my old hot rods revving up during a drag race. I could handle this!

Then, startled, I yelled at the top of my voice, "Holy shit." The whole bottom had dropped out from under us.

Everyone was yelling, and Tony puked on his shoes. The damned plane had just driven off of a cliff! One minute we were on solid ground, drag-stripping it along, and the next minute, there was a tremendous drop…and then nothing!

We were flying, but I had never heard of such a takeoff. I had been looking out window when the grey asphalt under us had instantaneously disappeared and been replaced by a valley that was about a thousand feet lower down. It was too much for me. I fell back on my seat, closed my eyes, and did my best to keep the liquid that had been my breakfast from coming up.

It seemed like just a few minutes before we were landing at Cubi Point. As soon as we were down, we were escorted to the chief petty officer's working lounge beside the airstrip, where we were separated into groups. The sailors stationed locally were released to go back to their duty stations, but there were ten of us who were going to ships that were underway. The ten ship-sailors that were left in the lounge were going to be flown to the aircraft carrier, USS *Hancock*, from which we would be transferred to our ships. We were told to just stay in the lounge and wait for a couple of hours until the *Hancock's* mail plane came in. The mail plane was going to fly us to the ship.

I found a comfortable chair and was about to doze off when someone opened the refrigerator in the lounge and shouted, "We got beer!" There were two cases of Budweiser in the refrigerator. We didn't want to steal it, but it was too tempting to pass up in our present condition, so we took up a collection, left payment and a note in the refrigerator, and proceeded to get drunker.

By the time we had done away with the beer, the mail plane arrived, and an ensign came to get us. We were all merrily blitzed by that time. We loaded onto the little plane and strapped ourselves in. We were soon aloft, without the drama of the Baguio takeoff. Again, I had a window seat.

When we got close, the pilot told us where to look, and we could see the *Hancock* on the horizon. It was so tiny that it just looked like a speck on the water. I knew that other ships were with her, but they were too small to see until we got very close. I remember thinking that it must be really hard to land an airplane on that tiny target, but I had seen it happen many times from the

Cogswell when we were escorting *Hancock*, so I wasn't particularly worried. Hell, we were all too drunk to worry.

Then we made our approach. At the last minute, we were waved off for some reason, and I saw the *Hancock*'s superstructure flash by my window as the pilot gunned the plane's engines and we headed almost straight up. That scared the hell out of me! I had no comprehension of what the pilot meant by, "We've been waved off."

I remembered pulling a pilot out of the water after a botched carrier landing during our last WestPac cruise, and I was certain that we would be in the water soon ourselves. But then we leveled off and circled the carrier as we waited for permission to come in again. The pilot came on the speakers and explained what was happening, and I calmed down again. But that had been a terrifying few minutes.

We were again far up and aft of the carrier. It was tiny again, and then we made another approach and watched the carrier get larger and larger. I have to admit that I was a bit tensed up this time, but we landed uneventfully, with all of us flying forward violently into our seat belts as the plane caught the hook on the carrier's deck, and we came to an abrupt stop. We were a bunch of very happy campers when we got off that plane.

The carrier had a contingent of Marines aboard and they were placed in charge of us as soon as we deplaned. By now it was evening and none of us had eaten all day, so they took us straight to the mess decks, where we had supper. That was probably a smart move, since it also sobered us a bit. Then they escorted us to the Marine Quarters, where there were enough empty bunks for us. I had a few words with a Marine corporal who insisted on treating us like prisoners. He backed off, but he certainly didn't like us. He let us know that he considered us to be some kind of scum, if not prisoners, and we had better not leave the immediate area or he would have us thrown in the brig. We were too tired to care and we soon settled in for the night.

The plan was for us to be transferred to our ships first thing in the morning by highline. This would be another adventure, I was sure. The highline process is a method by which people or materials are transferred between two ships steaming alongside each other. The transfer is accomplished by stringing ropes between the ships, with crews on both ends keeping the ropes taut. People ride across in a cage with a seat in it as the crews pull the lines to drag the cage between ships. If the lines get slack, for any reason, the rider gets dunked at a speed of around twenty knots! It's a much more exiting ride than any theme park could possibly imagine!

Since there were six of us from the *Cogswell*, we were scheduled to be the first group transferred in the morning. So as soon as we had eaten, we showered and went to bed, knowing that we would be up very early to be high-lined between the ships. Since we were only aboard for the night, we didn't have lockers. We just piled our belongings on the floor beside our bunks.

At 5:00 a.m., we were awakened by the same Marine that had been such a hard-ass the night before. Apparently he had been on some type of night watch, because as soon as we were all up, he went to bed and was soon asleep in a bunk in our area. We were quiet and went about getting cleaned up and dressed. Suddenly, I realized that my beloved Hong Kong No-Squeak Boots were missing! Someone had stolen them from the stack of clothes beside my bed! I told my friends, and we searched the entire compartment looking for them. We made a bit of noise doing this, and the corporal woke long enough to yell at us, "Will you good-for-nothing asshole Swabbies shut the fuck up?"

Then he made a big mistake. He turned his back on us and went back to sleep.

I turned to my friends and told them, "Don't worry about the boots. I found something to wear." Then I bent over and took the corporal's shiny cordovan dress shoes out from under his bunk. They were a bit big, but they would do the job. We quietly gathered our gear, muffling our laughter, and headed for the mess decks for breakfast.

We had just eaten when the ship's speaker system came on and told us to go to the highline station. We did that and got there just in time to see the cage coming over to us from the *Cogswell*. We had agreed that I would go first, since I had a good reason to get off the *Hancock* as soon as possible. So I got into a lifejacket and stood by, waiting for the cage to be readied.

It dawned on me about that time that the lifejacket was a lot cleaner than the clothes I was wearing. They showed the wear of days of partying and the trip from Baguio to the *Hancock,* not to mention a sizeable group of stains left by pigpen mud. I was almost expecting to be put on report as soon as I came aboard the *Cogswell*. I was certainly not looking like a third class petty officer in my grubby civvies. Plus we didn't know for sure that our escape from Olongapo had not been reported by someone. We were worried, but we had decided to put on our best faces and try to bluff it through.

I got in the cage and sat down. The bos'n in charge of the highline station checked to make sure that the cage was secure and my safety belt was tight. Then he gave the signal and I was on my way! It was quite a ride, with the chair bouncing about thirty feet above the water as the crews heaved around on the lines. The salt spray whipped at my face, but it didn't bother me nearly as much as the sight of the white water churning below me as the two ships sped, side-by-side, across the ocean.

My back was to the *Cogswell,* and I was watching the *Hancock's* crew working the line that was feeding me across this canyon of raging waters when suddenly I saw the corporal! He was in his skivvy shorts and uniform shirt, with his corporal stripes showing, standing on the highline station waving his fist at me. He was obviously shouting something, but I couldn't hear anything. I gave him a cheerful wave and a big grin. He was so pissed that he was literally jumping up and down. It was truly a sight to behold.

I finally got to the *Cogswell* and climbed out of the cage. The ship's highline station was on the Foc'sle, and it was rocking pretty badly from the waves buffeting the ship. I have to admit that my legs were a bit shaky after that trip over the open water, so it was a bit hard to stand at first—but I was in one piece, and that was a very good thing.

Bos'n Cowell was in charge of the station, and he was preparing to send the cage back when I stopped him.

I said, "Just a second, Boats'. I have to make the Marines happy." I took off the now-salty cordovans and tied them to the inside of the cage. Then I gave Cowell a thumbs-up, and he sent the cage on its way back to *Hancock.*

I started to leave to go change clothes when the station phone-talker stopped me, saying "The Captain wants to see you on the bridge."

That was not good news. I looked up at the bridge above me and saw Captain Moore looking down from the bridge wing. He motioned at me to come up to where he was and I nodded. It took a few minutes to get there. I was a bit slow because I was in my stocking feet, and the ship's ladders were made of corrugated steel that dug into them, but I made it, and came to attention beside the Captain's chair.

He slowly looked me over, from head to toe. I must have been quite a sight, standing there shoeless in my bedraggled and semi-sodden civvies.

He said, "Where's your uniform, Noonan?"

"We lost them in the hassle of getting out of Baguio, Captain."

A long pause and then, "Okay. Now what's the story with the Marine's shoes?" The Captain had a set of binoculars around his neck, and he had obviously seen the half-dressed corporal jumping up and down at the *Hancock's* transfer station.

I said "Captain, they kept us in Marine quarters, under guard, last night. There was one Marine Corporal that was an absolute butthead to us. Then this morning, when I got up, my Hong Kong No-Squeaks were missing. One of the Marines had to have stolen them." I went on, "The butthead corporal was asleep when we left there this morning, so I borrowed his shoes in a kind of a trade."

The Captain's normally ruddy face took on a redder hue suddenly, and his lips compressed into a thin, bloodless, line across his face. To me, he looked mad as hell. He asked, "Why didn't you keep the shoes, if you were trading with the Marine?"

I replied, "Captain, the darned things didn't fit."

That did it. He exploded with such laughter as I had never before seen from an officer. He was doubled over in his chair when he gasped out, "You're dismissed, Noonan. Go below and get a uniform on."

Thus ended my great Baguio adventure.

CHAPTER SEVENTEEN

Bar Battles, Russian Ladies, & Binjo Ditches

It turned out that the Navy had sent far too many ships to the Laos area this time. There were ships everywhere. Within a day of my return from Baguio, the *Cogswell* and several other ships were detached and sent back to port. But this time, instead of going to Subic Bay, the ship pulled into Manila.

While I had been in Baguio, the Navy had approved the reenlistment applications for Fred and me. Our reenlistment was scheduled for the later that week, the day before we were getting underway from Manila.

Entering Manila Harbor was like a tour back in time. Historical artifacts, primarily from World War II, were everywhere. Ships from all over the world were in the port and it seemed like most of them were underway in a chaotic bustle that, more than once, threatened to run over us. Only a very alert Captain Moore on the bridge saved us as he carefully threaded our destroyer through the melee.

A group of us went ashore the first day in Manila, but we didn't particularly care for the town. It was a huge, bustling city, much as Hong Kong had been, but there was very little shopping and the few bars that we did find seemed somehow unfriendly after our experiences in Olongapo and Baguio. So we came back to the ship very early that evening.

The next day, some of us we signed up for a historical tour of Manila, which turned out to be a lot more interesting than I had anticipated. We saw everything from old Spanish churches to the POW camps where the Japanese had held our soldiers during the last big war. We learned a lot about World War II from our Filipino guide during that tour. In 1960, the Filipino population still had not forgiven the Japanese for some of the things that happened during that war. Our guide, who was an older lady, was not shy about her opinions. I had read books about the Bataan Death March and the return of MacArthur to the Philippines, so I enjoyed the tour very much.

A few days later, we reenlisted. Fred and I stood on the ship's quarterdeck in our dress white uniforms, with our right hands held high, as Captain Moore swore us in for another six years' service. I had only been in the Navy for twenty-seven months, but I knew that this was my future. This was just one more step in my escape plan.

The next morning, we got underway for Hong Kong. When we arrived, it looked exactly the same as it had the year before. The harbor was still bustling with everything from big freighters and junks to thousands of little bum-boats. The British police came aboard and gave us the same pitch as the previous year, and we caught what looked like the same water-taxi when we went ashore.

Once ashore, I made a bee-line for the Hong Kong No-Squeak Shoe Company. This time, I bought two pairs of the tailor-made boots. They were the most comfortable shoes that I had ever owned, and I was not taking a chance of losing them this time.

After I had the boots ordered, I went to the tailor that I had worked with last time and ordered a couple of pairs of slacks and some shirts. While I was doing this, I ran into some other sailors from the ship. We talked a bit and decided to go to the China Fleet Club (the British pub and restaurant for military personnel) for something to eat. We picked up a couple of other *Cogswell* sailors on the way. When we got there, the place was crowded with British and Australian Sailors from two ships that we'd seen in the bay. There were about ten Americans with us by now, all from the *Cogswell*, and we had a bit of trouble finding enough tables, but we finally settled in at two tables not too far from the door.

We ordered our food and, of course, beer for everyone. After we ate, we relaxed, had a couple more beers, and talked a bit with the Aussie sailors at the next table. We were getting along fine with the Australians, but for some reason, the British sailors were giving both the Americans and the Aussies a hard time. They threw a lot of cheap comments about how nice it was that their government built nice clubs like this and let people from "the Colonies" use them. It was a little intense, but I was proud of my friends. We just ignored the Brits and their comments. The Aussies were a bit more responsive, but I thought that they were rather restrained too, in spite of their reputation as brawlers.

Finally, we finished up and paid our bill, getting ready to leave. I stood up and turned to the table next to us and said a pleasant, "Goodbye" to the Aussies at the next table.

They seemed startled that we were leaving. One big petty officer looked up at me and said, "But the fun hasn't started yet, Mate!"

I didn't understand, so he said, "Wait a minute." He stood up, picked up his chair and threw it at a big table full of Brits. At the same time, he yelled at the top of his lungs, "Fuck the Bloody Queen and the fucking horse she rides on!"

The place erupted.

I found myself standing right next to a big *Cogswell* gunner's mate named Johnson. We got back-to back and started heading for the door. We yelled at the rest of the *Cogswell* crew, and they merged with us, forming a kind of phalanx headed for the outside. We took some tough hits. I got nailed with a solid smack in the gut, then a kick that almost dislocated my jaw, but I stayed upright and gave back as much as I could. Johnson caught a beer bottle on the top of his head, but he kept going with blood streaming down his face. There were a crowd of Brits guarding the door, but we bulled through them and finally made it to the outside world.

Fighting just wasn't in our plans for that day. The Brits and Aussies could kill each other if they wanted to, but this was not our idea of fun. As we got out into the air, we could hear sirens headed our way, so we sprinted down the street further into the Wanchai District, found a bar, and ducked into it. That got us clear of the fight area and the police who were descending on the pub, so we proceeded to fix our hurts and have another beer or two. It turned out that Johnson was the most injured of us, and after the tender ministrations of a Chinese bar-girl who washed and bandaged his wounds, he was up for a few more beers. All-in-all, we had been lucky. If we had been seated further towards the back of that place, we would have been in real trouble.

So obviously we had to celebrate our good luck.

I got back to the ship at about ten that evening and went immediately to sleep. When I woke, I had a horrible hangover and some very sore ribs. But, all told, I was in better shape than I had any right to be.

The story of the fight was all over the ship for the next few days. Johnson and I were the heroes of the story because we had led the phalanx to the door. We tried to tell everyone that we were just trying to escape, but it was no use. The crew apparently needed heroes, and we were temporarily elected. With the story of this fight added onto our recent escapade in Baguio, which the rumor mill had blown to incredible proportions, I was really getting a reputation on the ship. I was amazed when even my Department Head, Lieutenant Dun, stopped me to tell me that he had heard that I "had done the ship proud" during the fight. It was actually pretty embarrassing.

I had a few dollars in my pocket thanks to my reenlistment bonus, so I did one of the more prudent things I had done in a while: I took most of it to the ship's disbursing officer and had it locked away in the ship's safe. Then I took a bit of it and headed for town again. This time I ended up in Kowloon with Fred and a few other guys. We had a ball there. It seemed that the bars and bar girls were the same on the Communist side as they were on the "free" side of town—except everything was less expensive!

The police had warned us about Kowloon, though, when they came aboard ship the first day. They told us that, since Kowloon was on the mainland and was officially Communist Chinese territory, we would not be protected by the US or Hong Kong governments if we went there. They specifically warned us about the "White Russian" girls in Kowloon. They were, purportedly, often spies who were trying to find out anything that they could about us, our ships, and our missions through the use of "feminine wiles." Well, of course, many sailors went looking for the White Russians as soon as they got off the ship. I guess they were curious as to what constituted feminine wiles in such a free-loving port.

On our first night in Kowloon, we walked into a bar filled with White Russian women. Naturally, there were some sailors there, but the USA didn't have to worry about our group giving away any secrets to these wily females. They were uniformly uggggllllyyyy! Wiles or not, they were not having their way with us. We left there rapidly and found a bar with a much more comely, if Asian, staff. Maybe they were also spies, but we didn't know anything anyway, and I don't remember any of them ever asking us any questions other than, "Buy me a drink, Joe?" So we bought them drinks.

We stayed on the Kowloon side for the rest of the week, partying and raising heck. We never had any problem with anyone and never saw anyone that even resembled the dreaded Communist Secret Police.

When the *Cogswell* left Hong Kong, it headed back to the South China Sea and more endless days of patrolling off the coast of Laos. We spent over a month there before heading back to Subic Bay for more standby duty. We were inport almost a month this time, and I stayed fairly close to the ship. Olongapo had lost its allure for me.

Midway through this period, I received a letter from Mom. In it, she told me that she had had a heart attack and had been in the hospital in Missoula for several days, but by the time she wrote, and I received, the letter, the news was several months old. She was home again and had recovered, so there wasn't much I could do. I did call her from the base in Subic to make sure she was all right. She made light of it and talked about how it was a "wake-up call" that would get her to slim down a bit. I asked her if she had been fighting with Dad when it happened, but she wouldn't answer, so I knew that it was another beating-related incident.

There was nothing I could do about it from the Philippines, though, so I dropped it, and we had a short talk about the kids and life there in Montana. The conversation was frustrating, because it had to be relayed through a short-wave radio station. In those days, that was the only way to get a telephone call from anywhere in the Orient to the States.

We did one more turn in the South China Sea and a short stay in Subic after that. On April 6, 1961, we left Subic Bay for the last time on that cruise, enroute to Yokosuka.

We were welcomed at the Sakura Bar as if we were long-lost relatives. Mama-San and her girls made us feel as if we were the most special people alive. It was a great feeling. We spent a week in Yokosuka, most of it at the Sakura. It was a pleasant, but uneventful time.

We also did a lot of shopping at the Navy Exchange, since that was widely known to be the best place in the Orient to buy presents for the folks back home. Since Mom loved her tea, I bought her a really beautiful tea service. I knew it would be a treasure. I got other presents for the rest of the family and stashed them in my radar room aboard ship.

I was leaving the Sakura one evening, headed back to the ship, when I ran into a shipmate wandering down the street. He was a second class petty officer named James that I knew vaguely. He was obviously pretty drunk, so I took him under my wing and got a cab for both of us. It turned out that my good deed was a bit misdirected. As soon as James saw the cab driver, he started yelling at him.

Apparently James didn't like Japanese people, because he was using every racial slur he could think of. He offered to fight the poor cabbie and even tried to hit him. He was sitting in the back on the passenger side and I was behind the driver, so I was able to grab James's arm and deflect the blow, but the driver was very upset. He stopped the cab and tried to get us out, but I talked him into continuing and got James shut up for a while.

James started up again a few minutes later. He called that poor cabbie every derogatory thing he could think of. From the sound of it, one would have thought that James was fighting World War II all over again. The driver was an older Japanese man, so he could easily have been a soldier in the war. James obviously thought so, and he made it known that he intended to "beat the shit out of that Jap bastard as soon as this cab stops." I physically restrained him so that he couldn't hit anyone, and the cab driver kept us headed for the Fleet Landing.

Finally, the cab stopped. I could see Fleet Landing a few blocks from where we were, but this wasn't the normal cab stop. But I wasn't going to argue with the poor guy, so I paid him, and told James to get out.

He opened his door and stepped out. I heard him scream, "What the fuck?" and then I heard a loud splash.

By this time, I was out my door and standing on the street. The cab took off with its tires screaming. The driver was yelling "Fuck You, Asshore!" out the window as he took the next corner on two wheels.

I was so startled that I just stood there and watched the cab disappear. Then I turned around to look for James. I found him about four feet below the side of the road, setting in a Binjo ditch, with the dark waters swirling just under his chin.

The driver had pulled up to the edge of that ditch when he stopped. When James had slid out the door, he had been looking back at the driver, cursing him. He had not even seen the ditch until he slid into it. Now he was just sitting there with turds bouncing off his chin. He was absolutely stunned.

I couldn't help myself. I just started laughing. This was one World War II after-action-battle that I had to admit, the Japanese had won, and for once, the right was on their side. James heartily deserved what he had received.

James crawled out and sat down on the edge of the ditch mumbling something. The smell was absolutely unbelievable, and the muck was all over him, even in his hair. I couldn't get within ten feet of him—and probably wouldn't have, even if I were able.

I told him to stay put, and I went to Fleet Landing and told the Shore Patrol what had happened and where they could find him. Then I got in a water taxi and went back to the ship. I had absolutely no desire to wait and ride back with James, for obvious reasons.

I saw James the next day on the ship. He didn't remember the trip back to the ship, but he had no problems admitting that he had probably "bad-mouthed" the cabbie. He actually seemed proud of it! Apparently, after I had left, the Shore Patrol had retrieved him and made him strip off his clothes. Then they had dumped buckets of salt water from the bay over him, and, when he was cleaned off enough, they put him in a ship's boat, nude, and sent him back to the ship. At the quarterdeck, the OOD had put him on report for being out of uniform and using foul language to the OOD.

A few days later, he was taken to Captain's Mast, where he was reduced in rank to from second class to third class petty officer by Captain Moore. It couldn't have happened to a nicer guy!

We left Yokosuka and headed for Guam on our trip home. Just as we had done a year earlier, we refueled there and then overnighted in Pearl Harbor before finally heading for San

Diego. Arrival in San Diego, with the band playing and the dependents screaming as they waited on the pier, was a lonely time for a single sailor. I have to admit that I truly envied the other sailors who had loved ones waiting on that pier.

CHAPTER EIGHTEEN

Goodbye *Cogswell*

Shortly after we arrived in San Diego, I received my official orders to go to a Navy School (Fire Control Technician Class "B" School) at Great Lakes Naval Training Center. I had to be there by the end of July, so I didn't have long to wait. I was granted thirty days' leave enroute. When this was combined with the travel time that the Navy allowed me, I was going to have about forty-five days off before I had to report to Great Lakes.

I had saved my reenlistment money to buy a car, so I started looking for one as soon as my orders arrived. Because I was skeptical of San Diego's used car dealers, I tried to find my car by going to the base newspapers and the bulletin boards posted around the various Navy bases.

Finally, by word of mouth, I ran into my dream car: a 1954 Mercury convertible that another sailor had taken to Tijuana and had customized. He had leaded in all of the chrome strips, had the upholstery redone in crème-colored leather, put a new convertible top on it, and then had given it a multi-coat bronze lacquer paint job. It was beautiful! But it had a problem: he had blown the pistons out of the engine by running it without oil.

I saw an opportunity. With all of my Montana experience fixing up old junk cars, I didn't think that turning this one into a real car would be a problem.

I bought the car for very little money from the disgruntled owner. Then I took it to the base's automotive shop and ordered a new engine for it. For the next few weeks, I spent every off-hour working in the base auto shop, changing out that V-8 engine. I finished it about a week before my transfer date. I'll never forget the deep throaty rumble of that engine when it started up for the first time!

It had cost me a bit more than I had planned to spend, but I had enough money with me to get home, and I had been sending money home to the savings account for over a year now, so I was in pretty good shape financially.

I had mixed feelings about leaving *Cogswell*. She had been my home for almost three years and I would be leaving a lot of friends behind, but I was excited to think that I would be seeing my family again. It had been a very long time and I did miss them very much.

The hardest goodbyes were to Fred Ross and Bob Lawler. We had become very close. Little did I know that I would never again see Fred, and I wouldn't reunite with Bob for another forty years. I don't think that I could have handled that knowledge when I left them. They had been my family for the past few years, in a very real way.

On May 29, 1961, I put the *Cogswell* behind me, leaving some of the best people I had ever known in my wake.

I was twenty years old, I had a cool car, I had forty-five days free before I reported to school, and I had a lifetime ahead of me. I would miss my friends when I had time to think about them, but right then, I was living an adventure and loving it! Life was good.

I truly enjoyed that trip. It was really anxious to get home, so I took the fastest route, which was through Death Valley, Las Vegas, Salt Lake City, Southern Idaho and into Montana. A few hours later, I was pulling into St. Regis. I was home!

CHAPTER NINETEEN

Montana at Last!

I came over the last mountain crest and found myself looking down on the valley around the little town of St. Regis. It was a gorgeous sight, the wide valley with two silver rivers winding through it and the little town nestled beside them. It was just too much for me. My eyes started watering, and I had to pull over. I hadn't realized how much I missed this place!

After I pulled myself together, I drove through town toward home, passing the place where Joe had picked me up to go join the Navy almost three years earlier. I passed the school and saw people outside that I knew, but in my fancy convertible with California plates, no one took much notice as I passed.

I pulled into the driveway at my home and just sat there for a minute or so. It seemed like nothing had changed, either here or in the town. It was as if time had stood still while I was gone. I don't know what I had expected, but so much had changed for me that I had somehow assumed that everything here would have changed also. Somehow I was a little disappointed— though I was very excited to be home.

I got out of the car and had just started for the door when it opened and Mom came through it at what seemed like a dead run. I don't think that I ever saw her move faster, either before or after that day. She scooped me into a bear hug, and I didn't think she would ever let me go. Over her shoulder, I could see two teenage boys in the doorway; my brothers, Tim and Lyle.

They had big grins on their faces as they, too, headed for us at a trot.

If the town hadn't changed, my brothers certainly had. Tim was now fourteen, a blond, stocky guy that looked like a high school wrestler. Lyle, a year and a half younger, was tall and rangy, with dark hair much like my father's. He already easily topped Tim by four inches. But the biggest change was in their faces. They were maturing rapidly. I guess the Noonan household had a way of making all of us grow up fast.

Mom was looking good and she had lost a lot of weight. I had been worried about her heart attack, but it didn't seem to be a problem. When I tried to talk about it, she just ridiculed it, saying that it was probably just a huge gas pain because she was feeling great now. It obviously wasn't slowing her down, so I quit worrying.

That evening passed in a blur. Mom put on a big hamburger barbeque. Kathy came home from work and told me about everything that was going on with the other people in our age-group. The younger kids seemed to just sit there, enthralled. Tim wanted to know everything about the Navy and my life, while Lyle, Eleanor, Jim, and Dan were content to listen to us. Patty even seemed happy to see me. I really believe that she recognized me, but in all honesty, it was hard to tell.

After dinner, I had to take the kids for a ride in the convertible. That was a really big deal as they rode around town, yelling proudly at anyone they knew along the way.

Dad didn't come home until about ten that evening. We were all in the living room talking. He was drunk and he just walked through us without any comment. I don't think he even saw us. Tim and I shared a look that I never forgot. It was becoming apparent to me that Tim and I thought a lot alike. Neither of us had much respect for the empty hulk of a man that our father had become.

I found out later that night that Tim had taken over the job of maintaining the bunkers that I had dug so long ago. He had closed one and filled it in when he thought Dad was getting too close to finding it. A second one had always had rainwater problems, and it hadn't been used much, but the one that we had always used the most was still functional and available.

After Dad's arrival, Kathy and I took the convertible and went downtown looking for friends. I reunited with a lot of old friends and we sat in the local café drinking Cokes and gabbing until the wee hours. Even that hadn't changed.

The next day was Saturday, and, when I got up, Dad and Mom were in the kitchen. Dad was now sober and looking a lot worse for the wear, but he seemed glad enough to see me. Then he said, "I have something that I have to tell you."

I had a sinking feeling, but I said, "What's that?"

He had a strange look on his face as he said, "I spent your money."

I just looked at him, and he continued, "I came home a couple of weeks ago and your mother was looking at some bank deposit slips, so I asked her what they were. She told me that it was your savings, but I didn't believe her."

Tim interrupted with, "He was so drunk that he couldn't see, and when he saw that Mom had money, he beat the shit out of all of us, especially Mom!"

He and Dad were glaring at each other, and I knew there was no love between them. But Tim stood his ground and went on,

"He forced her to sign a check for all of the money in the account, and we never hardly saw him again until last night."

I looked at Dad and asked, "Is this true?"

He was slumped down on the chair and seemed to get smaller as I looked at him. He said, "Yes."

I turned to Mom and asked, "Is there anything left?"

"Only the last allotment that came in after he took all the other money," was her answer.

"Dad, do you have any of it left?"

"Naw, it all went." Then he actually looked at me and grinned, "No big thing. You swabbies don't work for it anyway. Everyone knows that the Navy's just one big welfare program!"

I thought for a minute. I wanted to smash that grin off his face, but that wouldn't get me anywhere, and it might make things worse for Mom later, so I held myself together. In honesty, I had realized that the loss of some of the money could be a possibility. I had thought that maybe Mom would have to take some of the money to survive, so I half-way expected to be short, but I had never considered that Dad would get his hands on it. Apparently, things had gone even further downhill since I had been gone.

"Dad, do you still work at the Diamond Match lumber mill?" I said.

"Yeah, but I can't get any money from them. They're strict about no advances."

I then said, "Okay, but I am here for the next month or so and I don't have enough money to get to my next duty station. So I need a job. Can you get me a job in the mill?"

"I probably could, but you couldn't do the job. Sawmill work is for real men, and you couldn't hack it."

I blew up then and called him a sneak thief and a wife beater, among other things. I told him that I was going to

Superior (where the mill was located) on Monday morning and I expected him to have made some contacts for me. I told him that I could do any job that a miserable drunk like him could do, and if he couldn't pay me what he owed me, he had better arrange for me to get work.

At one point in my tirade, he got red in the face and started to get up from his chair, glowering at me. But Tim and Lyle, who had both been watching from across the room, stepped forward and stood at my side.

Tim said, "Not this time. There's three of us here now."

Dad glared at us, but he was sober, so he sat back down. He agreed to talk to the sawmill manager first thing Monday. I told him that I would be at the mill office at 10:00 a.m. on Monday. Then I left the house.

I was really pissed this time. Over that vacation, Dad finally cut his last bond with me. I just couldn't imagine anyone so cavalierly spending someone else's money! And he didn't even have the decency to say that he was sorry.

I checked my money and discovered that I was better off . than I had thought. I had some cash on me and the recent allotment was still in the bank. Plus, I would receive another allotment check the day before I had to leave for Great Lakes, so I relaxed a bit. I was still short if I wanted to have any fun while I was home, but I would survive.

I was a bit lost when I went out to visit my friends. Joe was still in the Navy. My other high school cronies—Dale, Whitey, and Ray—had all joined the Air Force, and Dave Bennett had moved away, so there weren't a lot of people my age around. I went down to the truck stop, ordered a hamburger, and sat there thinking about the next month and trying to decide what to do. I was about ready to just leave and go to Great Lakes early. The past twenty-four hours had just reminded me of all the reasons why I had left in the first place.

Then an old friend, Teddy, who was about a year younger than me, walked into the café and we started talking. He was bringing me up to speed on all of the people in town and what had been happening in the area when my old friend, Sue, came in with her little girl in tow. She gave me a big hug and started blurting about the reasons she had sent me that "Dear John" letter when I was in Boot Camp. I stopped her and told her that it was old news now, and she didn't have to explain. The three of us got a table and talked for a couple of hours.

It turned out that Sue was living in Idaho, about fifty miles west of St. Regis. She had come home to visit, but was supposed to go back on Sunday because she had to work on Monday. She had a steady boyfriend in Idaho, so any thoughts that I had in that direction were quickly quashed. But we were still friends and we talked for a long time.

Then Teddy popped up and told me that he had a girlfriend in a place called Kellogg, Idaho, almost where Sue lived. He said that he could get me a blind date over there if I wanted to drive over with him.

That sounded good to me, so I waited while he made a call and set it up. While we were waiting for him to make the call, Sue decided to ride over with us so we could talk some more.

Teddy came back with a triumphant grin on his face and announced that he had come through: "We have a Drive-In Movie date for tonight. Your date is a real beauty! But I had to promise that, if we go out with them, we would go to church with them tomorrow morning. We can stay tonight at my girlfriend's parents' house—on the couches."

I was a little leery, but any date was better than no date, so we were soon on our way to Idaho.

166

We had a great ride over Lookout Pass into Idaho. Sue's daughter was a nice kid, and the four of us had a good time on the trip over. I dropped Sue and her daughter at their home and went on to the blind date with Teddy.

I was really appalled at Northern Idaho when I got there. It was a true environmental disaster in those days. The smoke from the ore smelters had killed all the vegetation, leaving mountainsides that were bare dirt with dead gray sticks where the trees had once been. The rivers and creeks were brown and thick with sludge from the mines. All of Northern Idaho looked like someone's idea of a barren alien landscape in a horror movie. Teddy, Sue, and I talked about it on the ride over, but Teddy warned me to not mention it when we were on our date. Apparently, the people who lived in this disaster preferred not to see it for what it was.

On the way to the blind date's house, Teddy asked if I had any condoms. When I said, "No," he directed us to a local drug store where (very bashfully, on my part) we purchased the required items. Then Ted allowed us to continue to his date's home.

Teddy was right about at least one thing. My blind date turned out to be gorgeous. She was as tall as I was (5'10"), blond, and busty. Her name was Alice, and she was really excited to be dating a "real sailor." I don't think the bronze convertible with leather seats hurt my chances either. After we were introduced all around, which included meeting the parents, we headed out. We went to the Miner's Hat Drive-In Restaurant, had burgers for dinner, and then drove around looking at the town until it was time for the drive-in theater to open.

We drove into the movie area and found a parking spot with a speaker. I stopped the car, turned off the key, and was immediately attacked in the best possible way. I was astounded at how uninhibited these Idaho girls were. We necked for a while, and I was thoroughly respectful with Alice. I didn't want to mess up a good deal by being too forward.

Finally, she said, "Jeff, check out Teddy and Doris." So I peeked over the back of the front seat and saw Teddy lying down on the back seat with Doris astraddle of him. Her shirt and bra were off, and her abundant bosom was bouncing madly as she rode Teddy for all he was worth.

This was all the encouragement that I needed, and soon I was in the saddle myself.

But shortly thereafter, I was interrupted by Doris, in the back seat. She was yelling "Do it, Teddy! Harder, Teddy! Please, harder!"

Alice and I had to muffle our laughter, but we soon got busy again.

After a while, we all composed ourselves, and I went for popcorn and some drinks. We ate and gabbed and then got busy again. Those girls had absolutely no inhibitions. It was definitely a double feature movie, in more ways than one.

I was a little leery about going to Doris's home to sleep, but the girls told us to relax. "We're good girls. No one will give you any problems if you're with us."

I was still a bit apprehensive, but it turned out, the girls were right.

The next morning, we got up and Doris's mother cooked us a really nice breakfast, while her Dad regaled me with stories about his time in the service during "The Big War." All was well.

Teddy, Doris, and I left a few minutes early for church. We picked up Alice at her home, as planned the night before. The girls were both prim and proper in their Sunday best, and we proudly escorted them into the church. It was my first time in a church in several years, so I held back a bit and followed Teddy's lead. It was a church denomination that I wasn't familiar with—one of those groups that Dad had always called "Holy Rollers."

We sat in a pew about half-way to the front of the church, with the girls seated beside Doris's parents, Teddy beside them and me beside him in the aisle seat. Soon the preacher came in and started his sermon. It was fire and brimstone, the like of which I had never heard before. I listened, fascinated. It went on for what seemed like hours, and I was really fidgeting in my seat when I started to notice people rising to stand and chant, swaying from side to side, bowing low, and then stretching toward the heavens...all the while chanting and mumbling. It got louder and louder. I was astounded. I had heard of this kind of church service, but I had never before witnessed anything like it.

Then Doris and Alice joined the others, standing and chanting. I could only understand part of what they were wailing, but it seemed to be a cry to Jesus to save them because they were sinners and needed salvation. Then Doris stretched to the sky, and her blouse popped partially open. Her bra came into view and all I could think about were her boobs bouncing wildly as she had ridden Teddy the night before.

I couldn't help myself—it was just too much to bear: last night, she had worshiped at the font of Teddy and had screamed even louder than she was today. Except then the words had been different.

I saw that Teddy was transfixed by the sight also, so I leaned over and whispered in his ear, "Do it, Teddy! Harder, Teddy! Please, harder!" Teddy erupted with laughter. He was laughing so hard that he choked and was coughing, gagging, and laughing all at once.

It was too much for me to handle and I went into peals of laughter. I was literally doubled over on the church pew, roaring!

The worship service came to a screaming halt. The preacher told someone to escort us to the doors, but we beat him to it and stumbled out the doors still doubled over, laughing uncontrollably.

We didn't wait for anyone else to leave the church. We headed for Montana. I pretty much laughed all the way home, but Teddy was a bit more reserved. He saw a good thing coming to an end for him and, while it really was funny, he schemed about how to get back in good graces.

I never went back to see anyone in Kellogg, but Teddy did. He was finally forgiven when he explained that "that uncouth sailor with had said something too funny to resist." He went out with Doris for several more months before they drifted apart.

Unfortunately, or maybe fortunately, "the uncouth sailor" wasn't welcome there any longer, so I stayed in Montana.

I went home early that night. I was planning to go to the lumber mill in the morning, and I wanted to be ready for whatever happened.

The next morning I was up early, but I held off on going to the mill because I wanted to let Dad do whatever he decided to that day. I had not talked to him since our blowout on Friday evening, so I had no idea if he would do as he had promised.

I stopped in the General Store and bought some heavy work gloves and then I drove to Superior and on to the Diamond Match Sawmill where Dad worked. I got there at ten sharp, went to the front office, and introduced myself to the lady at the front desk.

She said, "Oh yes, we were expecting you," asked me to take a seat, and went to get the manager.

When the manager came out, he got right to the point. He said, "Your Dad was in here this morning and explained what you need. You must be just like him if you've already blown your money and can't get to your next Duty Station. But he works hard, and he says you do too, so I'll give you a chance. But I'm only doing this because you're in the service and need help. I'm going to give you one of the shittiest jobs in this mill. If you can handle it, you can stay until you have to leave, but if we find you goofing off, even for a minute, that will be the end of you. Do you want it?"

"Yes Sir." I had a job, and that was all that mattered. Dad had obviously lied about the reason that I needed the job, but I could accept that. He had to live with these people and I didn't.

The manager turned me over to a foreman that I knew by reputation. He was a mill foreman during the week and a preacher on the weekend. So, keeping in mind my faux pas at the Idaho church, I was respectful and didn't even curse a little bit around him. He had me fill in all of the standard employment paperwork before taking me to the mill site.

Much of the mill worked on a kind of an assembly line. The logs were sent down one conveyor to the big stationary saws. Then the green, wet, slabs of lumber were cut from the logs and dropped onto another conveyor along with big chunks of waste wood and bark. After that, it was routed to another saw that trimmed the sides off the slabs, producing identifiable lumber. The lumber and waste, still together on a conveyor, were then sent directly to the station where I worked. As the lumber and chunks of wood went by me at full speed, it was my job to grab the waste wood from both sides of the new board and hurl it onto another conveyor that transported it off for disposal. This process of separating the waste from the good boards was known in the sawmill world as "picking stickers on the green chain." That was my new job.

For the remainder of the morning, the foreman had me work under the supervision of a big guy who had been doing the work before me. Then at noon, the big guy was sent to another job, and I became the Diamond Match sticker-picker.

At first, I didn't think it would be too bad a job. It paid $2.25 per hour, and that was good money from my perspective. Initially, the "stickers" didn't seem to be a problem. But they sure came fast. I was moving continuously, trying to keep up with the conveyor. A couple of times, I got overwhelmed that first day and the conveyor had to be stopped while I caught up. But by the first evening, I had it under control. The only real problems came when a big knot in the waste wood would require both hands and all of my strength to get it up and over to the other conveyor. But I got it done.

It was a tremendous relief when the evening whistle blew, announcing the end of my first shift. The continuous motion and the lifting of the waste wood had overtaxed every muscle in my arms and back, but I wasn't about to admit that to anyone. I walked out to where I had left my car and drove home. Hardly anyone had said a word to me all day, but I figured that was normal, because my job was on a station surrounded by conveyors with no one else in the immediate vicinity. I had seen Dad in the distance when we took a ten-minute break halfway through the afternoon, but he had ignored me, so I had said nothing to him.

I went home and let Mom cluck and worry over me for a little while, but I was determined to keep my cool, no matter how much my body ached. I cleaned up a bit and was leaving to go downtown when Dad came home. I thanked him for talking to the manager for me and didn't bring up what the manager had said about my reasons for working. He then surprised me by telling me that we should carpool to work starting the next day. I said "Okay," and then went on downtown.

The next morning, Dad was quiet on the ride to work. We had agreed to alternate cars and he was driving that day. He did ask me how I was feeling, and I lied and told him that I was fine. In fact, I was hurting so bad that I wasn't sure if I could do the job that day, but I was not about to tell him that.

It was actually better that day than I had expected. I was in agony for the first few minutes when the conveyor started, but as the day wore on, my body loosened up and I was able to keep it going. I noticed Dad and a couple of his cronies watching me from a distance, off and on, all day. Again, no one said much to me, but I did notice a bit of a thaw when we broke for lunch. I had bought some lunch meat and bread the night before and Mom had fixed a lunch for me, so I ate with the other workers and listened to the banter between them. I knew a few of them slightly from years past, but they were all a lot older than me. Their talk was mostly about the local bars and the women they were chasing, so, even if they had included me, I didn't think that I'd have much to contribute to their conversation.

When the day was over, I got in the car with Dad. He was much more talkative now. He told me that the foreman had told him that I was doing a good job. He said, "I didn't think you could do it, but you fooled me. You must be a lot tougher than you look."

I didn't say anything. Then, about a quarter of the way home, he pulled the car over in a wooded area. I thought that he had to pee, which would have been acceptable in that location and time period. But instead he went to a brush pile, reached under it, and pulled out a half-gallon of port wine. He took a couple of huge draws on the bottle, put it back and got back in the car. "You didn't want any, did you?" he asked.

I said, "No," and we proceeded on down the road.

A few miles further, he pulled over and did the same thing all over again. He repeated this twice more before he got home.

I got cleaned up and went downtown to hang out with my friends.

The next morning, we started out in my car. When we got to the place where he had stopped last the night before, he insisted that I stop the car, so I did. He then went through the same four stops that we had done on the way home. He had to have been drunk before we got to work, but it never showed.

I did my job that day, and we went through the same ritual on the way home.

This went on for a week or so, with me getting stronger and more able to do the job every day. After a week, I was handling the job as if I had been doing it my whole life, and the other mill workers were much friendlier. One of them told me that, before I had started work, Dad had told them not to expect much from me, so they had all kept their distance on purpose for the first few days. But since it looked like I was "hacking it," as they phrased it, they had gradually put aside Dad's words and begun judging me as just another new hire. I was becoming accepted.

On the way to work one morning, Dad had lingered a little longer than usual in his wine spots. I was really worried about him when he left me to go to his lumber grading station. I was right to worry.

When we stopped for our mid-morning break, the Foreman was waiting for me. He said, "Your father fell down the stairs this morning. We took him to the hospital, and they gave him some stitches and put him to bed. He asked me to tell you to pick him up at the hospital when you get off work."

I said, "Okay," and the foreman left.

The guys then told me that there was a lot more to the story than just a little fall. Dad had apparently been belligerent and obviously "staggering around" after he fell. The sawmill manager had been there, and he'd given Dad a warning before sending him to the hospital. If there was one more problem, of any type, Dad would be fired. The only thing that saved him this time, according to the other workers, was the fact that the mill didn't have any choice. They didn't have another certified lumber grader available right then, and the certification was important to their operation.

I picked Dad up at the hospital that evening. He was surly and didn't even try to explain himself. As usual, he directed me to stop at the first brush pile, just outside the Superior city limits.

I stopped, but I told him to wait in the car while I got the jug. He waited and I walked over to the brush pile, picked up the bottle, and held it high over my head so he could see it clearly. Then I threw it onto a big boulder and smashed it.

Dad screamed at me, "You Sonofabitch!"

I climbed back into the car and faced him, saying "Are you so far gone that you can't see what this is going to do to you? Your job is the only thing you still have, because this crap has ruined every other part of your life; and you're going to lose it if you don't quit drinking. At a minimum, you should quit in the mornings so that you can at least pretend that you still are doing a job. You need to keep bringing home a paycheck to support your family!" I was pissed, but I knew that I was not doing any good. He was too far gone.

I stopped three more times on that ride and smashed three more wine bottles.

Dad didn't say a word until I stopped the car at home. Then he said, "From now on, you take your car, and I'll take mine."

I said "That's fine with me," and we went our separate ways.

When I was a youngster, Mom and I had often had long conversations about life and, usually, what life would hold for me later on. This night we restarted the tradition, but this time we talked about her life and her future. I stayed home, and, when things were quiet after the little ones had gone to bed, we started talking. It went on for hours. I told her that I was very worried about her and the kids and I told her what had transpired with Dad at work.

She wasn't surprised at all. She had been hearing similar stories for years. She even told me that she could not remember the last time she had seen Dad without smelling wine on him.

I told Mom that I was leaving the allotment in place. She thanked me, but asked me to drop the additional part that I had been sending for savings. She also told me that she would not allow me to continue sending money to her if I ever got married. "At that point, you have to do for your family, and I won't have this mess be your responsibility. You deserve some happiness in your life."

Of course, I protested that I was plenty happy anyway and all of that. But she was adamant on this point.

Then we talked about Patty and the fact that Mom couldn't get out of the home to work as long as Patty was home. No one in town would babysit Patty. She needed specialized care and people were afraid to try taking care of her. Mom had looked into putting Patty in a state home, but she didn't want to do it. She told me, "Jeff, I'm able to squeeze by right now with the help I get from Ida and the other grocers. But if it gets to the point that I can't take care of the other kids, I'll have to put Patty in a home and hope for the best. I don't want that, but I just don't know how long I can hold out. Frankly, it all depends on how long it is before Dad loses his income—and we all know that's going to happen eventually."

Mom was in a really tough place in those days.

The next night, I went down to the truck stop and was in the café, talking to the owner of the garage next door, when one of my coworkers came in. He came over and talked for a few minutes, and then he said, "Why don't you come with me. I'm going to meet some of the guys from work at the Stag Bar."

I said, "I'd love to, but I'm not twenty-one yet."

"That's bullshit, this is still Montana!" he said. "If you're old enough to get shot at, you're certainly old enough to have a drink." I went with him and, sure enough, no one even asked for an ID, even though I had known Florence, the lady that owned the bar, for years. She just wanted to know all about the Navy and pumped me to tell her all about the places I had been and the sights I had seen. After a couple of drinks, I told them the story of my great Baguio adventure. After that, I was one of the in-crowd at that bar. *Thank God!* I had really started hating the downtown teenager scene. I had outgrown it.

177

I only stayed for an hour or so. I had to work the next day and I didn't want to even think about picking stickers with a hangover.

The next morning, I went to work by myself, but I ran into Dad when I got to work. He was walking straight and was obviously sober. I just wondered how long it would last.

The rest of my time at home was uneventful. I would go to work in the morning and come home at night. I spent the evenings at the Stag Bar, shooting the breeze and relaxing. Some nights, I didn't even drink. I didn't care for beer, and, unless there was a big party, a lady to chase, or something else happening, I just didn't bother drinking. I was just as happy with a glass of 7-Up, to tell the truth. I was also very determined that I was never going to end up like my father. I kept thinking about that during those days, and its been in the back of my mind continuously since then.

On the weekends, I tried to do things with the family as much as possible. Kathy, Tim, and I went swimming in the river several times. A few times, we took the smaller kids with us. Danny, Jim, and Eleanor seemed to enjoy these trips, and being with their big brother and sister. Only Lyle didn't seem to really be interested in hanging out with us. He had his own friends and didn't seem to want to be with the family. Of course, Patty couldn't join us, although somehow she always seemed to show up in the same room with us whenever we were home.

Kathy and I went joyriding with some of her friends a few times, and we went to the movie in Superior regularly. I hardly ever saw Dad, except at work. All in all, it was a relatively quiet, nice, vacation with a lot of family bonding.

The time to leave came around, and Mom held a big barbeque the night before I left. The family was almost all there. Dad never showed, but the rest of us had a grand time, joking and having fun with each other. I had quit my job the day before and had been invited to come back and work there "anytime that you want to," by both the foreman and the sawmill manager, so I was pretty proud of myself.

I got a good night's sleep and was out of there early the next morning.

CHAPTER TWENTY

Great Lakes

I remember that trip, from Western Montana to the Great Lakes Naval Station as being one of the really pleasant times in my life. There was no interstate in those days, so all of my driving was on winding two-lane highways. I cruised across the states with the top mostly down and the warm breeze blowing around me. I had been home and everything there was as well as it could be. And, thanks to my sticker-picking job, I had plenty of money for the trip. I stopped every night and got a motel room. It was pleasant. Then the part of the trip that I remember best happened.

I was driving across the hills of South Dakota, almost to the Minnesota border, when I spotted a girl on a hillside above the road ahead of me. It was one of those classic pictures, with the girl in a long, flowing dress, walking along the hillside. The dress and her hair were blowing behind her in the breeze as she walked in my direction. She must have seen me looking, because she waved at me, and I waved back. I couldn't help myself. I had passed her, so I stopped the car and backed up until I was a few yards below and ahead of her. I got out and walked over to the fence and waited for her to come to me. When she got there, I just looked at her and said, "Kiss me, please?"

She smiled and leaned over the fence and gave me a very tender little kiss on the lips. I backed up and looked at her.

I said, "This is magic. I'll never forget this."

Still smiling, she replied; "I don't think that I will either."

I got back in the convertible, waved, and drove on. I never forgot that sweet moment.

I often wonder what happened to the beautiful girl in that long, flowered dress.

Unfortunately, the magic had to end. Eventually, I arrived at the Great Lakes Naval Station, where I checked in a day early. I rapidly became inundated with the day-to-day make-work projects typical of any military base.

I received my class schedule as soon as I arrived. Much to my chagrin, it said that the first eight weeks of my school were totally devoted to mathematics! In eight weeks, going to school forty hours a week, we were scheduled to go from something called "Mathematics for Electronics" through Algebra and Trigonometry with the eighth week being totally devoted to Differential Calculus. This was foreign territory to me. I had not had a single math class in over nine years. Anything past eighth-grade arithmetic was totally new, and very scary, territory.

If I made it through this school successfully, I would be promoted to second class petty officer (E-5) and would be sent on to another school. But if I didn't pass, I would be going back to the Fleet, and the possibility of a Navy career would be doubtful. I had to get this done if I was going to make that escape that I'd planned for so long.

If I could make it through the eight weeks of math, the next twenty-eight weeks was going to concentrate on advanced electronic theory. That part didn't scare me. But I had to get through the first eight weeks, and that was going to be pure hell!

As I expected, when the school started, I was immediately overwhelmed. They gave us a test to see where we were in mathematics, and my results were abysmal. The instructor took me and two other guys aside after the test and assigned us to a remedial night school that was being held for extreme cases like us. That meant that I would be going to regular school for eight hours during the day, and then I would come back for three more hours in the evenings, plus eight more hours each Saturday. All in mathematics!

That first eight weeks was as close to purgatory as anything that I had ever known. Day by horrible day, night by agonizing night, I worked. With painful steadiness, we moved through basic arithmetic, advanced mathematics, algebra, trigonometry, and finally, calculus. Somehow I made it through the eight weeks. I studied every day and never left the base, even on Sundays. My final grade going through this segment of the school was 68 percent. A passing grade was anything above 67.5 percent. The other two guys that the instructor had singled out had flunked out and had been sent back to the Fleet. Three others in my class (of seventeen people total) had been sent back to repeat the segment. But somehow, I had made it through.

As soon as I completed the math phase of the school, and we moved on to electronics, I was good. Somehow all of the electronics theory made sense to me, where math never had. I went back to an eight-hour day, and my grades were in the top of my class. I even worked three nights a week as a pin-setter in the base bowling alley to put some money aside. Life became reasonable again.

Interestingly enough, I never used any of the advanced mathematics, in any way, through the remainder of the school. Nor have I ever used it since then.

Because my entire life had been wrapped up in the school, I had not gotten to know any of my fellow students beyond a simple "Good morning." Initially, my fellow night-school students and I were a bit ostracized, since we were known to be the dummies that would end up going back to the Fleet. When I broke the mold and didn't get shipped out, it took a while for people to warm up to me, so I didn't have any real friends when it came time to celebrate my twenty-first birthday.

I had a long weekend free when my birthday rolled around, so I decided to just take off and go north into Wisconsin for the weekend. I had really enjoyed my trip across country, so I figured that I'd just get on the road and celebrate wherever I happened to stop for the night.

I made it to Madison, the home to the University of Wisconsin, that day. After driving around town for a few minutes, I decided that this was as good a place as any for a birthday bash. It turned out that it was a good choice. I don't remember a lot about the evening, but I woke up (fully dressed) under a blanket on the floor in a sorority house dorm room, with a (also fully-dressed) coed on each side of me. It was warm and cuddly, but my left arm was asleep with one of the ladies' heads resting on it; the other lady had flung her leg over my bladder, and that was fast becoming a problem. I have absolutely no idea how I got there, but it must have been a lot of fun.

The girls snuck me out without setting off any alarms, and I went back to my motel and slept for several more hours before heading back to the base.

All in all, I considered my twenty-first birthday to be a rousing success.

A few weeks after my birthday, my mother sent me the address of an aunt and uncle who were living in the Chicago area. Aunt Mary, my dad's sister, was married to my Uncle

Wayne. At that time, they had six children, ranging in age from two to twelve. Mom told me that Uncle Wayne was an Army colonel, so I was a bit intimidated, but I decided to go see them anyway.

I couldn't remember ever meeting Aunt Mary or any of her family before. I knew that she had joined the WACs during World War II as an Army nurse and had married Wayne shortly after the war. But that was everything that I knew about them. I did remember that Aunt Ruth, in San Francisco, had talked to me about Mary and their childhood, but those memories were vague and fading fast, so my visit was really a blind one.

Aunt Mary, Uncle Wayne, and their family turned out to be wonderful. I stayed with them for the weekend, and they treated me as if I were a long-lost family hero. I never saw Wayne in uniform, and I was in civvies, so the difference in our ranks didn't enter into anything. The fact that they were a career military family was very interesting to me, and I did get a lot of encouraging advice from them. They were totally supportive of my plans to make the Navy a career. In fact, I got the impression that anything that I decided to do that would keep me away from my dad was fine with them. I was never told the specific reason, but Mary didn't seem to have anything good to say about her brother. She didn't badmouth him. She just clammed up and had a tight look on her face whenever his name came up. But, even with that, I had a great time with them that weekend, mostly talking about my grandparents, about whom I knew nothing, and military life.

School was going well, but it had become boring. Now that I was able to have a bit of free time, I began to make some friends. Soon there were five of us who went places on the weekends and had a good time together. We were all classmates, and we ranged in age from me, at twenty-one, to a really nice guy named Roy who was in his mid-thirties. Only I and one other guy, Bob, were third class petty officers. Roy was a first class (E-6), and the others were all second class.

One of my new friends, Mike, was from Seattle and he was making plans to drive home for Christmas, so I signed on to ride with him as far as St. Regis. He found three other guys who would share in the cost and who he would drop off in Idaho and Washington, and we had a plan. We all put in for leave during the school's shutdown period from December 20th until January 3, and it was approved. I was going home for Christmas for the first time in three years! I think that I was more excited by this than I had been even about the forty-five day leave that I had just completed.

When the leave period started, we got in Mike's car and drove straight through; taking turns behind the wheel and catnapping in the back seat. We made good time, and I was home on the afternoon of the 22nd. Mike and the guys dropped me at home and took off immediately.

CHAPTER TWENTY-ONE

Home for Christmas

Nothing much had changed at home since I had gone away the previous July. Mom was really interested in my Navy school, so I spent some time telling her all about it. She had a big grin when I told her about the hell that I had gone through over the mathematics. She couldn't resist a big, "I told you that not going to high school would catch up with you!"

I realized then that I had not told her about the deck force and the hell that I had lived through for months because of my lack of a diploma. So we spent most of the first evening that I was home talking about this.

Tim, Lyle, and the smaller kids listened raptly and I really laid it on all of them about staying in school and studying hard. They all eventually made it through high school, so I like to believe that a little bit of this talk may have stuck with them.

Tim and Lyle had cut a Christmas tree and brought it home a few days earlier. They and Kathy had had a "decorating party' the day before I came home, and now we were sitting in the living room with the tree lit up for the holiday. It was a really comfortable evening.

Dad came in at about ten. He was drunk and looking for a fight. He threw a curt "Hello," my way and went past into the kitchen. We could hear him stumbling around in there, and we all just sat still, waiting for the other shoe to drop. It did.

"Where the hell is the bread?" he roared.

Mom started to get up and go get it, but I stopped her. I knew that, if she went into that room, he would find a reason to start hitting her. "Mom, where is it? I asked.

"In the bread box on the table," she told me.

I got up and walked into the kitchen. I took the bread out of the box and put it in front of him without saying anything. He stuck his face inches from mine and said, "Think you're pretty smart, don't you?" I just looked at him, turned, and walked back to the living room where we had been talking.

I remember thinking, "My God, I am as tall as him now!" That astounded me. Of course he still outweighed me by at least eighty pounds, but the fact that I could go eye-to-eye with him was something special in my mind.

Mom and the kids and I continued talking while Dad fumbled around in the kitchen. Finally he came back in to the living room. He looked at us, all contentedly gabbing, and then screamed at us, "This place is a pigsty! All of you get up and start cleaning, right now!"

Everyone started to move, but I held up my hand and said, "Stop." I looked at Dad and, still speaking calmly, said, "You're drunk, Dad. It's late, and the time for cleaning is long past. Why don't you go to bed and let us relax for a while?"

He had a half-eaten sandwich in his hand. He threw it at the wall and then turned threateningly toward where I was setting. I just sat there looking at him. Then slowly he turned and went to his bedroom. We never heard any more from him that night.

The next day, I rode around and checked to see if any of my friends were home for Christmas, but without much luck. Since I was now of legal drinking age, I stopped in all three bars in town and ran into some of my old teenage cohorts. We ended up closing the Stag Bar later that night, having a great time reminiscing about "the good old days."

On Christmas Eve, I stayed close to home, gabbing with Mom and helping Tim and Lyle with their chores. Actually, it felt good to cut wood for the stoves again and stretch some of the muscles that hadn't seen much use since working at the lumber mill the previous summer. It was a pleasant day.

Dad came home after we were all asleep, so there were no confrontations that day, but we knew that there would be problems the next day. No holiday was safe from his temper any more.

The little ones got us up early on Christmas morning. It was a fun time, made special for me because of the last few years that I had been away for this day. I had brought presents for everyone, and so had both Kathy and Mom (although hers were disguised as Santa Claus's). Even Dad got into the spirit, sitting by the Christmas tree, passing out the gifts to everyone. It was almost like old times in our home—old times that I remembered and missed very much.

That Christmas was one that I cherished for many years. It was great. Dad did not get drunk for the first time any of us could easily remember. He was almost his old self. He carved the turkey without incident, and we all enjoyed a real Christmas dinner. He even got out his guitar in the evening and sang some of his Western songs while Patty and the rest of us listened.

This was always Patty's favorite time. She would crawl up to Dad's feet while he played and sang and would sit there in rapt silence. We never did anything that would interfere with Dad when he was playing that guitar, mostly out of respect for

Patty. This was her time; the only time that we ever saw her showing real enjoyment.

With a successful Christmas under our belt, we had high hopes of an enjoyable holiday vacation. But that was too much to ask. The next day, Dad was gone when we got up. I hung around the house, talking to Mom and the kids, munching leftover turkey, and just being lazy most of the day.

That afternoon, I went up to the Stag Bar and had a drink with some locals, but nothing was happening, so I decided to go home and hang out with the family.

I had just walked onto the front porch when I heard Lyle calling to me from out in the yard, "Jeff! Jeff! Don't go in there!"

I turned to look at him, and that was a mistake. Dad came out the door and lunged at me, landing a huge right fist on my right ear and temple. It was so hard that it picked me up and knocked me completely off the porch. I remember being massively confused when I landed on the path at the bottom of the stairs. My face and my shoulder where I'd landed were hurting, but I just couldn't figure out what was going on.

I struggled up onto my hands and knees and then to my feet, just in time to catch another fist—this time to the left side of my rib cage. I went down again, gasping for breath. I remember thinking that I must be dying, because I couldn't breathe and I was hurting so horribly. Then his foot hit my solar plexus hard, and I must have blacked out.

The next thing I remember was Mom washing my face with a wet cloth. I was still lying in the pathway in front of the porch stairs.

I sat up quickly and looked around, trying to find Dad to make sure I saw him coming this time, but he was gone. Lyle and the younger kids were there, watching, but Dad was nowhere in sight.

Mom was crying and I could see that she had been beaten again.

I asked, "What happened?" and they told me that Dad had come home a little while before me and had been screaming at Tim and Lyle.

When Mom tried to intervene, Dad had hit her, and Tim had run out the back door, taking the other kids with him.

Lyle had seen me coming in and had doubled back. He was crying as he told me, "I tried to warn you." He repeated this over and over.

I stood up, saying, "Lyle, I know that you tried. This isn't your fault. Believe me, it isn't your fault." I tried to put my arm over his shoulders, but I found that it hurt my ribs too bad to raise the arm, so I just patted his arm and repeated that it wasn't his fault.

I went to the bathroom to wash my face. I was a mess. My ear and cheek were both cut badly, and blood was everywhere. It hurt to breathe, so I knew that I had some rib damage. My shoulder was scraped and bleeding where I had landed on it.

I also had a strange buzzing in my ears that bothered me, but I didn't think that was serious, so I ignored it as much as possible. (I still have that background sound, that buzzing in my ears, even today, after all the years that have passed. It has never gone away.) This was the worst beating that I had ever had. Dad was escalating.

I washed up, and Mom wrapped my ribs with some gauze strips. Then she made some hot tea, and we sat and talked, calming the kids as best we could. Mom did some cleanup of the mess that Dad had made of the kitchen, but none of us were in any shape to do any meaningful work, so we mostly just sat and talked. After awhile, Tim came back from where he had been hiding in the woods. He cried hysterically when he saw me, but we finally got him calmed down. We slowly came back to sanity. After all, this was not a totally unusual day in this household. Eventually, everyone drifted off to bed.

We never saw Dad for several days after that. I stayed home the next day, both to heal a bit and to be there just in case he returned, but he didn't. I don't know where he was, because he never showed up in St. Regis. Kathy was working at Tilly's Café, beside the St. Regis Bar where Dad sometimes drank, and she reported that he never showed up there. At the time, I just didn't care where he was, as long as he wasn't hurting my family.

The rest of my Christmas time at home was fairly uneventful. I spent a lot of time in town, either playing pool with friends at the Stag Bar or hanging out in Tilly's, gabbing with Kathy. Dad finally showed up a couple of days before I had to leave, but he never mentioned what had happened, and he seemed to be a lot more sober than he had been. I hoped for the best.

Then Mike and the other guys showed up, just as a snowstorm was starting. Mom insisted on feeding everyone dinner, but then we headed out, planning on driving around the clock again. The guys wanted to know, of course, how I had managed get so badly beaten up. I told them that it was just a bar fight and warned them that it was never safe to screw around with a Montana logger's woman. They were good with that explanation.

We made it across Montana and into South Dakota before we started seeing some really bad weather. We were in a rather desolate stretch of highway somewhere in South Dakota, when a real blizzard came down on us. We were driving about ten miles per hour and couldn't see anything. The farther we drove, the worse it got, with the road almost totally obscured at times. Apparently, other drivers had received some warning, because there was no one on the road other than us. We had no option but to keep going and hope for the best. We drove like this for several hours before we finally saw a small town. When we spotted a motel, we pulled in. There was no way we could go further.

We took the last two rooms at the motel and were very happy to have them. Mike and I doubled up, and the other guys took the other room. Once we were settled, we decided to try to get something to eat. The motel clerk pointed us to a combination bar/restaurant that was just across the street, and we set out to get some food.

The wind and snow howled around us as we walked across to the restaurant, all very happy that we had found shelter. It could have been a bad scene if we had stayed on the road much longer.

We had a bit of a surprise when we got to the little café that we had been directed to. It adjoined a bar, and we entered through the bar and went on through a door to the café. In both establishments, we were the only Caucasians. Apparently we had stopped on, or near, an Indian reservation; the people in both the bar and the restaurant were all Native American.

We sat down in the café and had dinner. After dinner, we went into the bar to have a drink and play some pool.

One of the guys, a fellow named Jim, started flirting with the bar maid. She was going along with it, and they were having a good time, bantering back and forth. As the night wore on, the bar started to fill up a bit. I was winning the pool games, so I wasn't paying attention to the other customers until one of them suddenly threw a pool cue onto the table as I was getting ready to shoot.

I looked up and realized that at least ten young Indian men were standing at the end of the table. The leader, a guy that would have made three of me, said, "You're not welcome here. We understand that you're snowbound, so you can stay in town, and you can eat at the café. But get out of the bar, and don't come back."

It was all very calmly stated, and I took it at face value and put my pool cue away. But Mike wasn't so accommodating. He asked, "Why? We aren't bothering anyone."

The big guy pointed at Jim and said, "He's bothering one of our women. You had your chance. Now get out and stay out!"

Mike started to say something, but I grabbed his arm and said, "We're leaving."

The big guy flashed a grin and moved aside to clear a path to the door. We took it. There are times when discretion really is the better part of valor, and I was convinced that this was one of them.

We went back to the motel and talked about it. Not one of us thought that we should have stayed. We would have ended up reenacting Custer's Last Stand.

It took three more days before the roads were clear enough to drive again. We had one terribly boring time hanging around the motel, but we stayed there.

It was obvious that we wouldn't get back to the Great Lakes Naval Base on time, so we called ahead to the Base Duty Officer and explained our situation. It turned out that we weren't the only ones. The blizzard had caused a lot of people to be stranded, and the Duty Officer just told us to get there as fast as was reasonable. In the end, we were three days late, but we were not even close to being the last sailors to get there.

I received some really bad news when I got back to the base. My car, which had been parked in a paid parking lot outside the gate, had been stolen. I reported it to the police, but it never turned up. I was heartbroken. I had really loved that old Mercury convertible.

The rest of the school went by uneventfully. I was having no problems with the course, now that the math part was over. It even got really interesting when they taught a week on a new subject, "Transistor Theory." I had heard about transistors, of course. After all, Transistor Radios had been the rage for a year or two. I was really excited to learn this new technology.

Then I received my orders to my next duty station. I was going to a twelve-week school in Virginia. The school was going to train me to maintain and operate an analog computer that controlled the guidance radars and missile launchers for a Terrier Guided Missile System. I was really excited, especially when I was told that the computer was totally transistorized. This was the Navy's most modern equipment, and, after working on an older destroyer for the past three years, this would be an incredible advance in technology for me.

It turned out that most of my class was going to this school, so all the single guys decided to drive down together in a caravan when we were scheduled to go. But first we had to complete the school at Great Lakes, which we did in February 1962.

Upon graduation, I was promoted to second class petty officer. I was really proud of that promotion. Three years earlier, I had been cleaning the ancient bathrooms of an old destroyer; doing one of the worst jobs in the Navy. Now I was an E-5, and I was on my way to one of the Navy's premier enlisted schools. I have to admit that I was incredibly proud of myself.

CHAPTER TWENTY-TWO

Never Pick a Fight with a Destroyer Sailor

The trip to Virginia was a lot of fun. We were given two weeks' leave, plus travel time, when we left Great Lakes. Since we had just been on Christmas leave a few weeks earlier, we decided to forgo the leave and just drive straight to Virginia. But we had lots of time, so we just drove a few hours each day, then we would stop at a likely-looking town and party for the day. We ended up spending three days in the town of Warren, Ohio, while we waited for one of our guys, Big Bob, to fall into and out of, love. Then we drove on to our final destination, the Navy Guided Missile Schools Command, at Damneck, Virginia.

This school proved to be both interesting and a lot of fun. The instruction included both classroom theory and hands-on lab work. I found that I learned much better and retained the knowledge better with the hands-on approach. We were taught to operate and maintain the Mk 119 Computer, a key component of the Mk 76 Terrier Guided Missile Fire Control System. This was the one of the Navy's most modern systems; one that being installed on the newest Navy ships.

The computer itself was like nothing that exists today. It was about six feet high, eight feet long, and two feet thick. The entire front of the computer was taken up by metal dials that were driven by about twenty electromechanical modules, each about a foot square. They, in turn, were driven by electronic signals emanating from small, transistorized modules located in the rear of the unit. The computer itself was electronically coupled with weapons control consoles in the ships' Combat

Information Centers (CICs) that transmitted target coordinates to it so the computer could point the fire-control radar at the target. When the radar locked on to the target, the computer then calculated data for the guided missile launchers and the missiles themselves. When the launcher was assigned to the computer and the missile was on the rail, the system was ready to fire. It was incredibly complex, yet for me it was very understandable. I really felt at home with this system and its maintenance as soon as I was introduced to it.

The school passed uneventfully. Since Damneck was an out-of-the-way location a few miles from Virginia Beach (which was way too expensive for us), we mostly stayed on the base at night. I did some studying and played some bridge, but there was really nothing exciting to do. Once in a while, a group of us would go out to a private club, the Fleet Reserve Club that was located near to the base. But it was mainly a family club, so we would just have a few beers and then go back to the barracks.

Then I ran into a real problem. Against my better judgment, I went with a group to the Base Enlisted Men's Club. We had dinner, and after dinner, we stayed and gabbed and drank beer. By this time, we were all old friends, having gone through Great Lakes and now the computer school together.

We were having a good time, joshing around, and we stayed far too long. Finally, the club was closing, the lights were turned up, and the bartender was telling us, "Wrap it up, Guys."

One of our group, Big Bob, was getting a bit obnoxious and was refusing to leave. He claimed that he didn't have to go anywhere because his beer was still full. So, in the cheerful mode of the evening, I reached over and poured ketchup in his beer and told him that he had to leave, because now all the beer was undrinkable.

Bob erupted and came for me. He tackled me, and we went down in a childish kind of wrestling match on the floor. Our friends immediately pulled us apart, and the Shore Patrol took Bob in tow. We explained to the Shore Patrol that we were friends who had just had a few too many, so they agreed to just hold Bob until the rest of us could get to the barracks before they brought him back to the barracks in their paddy wagon. With that understanding, the rest of us headed home to the barracks and bed.

I was asleep in my top bunk in the barracks when Bob was brought in. Apparently, he waited until the Shore Patrol left, and then he started hunting for me. He was still drunker than a skunk and was really pissed that I had ruined his last beer.

I was sleeping on my side, with my back to the aisle, when he found me. He immediately started pounding on my side and back, hitting everything he could reach.

I woke up, totally startled, and sat way up on my bunk. In what was purely a reflex, my right hand shot high in the air above my head, and then down with all of my strength to hit him right in the eye. The punch was so hard that it split both my knuckles and his eyebrow. He went down, bouncing off the bunk across the aisle from me. I jumped out of my bunk and grabbed him in a headlock as he was getting up. He was none too stable, so I was able to hold him there.

By this time, the lights had come on in the barracks, and everyone was shouting and milling around. The Duty Petty Officer came to see what was going on. As soon as he figured it out, he called the Shore Patrol back to the barracks.

I was still holding Bob in the headlock when the Shore Patrol got there and took charge. They took Bob off to the Base Brig for the night, but not before they put both of us on report.

Some of my friends tried to talk them out of writing me up, but it was no use. They explained that it wasn't their job to judge the situation; it was their job to document it so the CO could do the judging. But they did leave me in the barracks, even as they hauled Bob away, still yelling obscenities at me.

The next day was Sunday, and we never saw Bob. The Shore Patrol kept him locked up for the weekend. That did bother me a bit. I'd just thought Bob was overly drunk and would probably be his old happy-go-lucky self by Sunday morning, but the authorities had apparently decided to give him a taste of the crowbar hotel.

Monday morning, Bob showed up in the barracks just in time to shower, change clothes, and go to class. He had one of the biggest shiners that I had ever seen! The whole side of his face was swollen beyond recognition.

Bob caught hell from our classmates. He was at least six inches taller and sixty pounds heavier than me, and he looked awful. But he took it in good humor and repeatedly apologized to me and the other guys that had been with us. He was a good guy. He had just exceeded his capacity, and now he was paying for it.

I caught a lot of comments from the group about how bad Bob looked and how unscarred I was, but I never told anyone that my one big punch was just a half-asleep panic reflex. If they wanted to consider me a giant-killer, who was I to argue?

But all was not sweetness and light for us. We had been put on report, and the School's Command did not take this fact lightly. We were hauled into the school's front office at the first break on that Monday morning and were royally chewed out by the Command Master Chief. He then informed us that we were to appear at the Base Executive Officer's Office on Wednesday at 10:00 a.m. for a "preliminary hearing" before going to Captain's Mast at a later date as scheduled by the Executive Officer.

I had been so proud of making it to second class petty officer! Bob and I had both been promoted at the same time, and we were both certain that we would both lose at least one stripe over this mess. Bob spent the next two days apologizing to me, and the rest of the group spent the next two days telling him what an asshole he was for doing this to us. It was not a fun two days.

Finally the day came and we were both standing in the outer office waiting for the Executive Officer to get done with some other offenders. I was shaking in my boots. The last time I had been this scared was when Sheriff Tamietti had caught me poaching the night before I joined the Navy. Bob was in worse shape than I was. He was noticeably shaking, and with that huge black eye and swollen face, he looked horrible.

The chief in charge of the office came over and told us, "When your names are called, march into the inner office and come to attention in front of the podium. Salute the XO, then go to Parade Rest and stay there. Only speak when spoken to. Understand?"

We both replied, "Yes, Chief."

Then we waited.

Finally our names were called. We did exactly as we had been told and ended up standing in front of the podium. The XO was there, but his back was to us. We still went through the routine and came to Parade Rest, waiting. Then the XO turned around, and I almost crapped my pants. It was Commander Moore, the *Cogswell*'s (apparently former) commanding officer!

My jaw must have dropped, but he ignored it. He stared right through both of us and gave no sign of recognition, even though I knew he must have known me. We had shared too many long bridge watches together for him not to have known me. It was only about a year ago that he had officiated at my reenlistment ceremony in Manila Bay.

Then I noticed that he had the personnel folders for both Bob and I on the podium in front of us. He knew who I was, but he obviously wasn't going to let that fact be known.

He came to the podium, sternly declared, "Executive Officer's Mast is now in session." and immediately asked us to describe the circumstances that had brought us there.

I looked at Bob, and he started talking. I have to give Bob a lot of credit. He told the straight truth and took full responsibility for everything that had happened. When he finished, the Commander looked at me, and said, "Do you agree, Noonan?"

I said, "Yes Sir, except that I deserve some of the blame. None of this would have happened if I hadn't dumped ketchup in his beer."

The Commander looked stern and talked a bit about the seriousness of the offenses that we were charged with, and really chewed us out for "disgracing our uniforms and not acting like petty officers." Then he, with a perfectly straight face, talked about both of our service records and the fact that neither of us had any prior offenses. I learned that Bob had been in the Fleet for four years, stationed on an aircraft carrier.

Finally, the Commander wound down. He told us both that, because we had been honest about the circumstances, and because we were both obviously remorseful, he was going to drop the charges. But, he added, "If you so much as step an inch out of line for the rest of your time here, I will resurrect this, and you will go to Captain's Mast. I guarantee you that the Captain won't be nearly as lenient as me. Understood?"

We said that we understood, and he dismissed us.

As we came to attention and prepared to salute, the XO turned back to us, looked at Bob, and said, "Did you get that eye in this fight, Sailor?"

Bob involuntarily touched his face and said, "Yes Sir."

The Commander went on, "You have only served on aircraft carriers, haven't you?"

Bob replied "Yes Sir."

Commander Moore then looked at him with a slow grin coming over his face. "Son, you just learned a lesson. You should never pick a fight with a destroyer sailor!" With that, he walked out the back door and left us there with our mouths open.

The Master Chief, who had been in the room the whole time, escorted us out of the office and told us how incredibly lucky we were. I agreed with him. But I never, ever, told anyone that I knew Commander Moore. I just let everyone think that we were the luckiest two sailors on earth. Maybe we were, at that.

CHAPTER TWENTY THREE

Bath, Maine

The rest of the school went well. Then about a month before we were to graduate, we received our orders. The rest of the class was going to ships on the East and West Coasts. But my orders were to a ship that was just being built in Bath, Maine. The ship, USS *Leahy*, was the first of its class, a brand new ship-type that was to have Terrier Launchers on both the bow and the stern of the ship. There were to be four of the Mark 76 Guided Missile Fire Control Systems (Mk 76 GMFCS)aboard, each with computers that were to be a whole generation newer than the one we had been studying.

This new ship concept was a bit of a shock to me, since I had only served on the one very old destroyer in the past. But I got ready for the challenge by asking the school to get me some documentation on the newer version of the computers. The documentation was all classified as "Secret," so I had to study it in the confines of a specific school classroom during the evening hours since I was still in the regular school during the days. My old experience at studying technical manuals on my own really helped with this project. By the time I graduated from school and left for Bath, I figured that I was as ready as possible.

I took a few days and wandered around the East Coast a bit on my way to Maine. I fell temporarily in lust in a small northern Pennsylvania town, but left when the new girlfriend turned out to have a daughter almost my age (who I liked a lot better than her mother). Then I wandered up through Boston and drove around in New Hampshire and Vermont. It was pretty country and I found myself really liking the older homes and the history of the area. It was as if I was really seeing the history instead of just reading about it. I liked that.

My orders stated that I was to report in to the administrative office on the Naval Air Station in Brunswick, Maine. This confused me a bit, since my ultimate destination was to be USS *Leahy* (DLG-16), which was under construction in the community of Bath. But I did as told and reported to the Air Station. I was absolutely astounded when they gave me a check for a month's "advance per-diem" and sent me on to Bath with instructions to find a place to stay and report to the *Leahy's* Commanding Officer the next morning.

I had to ask someone, "What's per-diem?" They explained that, since the ship was still under construction, and there were no Navy living quarters in Bath, we had to live in town, wherever we could find a place to stay. The per-diem check was for $12 per day to cover our living expenses. I thought that I must have died and gone to heaven! $360 per month was a fortune to me at that time.

I went from Brunswick to Bath and looked for housing. I was directed to a beautiful old mansion that had been converted to a hostelry called the Sedgewick Hotel. I went in, got a room, and paid for an entire month up front. I loved this place. It was an old, obviously historic, building and it had a very stable and distinguished air about it.

I have to admit that I was a bit intimidated by all of this. Everything that I had heard or read about New England told me that it was a very staid and formal place to live. I figured that it was the kind of place where the kids all wore formal uniforms to school and courtship was still carefully managed by the parents of the virginal bride. The atmosphere in the lobby of the Sedgewick Hotel just reinforced this concept. So when I got unpacked, I showered and then changed into my most formal clothes—slacks and a nice shirt under a cashmere sweater that I had bought during a weak moment in Hong Kong. Then I went down to the Sedgewick's dining room and took a seat for dinner.

A motherly waitress in a starched linen outfit brought me a menu. The prices startled me, but I decided to play the role and go with it for the night. Obviously, I wouldn't be able to eat all of my meals there and stay under my per-diem budget, but, I figured I could live with it for the evening.

I ordered a Manhattan, which I thought would be acceptable in staid New England, and then a steak dinner. I had never even seen a Manhattan before and it gagged me. But I fought it down as I maintained my dignified composure and ate the dinner in the style in which I was sure that every New Englander was accustomed. When I finished, I had a Baked Alaska for dessert, because—although I had never seen one before—I was sure that this was the kind of dessert that New Englanders routinely consumed. I was not about to embarrass myself, or Montana, in this new environment.

When I was paying the waitress, she leaned over and quietly asked me if I was with the Navy. I said, "Yes, Ma'am," and she told me that they had a lounge in the basement where I could probably find some of my new shipmates. She pointed out the door, and I gratefully thanked her.

I went through the door and down a set of stairs and walked into a fairly typical hotel lounge area. There were several people sitting around and the jukebox was blaring. I sat at the bar, ordered a beer, and settled in to see what was happening.

I was within a couple of feet of a table that had two older guys and their wives or girlfriends. I heard them say a few things about "the ship," and I assumed that they were senior petty officers of some kind that were attached to the *Leahy*. But I was still not sure of the protocol here in staid, stable New England, so I didn't approach anyone or try to make conversation. I was too busy making sure that I didn't disgrace myself.

One thing that I noticed was that all four of the people at the table had individual pitchers of beer in front of them. The two men had relatively empty pitchers, and the two women had full pitchers. Time went on as I took in my surroundings. Then I saw one of the men pour a glass of beer from the neighboring woman's pitcher. What happened next totally took away any fear that I had ever had about embarrassing myself in New England.

The woman said, "You motherfucker! Get your fucking paws off of my beer. You buy your own damned beer!"

These two F-words were the first F-words that I had never, in my entire life, heard a woman utter. In my wildest dreams, I couldn't imagine that a woman would even know those words, let alone say them in mixed company!

But there was more: next, she reached in her mouth and took out a complete set of false teeth, which she proceeded to drop into her pitcher. "There, you cocksucker," she said (*another* word that I had never heard a woman utter), "try drinking my beer now!"

I decided that there was something amiss about my understanding of New England. This was just too much to digest, and the day had been too long already. I went up the stairs to my room and went to bed.

The next morning, I put on my dress blue uniform, skipped breakfast, and walked to the building downtown where the ship's crew was temporarily located. I was surprised to find them working in an older storefront, with a haphazard bunch of desks scattered around the old display floor. I walked in and was immediately approached by another second class petty officer that I recognized from Damneck. He had been in a computer class that graduated a couple of weeks ahead of mine. His name was Dan Prateau, and it turned out that he had been waiting for me to show up.

With Dan guiding, I reported to the ship's personnel office (which consisted of one older yeoman sitting at a desk in a corner of the floor) and got the necessary check-in sheets. I found out that only a small portion of the crew was located in Bath. The rest of the crew was in training in Norfolk; they would arrive when the ship's construction was completed and they could go directly aboard the ship to live.

I was taken to see my new division officer, a Navy lieutenant. From his appearance and the rack of ribbons on his chest, it was obvious that he had well over twenty years in the Navy. His name was Cohen, and he seemed to be fairly friendly for an officer. He took me to meet the Commanding Officer, a Navy captain.

The Captain was obviously a spit-and-polish, by-the-book, kind of guy, and I reserved judgment on him. He gave me a welcome aboard speech that made a huge deal out of the fact that this would be the first ship of its kind and would be "watched very closely by the Navy, including the Fleet Commanders. So we had better be on our best behavior here in Bath, and we should plan on keeping a taut and immaculate ship."

I made a comment about being happy to be there where the Navy's newest guided missile systems would be tested, and he flatly told me that the main priority on this ship would be on its appearance. He seemed annoyed that I even thought about such a mundane subject as missile systems. I decided right then that this guy was nothing like Captain Moore.

When we left the vicinity of the captain, Lieutenant Cohen seemed to relax a bit. He talked to me about my background and what he expected of me while we were in Bath. He wanted me to be primarily concerned with the computer systems and the rooms that the computers were located in, the Missile Plotting Rooms. He wanted me to watch the system installations and report anything that I considered deficient in the installations. He also told me that we had "a pot of money" that we could use if we saw something that was needed but was not on the ship's plans. Our job was, in short, to make sure that our workspaces and our equipment were put together in such a way that we could maintain them when they were turned over to us.

The Captain had made a really big deal to us about ship cleanliness. I was confused about this, since we did not own the ship, and the shipyard people were responsible for it now, so I asked the Lieutenant about it.

"How are we supposed to keep the ship clean, when the shipyard still owns it?" I asked.

The Lieutenant smiled at me, "I'm glad that you had the sense to ask me that. You aren't. We have absolutely no control over the yardbirds or any of the messes they make. The Captain knows this, but I think he just wants to emphasize that he intends to run an immaculate ship, and he's preparing us. But as long as the ship is in the shipyard, we're just guests of Bath Iron Works. We've got to be diplomatic, and telling them to clean up after themselves ain't diplomatic. But I'm not worried about any of that. Just make sure that your spaces and equipment the best that they can be technically, and we'll get along fine. Do you have any questions?"

I replied, "No, Sir."

I was amazed at the ship when I got aboard. Compared to my previous ship, the *Leahy* was huge. Where the old *Cogswell* had displaced 2,100 tons of water when afloat, the *Leahy* displaced 7,800 tons. When I arrived, the physical construction was almost done, and the ship's systems were in the early stages of testing, so it actually looked like an operational ship, except for the hordes of shipyard workers aboard.

Dan Prateau showed me our spaces aboard the ship and introduced me to some of the workers who were testing and upgrading the new systems. There were a good number of engineers aboard, some from the Navy Guided Missile Station in Port Hueneme, California. Others were factory representatives from the companies that had made the equipment. The computer center had engineers from Ford Instrument Company (no relation to the Ford automobile company) and the radars were being worked by engineers from Sperry Gyroscope Corporation. Other engineers, from a company called Vitro Engineering, were responsible for the interface between all of the different equipment. There were also engineers from Western Electric and a host of other companies.

After a day of walking around and meeting the people working with these missile systems, I decided that I had really stumbled into a big deal. I had never before seen such an assemblage of obviously intelligent, talented, people in my life. If this number of these types of people could dedicate themselves to this equipment, it was obviously the most important project that I had yet been exposed to.

Mom had told me a million times that, if I wanted to escape from the old life, I had to find something important and then work my butt off to become a part of it. "That's the only way that you'll escape, Jeff—by finding something that interests you, then working your fingers to the bone. If you use your brains and work harder than anyone else," she had promised me, "you'll escape. If you don't, you won't."

I decided that I had finally found the thing that she had been talking about—the thing that I could put my teeth into and make mine. At that time, I couldn't imagine a better life than being one of these engineers, doing something as important as this with my life.

The next few months were intense. The engineers and technicians working on the missile systems were working twelve-hour shifts, five days a week. I stayed with them aboard ship as much as possible, watching their work, studying how they accomplished their testing and how they troubleshot and fixed the problems they encountered. I spent hours listening in on their conversations on sound-powered headsets as they worked, trying to follow their work in the system technical manuals. At the same time, we had other work to do to get the ship's documentation ready for the crew to come aboard. I also submitted a lot of change requests to the shipyard for such things as lockable bookcases for technical manuals, storage for test equipment and tools, and similar things.

The days were very busy, and so were our off hours. I continued to live at the Sedgwick Hotel and as I got to know my way around the town, I made some very good friends, both with other *Leahy* sailors and with some of the local townspeople. Bath, Maine, was a small town. Not as small as St. Regis, but close enough that I felt at home there. The local people were wonderful to us.

The only cloud on my horizon was a master chief who was my leading chief petty officer. His name was Martinez, and he was a total ass. He had converted to fire control technician from boatswain's mate as a master chief and had not bothered to learn anything about his new job. He was an absolute disaster, a little man with a Napoleon complex who saw his job in the Navy as one of keeping ships clean and sailors in constant fear.

I had a continuing series of run-ins with Martinez while we were in Bath. He just couldn't seem to get the fact that the Navy did not own the ship yet and we were not in charge of the shipboard spaces. He wanted us to clean the shipboard spaces even while the shipyard workers were working in them. Of course, we couldn't do it, and when it didn't happen, he would get mad. He was on my case all the time, and I didn't have sense enough to ignore him. When, after one particularly bad session with him, I pointed out that the Navy had not even issued cleaning gear to us yet, he flamed out on me and put me on report for insubordination. Lieutenant Cohen squashed this, but Martinez was after me in a big way after that.

Staying involved in the work aboard ship kept me in close contact with the shipyard workers. One of them, a shipyard computer technician named George Lacroix, became a good friend, and we often left the ship in the evening and went to a nearby bar/restaurant for dinner and drinks. George was a single guy who never seemed to be without an entourage, including a girlfriend or two, so I did get to know a lot of Bath's single people. One of them was a widow at least fifteen years older than me named Linda Bauer.

Linda seemed to almost literally adopt me. She was going out with another local guy, but she thought nothing of inviting me to her home for dinner and taking me along with her family when they went to a nearby lake for a holiday. She was a nice person and a great mother who had three children between the ages of ten and fifteen. I spent some wonderful days with them lying on the beach at the lake and going to their beach club in the evening.

She and her two young daughters would not accept that I didn't know how to dance. They taught me to two-step and do the Twist, which was hot in those days. They didn't let up until I was able to hold my own on the dance floor.

I honestly felt like a big brother in this little family. To this day, I don't understand why they took such an interest in me, but I really do appreciate the fact that they did. It was a very good memory to take away with me.

While we were in Bath, I got a letter from Mom telling me that my sister, Kathy, had been married. She had married a St. Regis logger that I knew slightly.

I was surprised. I hadn't known that Kathy was even dating anyone seriously, but I was happy for her. Her new husband, Don, was older than Kathy, but he was a good guy from all that I had seen, and I thought that he would be good to her.

Actually, my first thought was, "Great! Kathy escaped!"

But all good things must end. After I had been in Bath about four months, the ship's construction was done, and we had to leave. We took *Leahy* to Boston Naval Shipyard, where it was to be outfitted with supplies and some final work was to be done before the official commissioning, scheduled for the coming August.

CHAPTER TWENTY-FOUR

It's Great to be a Bar Hero!

Master Chief Martinez did a number on me when we arrived in Boston. Upon arrival, the ship was required to furnish one person to the Armed Forces Police in Boston. Martinez volunteered me. It was to be a three-month tour, after which I would return to the ship.

I wasn't too happy with this idea. There would be a tremendous amount of technical work done on the missile systems during this three-month period, and I didn't want to miss it. But the Chief didn't understand the amount of work coming up and he wasn't particularly interested in it anyway, so I had no choice.

I left the ship within a day or so of its arrival in Boston, a bit excited by the impending adventure. I had done some one-night Shore Patrol assignments when I was on *Cogswell* in WestPac, but the Armed Forces Police, where I would be working for the next three months, was something new to me.

I had a weekend off before I had to report, so I decided to get a room and relax for a couple of days before reporting to the new duty station. I checked in to a downtown hotel, within walking distance of the Westerner Bar, which I had visited the night before with a group of my friends. Then I got cleaned up and went out for some dinner.

The Westerner Bar was in a Boston neighborhood that, in 1962, we called "The Combat Zone," but it was nothing like the freewheeling mess that was created in the same area a few years later when the city tried to corral all of its sleaze in one central area. The Combat Zone of 1962 was only a three-block area that had a group of bars and restaurants that catered to young people—primarily college students and military personnel—who wanted a place to hang and dance at night. It was well-patrolled and safe, but exciting.

It was about nine in the evening when I walked into the Westerner and got a seat at the bar. A Country-Western band (what else?) was just warming up, and the evening's customers were slowly wandering in. Most of them got tables close to the dance floor, but, since I was alone, I stayed at the bar and just watched the people.

I had been there about an hour when a woman came in and sat next to me. I recognized her as someone that had danced with my friends and me the night before. She was about ten years older than me, but still quite attractive for an older woman.

She said "Hello," obviously remembering me, and I did the same.

I said, "I remember you from last night, but I don't remember your name. I'm sorry."

She said "I'm Delores and I think that you're Jeff. Am I right?" She had me there, so I bought her a drink, and the evening was off and running.

We soon joined a group of her friends at a table and danced the night away. Of course, I gave her a ride to her apartment when the evening was over and ended up staying for the weekend. Boston was starting out with a bang!

On Monday I reported to the Armed Forces Police Headquarters, which was co-located with the Boston Police in a downtown police station. I was surprised to find out that I would, once again, be on per diem while I was assigned there. I was to get a hotel room and live "close to where the action is." The theory was that we would always be on call in case of serious trouble, so we had to stay nearby. We were to work four days and then have three days off, on a staggered rotation. Our work hours, during our "on-shift" days were from three in the afternoon until three the next morning.

The first day, I was taken to a small-arms range and went through a firing test with a .45 caliber pistol, and then I had to take a physical at the Naval Shipyard Dispensary. While I was at the shipyard, they had me fill out about a million forms, after which they gave me my per diem check and told me to find a hotel room and report to the police station at three the next day for duty. They gave me a choice of two hotels and sent me on my way.

I checked in to the Bradford Hotel that afternoon and got my gear ready for the next day. Then I drove over to see Delores for dinner and a quiet evening at her place. We had a quite a talk that night, and we decided that we would become "friends with benefits" because we enjoyed each other but had such an age difference. We both agreed that we would pass each other by if we ran into each other when we were with dates or anything like that. We also set up a telephone code so I could call and see that the coast was clear before I came over to her place in the future. I have to admit that I really liked this arrangement!

The next day was a bit of an adventure. I reported to the police station a few minutes early and ran into my fellow Armed Forces Policemen, a group of about twenty people from all the services. Almost half were sailors from ships being worked on in the shipyard. The rest were from all types of military bases in the Boston vicinity. At 1500 hours sharp, we assembled in a police briefing room and waited for our assignments.

A Marine gunnery sergeant came into the room and took the podium. He went through some housekeeping items and general information and then he discussed the patrol assignments for the day. All of the assignments were by teams, since all patrols were two-man efforts. He made a special point to remind all of us that we were only there to ride herd on military personnel. "If there is trouble, but no military are involved, call the cops, but stay the hell out of it!"

He began giving out the assignments for the night. Several teams of people were called out and their patrol areas assigned. Then I heard my assignment, "Washington and Noonan, Roxbury."

I looked around for Washington and spotted his name tag. He was the biggest man in the room, a huge black sailor wearing the uniform of a first class commissaryman (cook). He spotted me at the same time and immediately shouted out, "Hold up, Sarge!"

The sergeant stopped and asked, "What is it, Washington?"

"You're saddling me with that skinny little kid and giving us the Roxbury beat. Not only is he a 150-pound midget, he's also a frigging technician. He's not going to be able to handle Roxbury."

The sergeant looked at me and started to say something, but I held my hand up, palm out, to stop him.

I said, "Sarge, please let me answer the man."

He nodded, and I turned around to face the giant cook.

Then I said, in a very firm voice, "First off, I'm not a one-hundred-and-fifty pound midget. I weigh a grand total of one-hundred and twenty-eight pounds, soaking wet. Second, I was a bos'n mate before I ever thought about becoming a technician and I am probably one of the meanest motherfuckers you've ever met. Third, I'm not sure that I am really comfortable with having a cook as a partner. You can't just deep-fry the assholes when they cause trouble." I paused and then said, "But if you're willing to give it a try, I guess I could bend my rules for you. If we do work together, I'll have your back—or at least the part of it that I can reach." I grinned and held out my hand to him.

The whole room cracked up. Even the sergeant was laughing. Finally a big grin broke over Washington's face, and he walked over to shake my hand. I had a partner for the day.

After all the patrol assignments were given out, the meeting broke up, and we went to the parking lot where paddy wagons were standing by to take us to our assigned spots. While I was waiting, Washington and I got a little better acquainted. It turned out that he was there on permanent duty, working his way through a two-year shore duty assignment. He had been there about six months when I showed up. He asked me if I had any questions, and I replied, "Yeah, just one. Where the heck is Roxbury?"

He looked at me and said, "Are you serious? You don't know about Roxbury?"

"I never heard of it."

He responded with a very discouraged, "Oh shit."

He didn't say anything else until we were getting out of the paddy wagon. Then he turned around and, grinning, said, "Welcome to Roxbury, Kid."

I looked around. The first thing that struck me was that I was in the middle of the most rundown slum that I had ever seen. The second thing I noticed was that I was the only white person in sight. Washington was still grinning. He said, "I tried to help you out, Kid. But your alligator mouth overloaded your hummingbird ass. Now you're gonna be in real trouble if you aren't careful. Stay behind and watch me, do what I do, and we may both survive this night." With that, he led the way down the street.

I followed.

The first few hours were uneventful, and I slowly gained some confidence. We mostly walked the sidewalks, stopping to talk to vendors and shop owners. While it was still quiet, Washington brought me into several bars and nightclubs that he told me were the trouble spots we would have to deal with later. We went through each of them in some detail, checking to make sure we had the layouts down and knew where all the doors and hiding spots were. I also went out of my way to say "Hello" and try to talk a moment with all the bartenders and waitresses.

As evening fell, the bar scene started to develop. Each of the bars he had shown me had bands playing and large dance floors. We modified our patrol; we were just walking from bar to bar now, but things stayed quiet for the evening. After all the buildup, it was almost disappointing, but everyone was great to us. After the first couple of times through the bars, the people just seemed to accept us and even joked a bit with us as we wandered through. I soon relaxed and started having fun along the way, cracking wise to the waitresses and generally having fun with the crowds. It wasn't that much different from other bars I had been in. Everyone was there for a good time, and no one wanted trouble.

The night was soon over, and we were walking back to where we were to meet the paddy wagon when Washington broke the silence, "You did real good tonight, Noonan. People really liked you, and that's important here."

I replied, "It's important everywhere, Cookie. These are just people like you and me; just people trying to have some fun in this old world."

Washington was silent for a time before he said, "Just people like you and me? I don't think that I have ever heard anything like that from a white man before."

A bit confused, I said, "It's the truth, Cookie. We're all alike underneath it all." He immediately came back with, "Noonan, you lied to me. You really ain't the meanest motherfucker that I've ever met."

I chuckled and we got aboard the paddy wagon.

That first week passed with no remarkable events. The daily roster gave us all alternating beats, so that we didn't get too friendly with anyone that we met while on duty. We would go from Roxbury one day to the Combat Zone the next, and then South Boston the next. Occasionally we would get Paddy Wagon Duty, but that was usually kept for the permanent staff people.

I spent my first free weekend taking care of my uniforms and doing some housekeeping chores. Delores and I ran into each other on Saturday night in the Westerner, and I stayed with her through Sunday and then went back to the hotel.

One day the following week, I was assigned to patrol in the Combat Zone with an older Navy machinist's mate who was so small that he made me look big. We did the normal afternoon routine and then went into patrolling the bars after the sun went down. The, about ten in the evening, we ran into what became my first real encounter on the police beat.

We were standing unobtrusively to the side in the Westerner Bar when an obviously deranged man suddenly appeared in front of us waving a big stick. He was a little taller than me and quite a bit heavier. He was yelling that he was a good Marine that had fought in Korea, and that we were harassing him. (We had not even noticed him until he started waving the stick in our faces.) He just crouched there in front of us, waving that damned stick and yelling taunts, "Come on you scum-sucking sailor bustards. Come on and see what a real man does to you!" and similar things. He had one of the most intense looks on his face that I had ever seen, with a wild stare that seemed to be all over us all of the time. He was either crazy or on something very strong.

My little partner was scared silly. He kept mumbling, "Oh shit...Oh shit," over and over again. He was an older guy, and this obviously wasn't his thing. He stayed half hidden behind me. That pissed me off, but I didn't have time for him right then.

I remembered reading somewhere that you shouldn't show fear to a guy with marbles missing, so I tried something that I wasn't sure would work. I started smiling at the guy in a friendly manner. He noticed and hesitated, but then started yelling even louder and more profanely. So I upped the ante and started laughing. The louder he got, the harder I laughed. After a few minutes, I was slapping my thigh and pointing at him, and he was screaming at the top of his lungs. It must have been quite a sight. Finally I stopped laughing, looked at him, and said, "That's enough. The show is over. We're leaving now."

He cocked his head to the side and looked startled. Then he dropped the stick to his side, said, "Okay," and walked away.

I was really relieved. We had no authority over civilians, and we could have gotten in trouble if we had been forced to hit him or anything. We were forbidden from aggressive action against any civilian, even one as obviously out of it as this guy had been. As soon as he moved away from us, I told my partner to follow me and I went to the bar, borrowed a telephone, and called the police. They found the poor guy and took him to a hospital for evaluation.

But that was not the end of the incident for me. At least a hundred bar patrons had seen the action, such as it was, and even the band had stopped to watch us. I had an instant reputation in the Combat Zone. I was "the sailor who laughed at the crazy guy." The story traveled fast, and, of course, the deed got bigger with each telling.

We left the bar on our rounds right after the incident, but when we came back on the next visit an hour or so later, a little waitress named Rosie that I had joked with earlier met me with a cool soft drink. Additionally, before we left the bar, I had a date for the next Saturday night with another girl, a tall brunette named Angela. It was good to be a bar hero.

The Saturday date with Angela turned into a good thing, and we were pretty much a steady item within a week or so. Delores was cool with it, so I kind of alternated between the two of them.

Then, one day, I was sleeping in my hotel room when I was awakened by a knock on the door, "Room Service" a voice said.

I mumbled something at the door and turned over to go back to sleep when the voice said, "I said Room Service, Jeff. Get your ass out of bed."

Startled, I went to the door and opened it a crack. Rosie, the little waitress from the Westerner was there, wearing a maid's uniform. She pushed her way right on into the room. "I got a second job here" she said, "Is that okay with you?"

Totally confused, I said "Sure," and jumped back into bed to cover up. She grinned and stretched, and, with a shrug, the uniform hit the floor. There was nothing under it.

It was really, really, good to be a bar hero!

The next two months on the Armed Forces Police were every young man's fantasy. Over time, Delores and I saw each other less and less, but we remained friends. Angela kept me busy in the evenings, and Rosie took care of me during the daylight hours. It was certainly a fantasy life, but I knew that it was temporary. As much as I enjoyed Delores, Angela, and Rosie, they were not people who would fit into my lifelong fantasy of a little cottage with a white picket fence and a couple of cheerful kids. None of the three was a settling-down kind of person, and I was not a forever-partying kind of guy.

I enjoyed it while it lasted, but nothing lasts forever. Soon my three-month Armed Forces Police gig was over. At about the same time, Angela and Rosie found out about each other. Judging by their reactions, I was no longer their favorite bar hero. Delores and I were still friends, but it was back to the ship and back to work for me. The fantasy life was over.

CHAPTER TWENTY-FIVE

My First Shakedown Cruise

When the ship left Bath, all of the ship's equipment, including the missile systems had been turned over to the ship's crew. The missile systems were still far from operational and were in need of extensive repair and modernization. While I was doing my police duty, the missile crew had been working night and day to get the systems together. When I returned, I jumped in with the rest of the guys. The next months were an incredibly hectic time for all of us.

While the ship was under construction in Bath, the shipyard had been responsible for the installation and checkout of the missile systems, but the shipyard's construction contract was several years old, and the shipyard was only contractually obligated to bring the systems up to a baseline operating condition that had been established when the contract was awarded. By the time the systems were turned over to us, this baseline was obsolete. In the years since the construction contract had been awarded, the Navy had authorized a host of equipment and system changes to fix problems that had been encountered in both laboratory and fleet environments. It was our job to tear the systems apart and install the changes and upgrades, which were known as Ordnance Alterations (ORDALTS). When we finished installing all of the changes, the engineers would be brought back, and we would retest the systems to ensure that we had everything put together correctly.

I was put in charge of the forward plotting room, with two computer systems. Dan Prateau had the after two systems. We had two third class petty officers working for each of us, and we both worked for a first class petty officer named McBee. He, in turn, reported to my old nemesis, Master Chief Martinez. Lieutenant Cohen was our division officer. With that organization in place, we took on one of the most grueling and heartbreaking challenges that I have ever encountered.

The computers and all of their associated wiring, cabling, and switchboards had to be completely ripped apart and rebuilt. We followed ORDALT instructions that reminded me of a set of Sears-Roebuck toy-assembly instructions, except that the ORDALTS were far more complex. Neither I nor either of my third class had ever touched one of these computers before, so just finding our way through them was a challenge.

My boss, McBee, was a good guy, and he had worked on these systems in the Fleet, but he had other responsibilities that kept him busy most of the time. The Chief was a total waste—a guy who knew nothing about the systems and didn't bother to learn. His biggest contribution was to come around about once every day, screaming at us because we couldn't keep the areas clean enough for him when we had the equipment torn apart and scattered all over the rooms. It was very obvious that his only function in life was to make life hell for those of us with a real job.

I became really good friends with a third class that worked on the Gun Fire Control Systems aboard. His name was George Kaplan, and he was always ready to go to town and have a beer or two with me. Whenever the Chief would get on my nerves too much, George and I would hit the town, usually drinking in the Westerner and other bars in the Combat Zone. I introduced George to Delores, and some evenings, we would just go to her place and play cards or watch television. George would sleep on the couch.

But we couldn't do this very often because of the amount of work that I had to do on the missile systems. The entire missile fire-control crew was on twelve-hours-per-day, six-days-per-week, schedules that were basically self-imposed. We saw the amount of work that was ahead of us, and we dug into it. We didn't feel that we had a choice. There was an engineer from Ford Instrument Company assigned to the ship, so he helped us with any technically difficult problems that we ran into and kept us pointed in the right direction when the workload got too big to handle.

Since we were on this kind of a work schedule, the Chief and his unyieldingly stupid demands were really getting to us. He was the worst leader that I encountered in my entire Navy career; a man that had no concept of the work that we were doing and just wanted everything shiny-clean all the time. It was impossible to make him understand us or what we were doing. If I tried to explain the technical work we were doing, he refused to even listen. Several times he walked into the room when we were in the middle of a system test—working via headphones with all the other elements of the missile system on tests that took days to get organized—and made us stop everything, get off the headphones, and swab the decks or shine the brass in the room.

Even the civilian engineers had a problem with this kind of thing, and they complained to the Commanding Officer that the Chief was interfering with their work. But it made no difference, and the problems went on.

I have never been one to suffer in silence, and I took my job, as well as my responsibilities to my men, very seriously. So I began regularly clashing with the Chief. He reported me regularly to our division officer, Lieutenant Cohen. The Lieutenant was a good guy who really did understand, but he couldn't get anyone else to appreciate the workload requirements of the experimental missile systems that we were trying to assemble. The Captain had set the standards for the ship, and his priority was to keep things spotless, whether they worked or not. The Chief was content to just keep the Captain happy, and the rest of us were caught somewhere in the middle, trying to make a fighting ship out of a showboat.

The Boston-outfitting period finally came to an end, and the ship was commissioned. After the commissioning ceremony, we had a short period remaining in the shipyard before the ship was heading south for its shakedown cruise.

It was during that period between the commissioning ceremony and our departure that George and I ran into some real excitement. We had gone to Delores's place for the evening and were playing cards on her kitchen table with her and one of her friends. I was idly staring out the kitchen window, waiting for one of the players to do something, when I thought I noticed something in the basement of the building across the alley from us. I looked harder, and soon we realized that the building next door was on fire!

Delores's apartment was in a six-story apartment building located in a group of similar buildings in an older and somewhat rundown neighborhood. Fire in one of those buildings was no small matter. They were old frame buildings that would burn like kindling.

We knew we had to move fast, and Delores didn't have a telephone, so George and I made a plan and moved. George ran to a nearby convenience store and called the fire department. At the same time, I ran next door and up the stairs to the top floor. I then started beating on doors, hollering "Fire, Fire. Get out now!" at the top of my lungs. People started emerging, streaming down the stairs wearing whatever they had on when I hit their door. I kept beating on doors, working my way downstairs a floor at a time until I encountered George who was working his way up to meet me. About this time, the Boston Fire Department arrived and took over. George and I went down to the street and ran into the people we had warned. The Fire Chief was with them and, of course, he had a group of reporters with him. They took our names and information and we talked to them for a few minutes before trying to go back to Delores's place. But the Fire Department had evacuated all the adjoining buildings so, after a while, Delores took off to stay at a friend's home, and George and I went back to the ship.

The fire gutted the first three or four floors of the building before it was under control. The building was permanently evacuated, and eventually, it was torn down. But no one was hurt.

By the time we got back to the ship that night, the land-line telephone on the quarterdeck was ringing off the hook. Every reporter in Boston was calling for us. We had become minor celebrities. We took one call that came in as we walked aboard. When we realized what was going on, we explained it to the OOD and asked him to just tell everyone that called that we were not onboard. He agreed, and we went below and went to sleep.

The next morning, we awoke to find that the local papers had carried the story of the fire, and reporters had been calling the ship all morning to try to talk to us. We decided that we didn't want this publicity, so we asked the OOD to just give them a "No Comment" if they called again.

The mayor of Boston wrote us a nice letter, thanking us for what we had done. The XO made sure that the letter went into our official personnel records. But, in all honesty, I was too busy, working too hard on the missile systems, for it to make much of an impression on me at that time.

A few days later, we left Boston, heading south for the *Leahy's* shakedown cruise.

The shakedown cruise for a new ship is a period designed to test the ship's equipment as well as train the new ship's crew. Most crewmembers on a new ship like *Leahy* have never been to sea, and, in this case, none of us had ever been to sea on a ship of this type, so intensive training was required. At the same time, the ship was still in the throes of trying to get all of the ship's systems operational. In the missile systems, we carried a full team of the type of engineers that had been with us in Bath. We were now working twelve-hour shifts, six days a week.

But the Command still had no concept of this effort and treated it as if it were an undesirable annoyance. The ship stopped at every major port on the East Coast, showing the local dignitaries our beautiful new ship. At every stop, we had to cease work and train our equipment centerline so that it had a more appealing appearance. In every port, the ship hosted an Open House so that civilians could come aboard and wander through the ship. At every stop, we were expected to have our equipment and the rooms it occupied spotless. In between, we were expected to stand underway watches and perform our military duties as if we had nothing else to do.

With all of this interference, the missile systems were not coming up to an operational state on schedule, and we were working longer and longer hours. The civilian engineers were

228

under the supervision of a very knowledgeable Navy officer from the Navy Missile Station in California, but, even though he complained loudly to his command, the ridiculous dog-and-pony-show atmosphere continued, and the systems got further and further behind schedule.

On one unforgettable Sunday morning, about two hours after we had stopped work after a straight-through thirty-six-hour work shift, Chief Martinez came into our berthing compartment screaming about what lazy SOBs we were. He wanted the entire crew to get up and get out so that our berthing compartment could be shown off for an Open House.

I tried to explain to him that the crew was exhausted and needed the rest, but the Chief made a snide remark about how we could do better if we "stayed off the beach and out of the bars."

I told him again that the crew had not been ashore—they had been working.

Apparently this fact was just beyond his comprehension. He started screaming at us again, "This is a direct order! Get your lazy asses out of those bunks, now!"

I lost it and told him, very quietly, to get out and let my troops sleep. He told me that I was on report, and he was going to make sure that I lost a stripe for insubordination. Then he charged out of the room.

I picked up the phone in our compartment and called Lieutenant Cohen and explained what had just happened. He thanked me and got off the phone as the Chief began pounding on the door of his stateroom.

The Chief was as good as his word. He put me on report for insubordination and dereliction of duty. I was restricted to the ship until the situation could be adjudicated.

The restriction was not a problem because we were working pretty much around the clock and straight through the week at the time. We were finding an incredible amount of problems with the new systems. The engineers were documenting them and sending daily missives back to the factories and the Navy guided missile centers. A senior engineer from Johns Hopkins University was now aboard, trying to sort out all the problems and coordinate their resolution. In the meantime, the Chief and most of the chain of command was engaged in the business of showing off the ship to anyone that would look at it. The ship's internal technical problems just weren't compatible with the command's desire for a showboat.

In a way, the *Leahy* reminded me of my old Mercury convertible when I first saw it. The exterior was beautiful, but the engine didn't work.

After a week or so, I was scheduled to go to the Executive Officer about the charges that the Chief had filed against me. I went to his office accompanied by Chief Martinez and Lieutenant Cohen. As protocol required, I came to attention, saluted, and went to Parade Rest in front of the XO. He then read the charges and asked the Chief for his comments and recommendations. The Chief described the situation that had occurred from his perspective, then said something like, "Petty Officer Noonan is a habitual malingerer, Commander. He is a prima donna who is always making excuses for not having clean spaces and his uniforms are always greasy and unkempt. In addition, he is regularly disrespectful. I consider him incorrigible and recommend that he be court-martialed, reduced in rank, and discharged from the Navy."

The XO then turned to Lieutenant Cohen, who had been listening to this quietly, "Do you concur, Mr. Cohen?" The lieutenant looked distressed and replied, "Absolutely not, Commander." He stopped to gather his thoughts and then went on, "Petty Officer Noonan is one of the hardest-working and most dedicated people that I have ever met in my Navy career. He has been one of the key people responsible for getting as much done on the systems as we have. Every engineer on the ship has complimented him for his hard work and intelligent analysis of our system problems. I recommend that we drop this whole thing and let him get back to work."

The XO was absolutely speechless for a moment. For a division officer to contradict a master chief was pretty much unheard of, and his reaction reflected that fact.

"Mr. Cohen, I don't understand how your assessment of this situation can be so radically different from Master Chief Martinez's. Can you explain this to me?"

"Yes Sir," the Lieutenant said. Then he looked at me and said, "But I would rather do it in private. I don't think that my explanation would be appropriate in front of Noonan."

The XO, who was a young, nuclear-trained, commander with very little actual leadership experience, was not buying this. "Ridiculous. We are in an Executive Officer's Mast right now. If it needs to be said, say it now."

So Lieutenant Cohen continued, "Commander, with all due respect to his rank, Master Chief Martinez is an idiot. He runs the troops like some kind of martinet and has absolutely no comprehension of the work that they are doing. If I had my choice as to which one of these two should be kicked out of the Navy, it would not be Noonan."

With that, the XO finally saw the light. He turned to me and said, "Petty Officer Noonan, please step out to the passageway and wait by the door until I call you back."

I waited in that passageway for what seemed like hours. I could hear voices being raised and heated discussions going on, but I couldn't make out any of the words.

Finally, the Lieutenant opened the door and said, "Come back in, Noonan."

I did, returning to my parade rest position. I could see that all was not well.

Both the Chief and the Lieutenant looked mad as hell, and the XO wasn't happy either.

"Petty Officer Noonan, we've discussed your case and come to a conclusion. We're going to give you a choice of punishments. You can go to Captain's Mast, and take a chance on having a serious offense on your Navy record, or you can accept an informal punishment for insubordination from me. The informal punishment won't go on your record. Which do you prefer?"

I thought for a moment, but the choice was obvious. The Chief was one of the Captain's favorite people—one of the few that continuously supported the Captain's showboating crapola. If I went to the Captain with the Chief after me, I could kiss my Navy career goodbye. "I'll take the informal punishment, Commander."

"Okay, Noonan. Here it is. You're to report to Master Chief Martinez daily at sixteen-hundred hours for one week starting today. You'll perform two hours of extra duty as assigned by the Master Chief each day. If I hear that you didn't do the work so assigned, I'll reinstitute the charges and you'll go to the Captain for formal sentencing. Do you understand?"

"Yes Sir." I said. I knew I was in a world of trouble. The Chief would use this to try to break me. My chances of surviving this were not good, but I'd do my best.

The XO then dismissed us and we went outside. The Chief was obviously pleased with himself, and at the same time, he was really pissed at the Lieutenant. He just kept glaring at Cohen, even as he told me to report to him at Chief's Quarters at 1600. I said okay, and he left the Lieutenant and me standing there. Lieutenant Cohen turned to me and said, "I'm truly sorry, Noonan. You don't deserve this, but it was the best that I could get for you."

I replied, "Please don't apologize. You saved my ass and I know it. It's up to me now. Thank you, Sir."

He said, 'I will watch this, Noonan. If he does anything that I need to know about, call me. Don't let him pull any crap on you." I thanked him again and went back to working on the computers.

My fellow workers were solidly behind me at this point. Without my knowledge, they got together and decided to have one person each day check on me whenever I was on this extra duty. They were going to watch, from a distance, so that there would be witnesses to whatever happened.

At 1600 hours sharp, I knocked on the door of the Chief's quarters and was admitted.

Martinez was waiting for me. He said, "Come with me," and he led the way to the Chief's berthing compartment, then on through it to their head. It was a horrible mess. The Chief said, "Clean this up. I will be back to check on you." He left me standing there.

I took a good look at the head and figured out what had happened. Multiple commodes were plugged up and had overflowed, with a liberal amount of feces in each of them. There was shit everywhere, and one of the toilets' flush-levers was physically blocked open, making that commode overflow continuously.

I quickly went to the overflowing toilet and stopped the flow. Then I just stood there and laughed. This just told me how badly the Chief had underestimated me. He had called me a "prima-donna" when he was talking to the XO. Apparently he thought that, just because we were working on the missile systems, we were the kind of people who thought we were too good for dirty work. That was fine with me. If only he had looked at my record, as a good Chief would have, he would have known that I had dealt with a lot worse than this during my deck force days on *Cogswell*. This obviously contrived mess was not going to be a problem.

One of my third class subordinates stuck his head in the door when I was laughing. I explained to him what was going on and he offered to help, but I ran him off. I could handle this.

The Chief came down to the head about five minutes before my two hours were up.

The head was sparkling, and I was just finishing up on polishing some of the brass fixtures.

He immediately started yelling at me again, "What the hell do you think that you are doing? There is no sense shining that crap if the shitters are broken! How damned stupid are you anyway?"

I looked at him and said, "They're all fixed, Chief."

His face turned an awful red color, and he went to each commode, flushing all of them. Then he looked around, dragging his fingers over the tops of mirrors and stalls, looking for dust. He didn't find any, and finally he said, "Okay. Report to me tomorrow at sixteen-hundred hours."

When I left, he was still standing there looking absolutely confused.

This type of thing went on day after day. After the stupid head trick, he kept trying, but he just couldn't seem to be able to find anything more rigorous or demeaning. By the sixth day, I was starting to feel like I would survive this after all.

Then, on the last day, he found something really tough for a little guy like me. He met me at the Chief's Quarters as usual, but this time he led me up to the main deck, in a partially hidden spot between the ASROC Launcher and the bulkhead under the ship's bridge. A gunner's mate met us there, carrying an old Springfield rifle. The Chief took the heavy old gun and handed it to me, "We're going to do some working out today, Noonan."

Then he had me hold the gun out in front of me, horizontally in both hands, with my arms fully extended.

I knew that he finally had me. I couldn't possibly do this for two hours. He just stood there with a nasty smile on his face, watching me. Every few minutes, he would tell me to raise the rifle over my head as far as I could reach. Then, when that got so heavy that my arms were shaking, he would have me hold the rifle out in front of me again. It was absolutely excruciating.

I was still determined, but my body was weakening fast. About forty-five minutes into this, my arms just wouldn't hold the gun up any more. It started sagging, and the Chief, standing there with a triumphant grin on his face, started yelling, "Noonan, this is a direct order! Get that rifle up in front of you."

I struggled to get it back to the horizontal, but it soon sagged again.

"Noonan, you're disobeying a direct order."

Again the struggle and, again, the inevitable drooping of my arms. Again the yelling. I kept trying, but I just couldn't do what he wanted. By now, he had a grin that was splitting his face. He was finally breaking me, at least physically, and he knew it.

Then he stopped talking, except to tell me where to hold the rifle next. I looked around, and saw that we were being observed. A group of about ten sailors, as well as two of the missile system engineers, had appeared, leaning on the ship's lifelines on the side of the ASROC launcher beside the Chief.

I was about at the end of my rope, with the rifle at a low angle and my knees shaking, when I saw the group assembling. They were all very quiet, but grim looking. They were a really mixed group that included some of my fellow missile system people, but also other sailors that I had seen around the ship as well as the two engineers.

The Chief told me to hold the rifle above my head, and he turned to them and told them to move on. "This isn't any of your business. Get out of here."

The sailors looked at each other and seemed a bit uneasy.

Then one of the engineers said, "I don't take orders from you, Chief, and I kind of like it here."

This was followed by an older boatswain's mate, who said, "I've gotta stay here to make sure my deck doesn't get fouled," and a gunner's mate who said, "I work on this launcher. I'm staying."

The whole group just stood there while the Chief's face got redder and redder. Finally he turned to me and said, "Okay, Noonan—take a break." He was beaten. He knew that he couldn't keep doing what he had intended to do. Not with so many witnesses.

I still had almost an hour left on my punishment period, but I made it through. After the group showed up, the Chief conducted the session as if it was just routine physical exercise. Interestingly enough, not one of those guys left until it was all over, and the Chief dismissed me. They just sat there on the deck and the bollards, quietly watching.

My shipmates had saved me. Every day, one of my friends had been following me, watching what happened. Today one of the missile radar crew had been watching and had seen what was going on. He had run back to the missile radar room and told the crew what was happening. The two engineers working on the systems at that moment had stopped work and told the sailors who were working with them to go get their friends and meet them on the ASROC deck. When they had arrived, the Chief had been yelling his threats at me, and they had heard him. That was all it took to make them take the action that they had.

My week of extra duty was over and I had survived, but I knew that it was only a matter of time before the Chief got to me. He had been humiliated by this incident, and he wouldn't forget me anytime soon.

Shortly after this, the ship arrived at Guantanamo Bay, Cuba for an eight-week period of Underway Training. We were scheduled to go to Roosevelt Roads, Puerto Rico, to fire our first Terrier Missiles as soon as we finished the training period and left Cuba. With the training exercises ongoing and the missile firings imminent, our work schedule went from bad to absolutely horrific. We went through continuous training drills during the daylight hours, with the crew learning how to handle all of the various battle conditions and damage control processes. Then, during the nights, we tried to get the missile systems to work.

In October 1962, just after my 22nd birthday, we arrived in Guantanamo Bay for training. Within days of our arrival, President Kennedy announced to the world that Soviet Missile sites were under construction in Cuba. The Cuban Missile Crisis was on, and we were in Cuba!

We were in a training status and had no real ammunition on board, so our contribution to the naval blockade that ensued was minimal. We were there, and we sailed impressively, showing the flag to all that would look, but the Navy wisely kept us out of all potential firing zones. We were told where to get ammunition if we were needed, and our training was accelerated just in case, but we weren't needed and the crisis passed us by.

But it was exciting to be on the cusp of history.

In the meantime, the work kept going. We were only able to catch an hour or two of sleep at a time, usually whenever we could sneak it in. In my computer room, we would cover for each other during the daytime drills, with each of us grabbing a couple of hours of sleep behind the switchboards while the alarms and the drills went on around us. Then we would work on the missile systems all night. It was the only way we could get our jobs done.

The engineers working on the ship's missile systems had only one objective during this time. They were under contract to bring the missile guidance systems on line so that the ship could take its place in the operational fleet. They didn't take kindly to all of the interference by the Command. They understood the need for the battle drills and tolerated them, but they weren't so kind about the unnecessary interference that they encountered on *Leahy*. The showboating was bad enough, but the Chief's continuous interference with the technical work was something they couldn't accept. They regularly mentioned this interference in their weekly reports back to their companies, with copies to the Naval Weapons Station in Port Hueneme, California.

We were almost through with the eight-week training period when the word came to us via the engineers' grapevine that Port Hueneme had sent a very strong message about our situation to the ship's command. Suddenly we were given more freedom to work the systems, and the Chief almost disappeared, just staying in Chief's Quarters all day. Lieutenant Cohen was around regularly, but he was always a help, not a hindrance.

Slowly we began to get ahead of the multitude of system problems that we had been working on for months. We actually started hoping that we might actually be ready to fire the missiles when we were scheduled to do it. We were still working around the clock, but we were able to concentrate on the systems

We finished the training period and headed off to Roosevelt Roads. Working around the clock, getting one system up at a time by cannibalizing parts from other systems, we did finally fire the missiles. It was not what any of us would call either a successful missile exercise or one without problems, but we managed to fire missiles under the control of each of the missile guidance systems, with a reasonable number of successful shots. By the time the last missile left the launcher, none of the missile crew, neither engineers nor the ship's crew, really cared anymore. We just wanted it to be over so we could get some rest.

When the last missile left the rail, the ship turned and headed north. We were going to Norfolk, to go into the shipyard for what the Navy called the "post-shakedown availability." The engineers all left the ship and headed back to their regular jobs with their work on *Leahy* finished. The entire missile crew saw them off, and then went to bed. I think that I must have slept for the next twenty-four hours straight.

When I came to, and we were back to work, Lieutenant Cohen called me to his stateroom for a meeting. I thought nothing of it, but when I got there, he had a very serious look on his face. He asked me to sit down, and then he looked at me and said, "Noonan, I've been very worried about you, so I've been making some contacts with friends of mine."

I was startled, and I asked him, "What're you worried about? I thought that I was doing a good job."

He replied, "You are, you are. In fact, you're doing a terrific job. That's why I'm so worried. There's someone aboard this ship who's out to get you, and you don't deserve his crap." He said it again, almost thoughtfully, "That's why I'm so worried."

He was so serious that I couldn't think of anything to say except, "Oh."

He leaned back in his chair and said, "I talked to my counterpart on the next ship leaving Bath, the *Yarnell*. We're old friends, so I could talk honestly to him. I told him the kind of bum deal that I thought you were probably going to get here. To make a long story short, between the two of us, we have some pull with the guy who assigns fire control technicians their orders back in the Bureau of Naval Personnel. If you want us to do it, we'll get you transferred to the *Yarnell* as soon as we get back to the States. Are you interested?"

This was a real surprise to me, but I knew where the Lieutenant was coming from. All of us knew that the Master Chief was just waiting for a chance to get to me. I also knew that the Lieutenant and my friends wouldn't be able to protect me forever. This transfer was probably the only way out for me, but I hated to run, and I also had some good friends on the *Leahy*, so it was a hard decision.

"Do you really think its necessary, Sir?" I asked.

"Yeah" Lieutenant Cohen replied, "I really don't know any other way. Off the record, that sneaky son-of-a-bitch is out to get you, and eventually he will—even if he has to trump something up. You and I both know it. I just don't have any other answer. If you're on *Yarnell,* you'll be out of his reach. But here, you're in his world."

I looked at the Lieutenant and replied, "Okay. Let's do it. I should be able to help on the *Yarnell*. I've learned a lot these past few months. But I sure hate the thought of doing all of this all over again!"

The Lieutenant smiled sadly and reached out to shake my hand, "I'm honestly going to miss you, Noonan."

"Me too, Sir," I replied, and I started to get up.

"Wait a minute," he said. "I'll make the calls to get this to happen, but I don't want the word to get out about this before · we have the official orders in hand. I don't want the Chief to have any warning of what is coming, and I don't want to give him any ammunition to use against me. Mum is the word, Noonan."

I replied, "I understand, Sir. Thank you again."

The official orders came through via message while we were still enroute to the States. I was to be transferred upon arrival. But I was not going to Bath this time. Instead, I was to meet the *Yarnell* in Boston when it arrived from Bath. The timing was such that I was not granted any leave enroute. Apparently they wanted me aboard the ship and working as soon as possible. That, I thought, was a good sign.

CHAPTER TWENTY-SIX

Goodbye, Little Sister

I was preparing for my transfer when I caught a real blow in the form of a letter from Mom. My sister, Patty, had died. It had happened over a month before I got the letter, but she was gone. She would never again sit on the floor in front of Dad while he played the guitar and sang to her. I kept thinking about that. I just couldn't get that picture out of my head.

It was a long letter, and Mom had poured her heart out in writing it. It was, at twelve neatly written pages, one of the longest letters that I had ever received.

It turned out that there was a lot that Mom hadn't told me about in the year that had passed since I had been home last. Apparently Dad had been laid off for the winter, and things had gone from bad to worse. He had gone on a weeks'-long drunk and had repeatedly attacked Mom and the kids. It had gotten so bad that Mom had gone to the Sheriff for help. He had talked to Dad and had given him a good scare, but there was no permanent solution to the problem.

But Dad's deterioration had one very real consequence. The family had no money, and Mom had no choice but to go to work. Her letter said that she had tried everything, but she just couldn't work and take care of Patty. Finally, she said, it had come to the point where she only had one option open to her, and she had done what she had to do in order to feed the family. She had committed Patty to the state home for the disabled in Warm Springs, Montana.

With Patty's care no longer an obstacle, Mom had found work almost immediately. She was cooking school lunches at the local school and working in a café downtown the remainder of the day. She said that with my allotment and her wages, the family was in better financial shape than they had been in years.

But, it had come at a cost. Patty was just eighteen when she went into the home. She died less than a year later, just after her nineteenth birthday. According to the doctors, she had died of natural causes related to her condition, but Mom was sure that the real cause was loneliness and a broken heart.

Reading between the lines, I could tell that Mom was devastated by Patty's passing and was blaming herself for it. That was, I thought, almost certainly the reason she hadn't written me sooner.

Mom said in the letter that she knew that I was very busy and probably wouldn't be able to come home for the funeral, so she was just sending a letter rather than having the Red Cross send a telegram. The funeral had been over for more than three weeks when I got the letter. I was devastated. Patty had been a big part of my life, and she was gone! Even worse, I had not been able to say any kind of goodbye. I had not even known that she was in the state home.

I hid in one of the missile equipment rooms, crying and thinking for hours. Then I wrote Mom a very nice letter, commiserating with her for her loss and being as cheerful as I could be. I never told anyone how much it hurt to not be a part of saying the final goodbyes to Patty. Somehow it was even more than not being part of the funeral. It was almost as if I had been told that I was no longer part of the family. I knew that this kind of thinking was silly, but the impression lasted for a very long time, and it hurt.

I guess that the fact that I was bone-tired when I got the news made it even worse than it would have normally. But Patty was my sister, and she was the first close relative that I had ever lost. It was hard.

Mom's letter went on to tell me that she had purchased two adjoining plots in the St. Regis Cemetery and had paid to have one headstone made for the two plots. The names on the headstone were Mary K. Noonan (Mom) and Patricia Robin Noonan (Patty). Mom intended to spend eternity with Patty, the child she had loved and cared for so unselfishly when she was alive.

CHAPTER TWENTY-SEVEN

My Second Shakedown Cruise

I was less than thrilled to be reporting aboard *USS Harry E. Yarnell*. Except for the number on the bow and the name on the stern, the ship was physically identical to the ship I had just left. The *Leahy* had been a nightmare for me, with all of the Command's showboating while we agonized over the missile systems. That had been my only experience with a new ship, and I was very afraid that all of them would be the same. But at least I was free of Master Chief Martinez.

I soon found that, although we had a couple of chiefs aboard *Yarnell*, they were there to get the job done. I never had a single problem with any of them. Our division officer was the man that Lieutenant Cohen had called to get me transferred to the ship. His name was Lieutenant Swan, and he was very much like Cohen in that he was there to help.

The most interesting guy on the crew was an older first class petty officer named Mark Wilcoux. He was in charge of the missile radars, and he had been doing this kind of work for several years. He had commissioned two ships previously and had taken them through their shakedown cruises and missile firings. He absolutely loved this kind of work. When I met him, he had been in the Navy for sixteen years, and, in my opinion, he could have made chief whenever he wanted to if he had tried. But he didn't want to leave his hands-on electronics work to become an administrator. He absolutely loved the challenge of working with the new, often experimental, radar systems.

I had only been aboard about an hour when Wilcoux looked me up. I was unpacking my seabag when he introduced himself. As the Division's senior petty officer, he was my immediate superior, but he didn't come from that angle at all. He introduced himself, shook my hand, and then told me, "I've been working with these new ships for five years, so I know the engineers they send on shakedown cruises. I've heard all about you and the *Leahy,* and from everything I hear, you're my kind of guy. You work hard, you know what you are doing, and you care about the job. If you take the computers, and I take the radars, we can make this into one of the best missile ships in the Navy—but we'll have to work our asses off to do it. Are you in?"

I just looked at him and grinned. I held out my hand, and we sealed the deal. That was the start of a good friendship that endured for years.

I was not aboard *Yarnell* more than two hours before I was up to my elbows in the computers. I had arrived just as the crew was getting into making the system changes that came after commissioning. They were a new crew, much as the *Leahy*'s had been, and they were struggling with the ORDALTS, many of which I had put in *Leahy* just a few months before. Suddenly, I was the old hand, a person with experience! I went to work with real gusto. Before long, I was directing the work on all four computers, and even people senior to me were looking to me for guidance.

I worked straight through the week, and when we reached a logical breaking point, I stopped the work and cleaned up the spaces. I figured that if I did that, maybe I wouldn't run into the kind of problems that I had encountered on *Leahy*...but it was just not the same Command or crew here. The *Yarnell* was totally committed to making the ship into a fighting unit. My leaders appreciated that I kept things as orderly as possible, but they, like me, were more interested in getting the missile systems up and running.

The ship stayed in Boston for another month or so before heading south. I was so interested in my work that I seldom even went to town during this period. I did go out to visit Delores occasionally, but I was really into my work, so the visits gradually tapered off.

Mark Wilcoux had his radar crew on a five-day, twelve-hour, schedule. On the weekends, Mark religiously went home to Vermont to be with his wife and children. He told me that he wanted his six kids to have a normal life and not have to move every few years, so he had left them at home. He volunteered for these new ships because he could be close to New England at least part of the time. I don't think that I've ever met a more dedicated family man.

Since Mark's crew was on the five-day, twelve-hour work schedule, the computer crew had to roughly follow the same schedule, as much of our work was interrelated. But I mostly stayed on the ship and worked extra hours on the weekends, so we were getting a lot of critical work done. I measured our progress against what we had on *Leahy*, and I saw us pulling way ahead of where we had been on that ship. I was really pleased with our progress, even before we left Boston. After we got underway, Mark matched me, and we worked straight through the weeks, so we pulled further and further ahead of the planned schedule.

By April 1963, our Boston shipyard period was almost over, so we went to sea for sea trials, a period when the work done in the shipyard is tested. We were at sea on April 10 when we received word that a new nuclear submarine, USS *Thresher* (SSN-593), was missing in the area. It had been at sea for sea trials, much as we were, when all communications with the submarine were lost.

We immediately stopped all other functions and steamed at top speed for the area where the *Thresher* was last reported. When we got there, we went into a search pattern, much as the *Cogswell* had done when we lost the men in the typhoon. We searched for days, but all we found was an oil slick and some debris in the water. The *Thresher* had gone down with all hands on board. The submarine's remains were later found at the bottom of the Atlantic, 8,000 feet underwater.

After we were detached from the *Thresher* search, we returned to Boston and prepared for the upcoming shakedown cruise. During this time, we did a lot of night work; doing a complete battery alignment on the ship's sensors and weapons systems. We also aligned the missile radar beams, a time-consuming, rigorous, and precise process called collimation.

When we left Boston, we headed straight for Norfolk, where we were scheduled to do some work in Norfolk Naval Shipyard. Since most of the work being done was on the ship's propulsion plant, we had a bit of slack in our missile work. When we could get off the ship, we often visited the local bars outside the shipyard gates on Crawford Street. Without a car, this was about as far as we could feasibly get. (Most of the single guys had put their cars in storage, or left them in Boston, for the duration of the shakedown cruise.)

Crawford Street was a two-block, free-wheeling area much like the Boston Combat Zone, except that the bars were smaller and only served beer. I never particularly liked beer, but since this was where the females of the species congregated, I decided to stifle my taste buds and enjoy it anyway.

I knew from experience that when we left the shipyard, the schedule would get much worse. The remainder of the civilian engineering team would arrive en masse, and we would have a tremendous amount of missile system testing and trials work. When this was almost complete, we would have to go through the Guantanamo Bay crew training period. Then it was on to Roosevelt Roads for the ship's initial missile firings. So I figured that I would take advantage of the slack period and get some studying done.

I had taken out several correspondence courses over the previous year and had been working on them whenever I had the time. But now, another deadline was looming on the horizon, and I had to get busy. That winter, I was going to have enough time in the service to take the exam for promotion to first class petty officer (E-6), and I had a lot of studying to do to prepare, so I started working on the courses and studying whenever I had time.

I didn't really have much hope of actually being promoted to first class in the near future. I had less than five years in the Navy and that was too junior to be even thinking about such a promotion. But I've always been a dreamer, so I couldn't see any reason not to try. I stuck my head back in the books and began studying seriously again.

The shipyard period was soon over. The missile system engineering team returned, and the serious work started anew. As usual, the team of engineers came aboard, led by a Navy lieutenant from the Missile Center in California. The Navy called this team the Ship Qualification and Training (SQAT)

Team. They were all missile system experts, with some being civil servants and the others all engineers representing the companies that had manufactured the missile system equipments.

When the SQAT Team arrived, they brought with them another group of system alterations designed to improve the missile systems. We installed the changes and then went to work testing and aligning the systems all over again. This time, the systems were in good shape to start with, so the work went smoothly. The primary problems that we encountered were in the radar areas, because of the inherent unreliability of the complex, high-powered radar equipment. In 1963, guided-missile system technology was still in its infancy and the radars reflected that fact. Very seldom did we have all four systems on-line and operational at the same time. But Wilcoux and his crews still got continuous accolades from the engineers. They did good work.

The next few months were almost an identical replay of the *Leahy* shakedown cruise except that we were somehow much more relaxed as we did our training and went about getting the systems ready for our first missile firings.

About halfway through the eight-week training period, we took a long weekend and sailed the ship to Ocho Rios, Jamaica, where we all had a weekend of fun and relaxation. In 1963, there wasn't much in Ocho Rios—just a huge jungle with a few plantations and a couple of primitive bars. We actually tied up to a bauxite shipping pier adjacent to the local bauxite mine, where, in later years, they filmed a famous James Bond movie. We went ashore in our dress white uniforms, which were red with bauxite dust before we left the pier. But we managed to raise a lot of hell and have a lot of fun before we had to head back to the training the next week. With a break like this behind us, we were more ready than ever to do our jobs.

When we finished the eight weeks of training, we proceeded to port in San Juan, where we took on supplies, made last-minute missile system tests and adjustments, and let most of the crew enjoy another Liberty port. The missile crew, including me of course, stayed aboard and agonized over last-minute missile system glitches as we prepared for our initial missile firings.

The *Yarnell* missile firings at Roosevelt Roads, in the days after we left San Juan, confirmed that we were on the right track with our efforts. We didn't hit every shot, but no one expected us to do that with dummy warheads and the guided missile systems of that era. However, we did better than just about any other new ship had in their initial firings, and we were ecstatic about our successes. When the results were put out in the official reports, the ship got messages commending us from both the Naval Missile Systems Center in California and Commander, Cruiser and Destroyer Forces, Atlantic, in Norfolk. It had taken some long, hard hours, but the payoff was worth it to us. We were one happy crew!

The *Yarnell* returned to Norfolk after the missile firings, and we immediately went into the shipyard in Portsmouth for our post-shakedown availability. For once, we did not have a tremendous amount of missile work to do, so I turned back to studying, and on weekends, several of us began raising heck in the bars on Crawford Street.

During the late 1950s and early 1960s, Norfolk and Portsmouth, Virginia, had some extremely hard-nosed police forces that generated a tremendous amount of revenue for the cities through their enforcement of "Blue Laws" on the sailors and Marines who were unlucky enough to be stationed there. We had many names for these police forces, but very few that are printable. One of the more popular names was the "Morals Squad." Whenever we were drinking in the areas, we always had our eyes peeled for any sign of the Morals Squad.

I had actually seen the Morals Squad arrest a sailor and a waitress because the sailor was seen giving the waitress a drink from his beer, so I walked a very careful line whenever we went to Crawford Street, or anywhere in the area, to have a drink. But it was for naught, because they did finally catch me, literally, with my pants down.

I had been wooing a young lady in one of the clubs for a few weeks, and I finally got a date with her on her night off. We went to dinner and a movie, after which we stopped at a bar on Crawford Street for a couple of drinks. Then, when the bars closed, she volunteered to make me some breakfast at her home. So we proceeded to have breakfast which, of course, led to other things.

I was peacefully sleeping when, at about 3:00 a.m., I was awakened by loud hammering on the door followed by two men charging through and coming into the living room only a few feet from where I was sleeping. "Get up and get dressed! You are both under arrest!" one of them shouted.

I sat up and groggily asked, "What in hell am I under arrest for?"

My girlfriend was also mad and was yelling that they had no business in her house.

One of them told her, "Shut up!" and then answered me with, "Look around you, Asshole! What do you think you are under arrest for?"

I sat up and looked at my surroundings. I was as naked as the day I was born, and so was my friend. We didn't even have a blanket over us. Worse yet, we were lying on her couch, the lights were on, and we were in front of a picture window.

"Oh shit," I said.

The bigger of the two Morals Squad cops grinned at me, saying, "Get up and get dressed. We're all going downtown."

I got up and started pulling on my clothing. When I got to my dress jumper, the cop stopped me with, "Jesus Christ, Kid! Are you really a second class petty officer?"

I replied, "Yes, Sir."

He and his friend looked at each other and went into an adjoining room, whispered to each other for a minute, and then came back.

"Do you have a car?" one of them said.

I replied, "No."

Then the bigger of the two said, "How would you like a sporting chance to get out of this, Kid?"

I jumped at the chance and replied, "Hell yes. What do I have to do?"

Both of them were grinning now, "Give me your uniform pants, and then get dressed—put the rest of your uniform on."

I did as he directed and stood up, looking rather silly in my white hat, jumper with neckerchief, skivvy shorts, and shoes.

He handed me my wallet and said, "Okay, Sailor. Get out of here. If you can make it back to your ship without being arrested, you beat the game this time. If you don't make it, we've never seen you before. If you aren't in jail in the morning, I'll deliver your pants to your ship. Good luck."

By the time I made it out the door, both he and his partner were roaring with laughter.

I didn't want to take a chance on them double-crossing me, so I broke into a dead run as soon as I was off the porch. To throw them off, I cut back in the direction away from the ship for a while, and then paralleled the shipyard fence from about a half mile away. It reminded me of the time that I ran through the pigpen in Olongapo, and I chuckled.

I found myself in a very poor, mostly black, section of Portsmouth. I cautiously navigated my way between rows of apartment houses. I went by one where an older couple was setting on the stoop.

"The Morals Squad is behind me," I said to them as I went by.

I got a big laugh and a "Run, Boy, Run! We won't tell them guys nothing."

I kept going.

Finally, my circuitous route took me to a point where I was directly across the street from the main gate of the shipyard. I hid behind a pile of junk in an empty lot as I checked out the entry. This was the only gate open to the shipyard at this time of night, and there was a Marine guarding the gate. The rest of the shipyard was surrounded by an eight-foot chain-link fence topped with barbed wire. I knew that the gate was my only real chance.

I waited and watched for a few minutes. I was about ready to head for the gate when I saw a black car slowly coming down the road, parallel to the shipyard's fence. I lay low and watched as my two favorite Morals Squad members slowly drove by, with a searchlight playing over the area.

When they got to where I was, across from the gate, they sped up and turned out the searchlight, apparently so they wouldn't blind the Marine at the gate. They obviously expected me to try to climb the fence and sneak around the Marine. They were planning to get me when I did.

I waited while they passed me by and started down the other side of the fence, with the light back on and searching. As soon as they passed the gate, I jumped up and ran across the road, directly toward the Marine gate guard. Out of the corner of my eye, I saw the black car stop and start a U-turn. When I was about ten feet from the guard, I slowed to a walk and approached him with my ID card in hand, as if everything was normal. He had a quizzical look on his face and was trying hard not to laugh.

I looked him straight in the eye, and said, "Not a word, Corporal...*not a fucking word.* I am not at my best right now." I grinned at him and kept going.

He just stared at me, but he let me through.

I walked about another twenty feet and then looked back.

The black car was stopped outside the gate, and the driver was looking at me. After a minute, he gave me a "thumbs up," and drove away. I walked back to the ship, crossed the Quarterdeck, and went to bed. The quarterdeck watch just laughed as I went by them.

The next morning, my pants were delivered to the ship by a police messenger.

The next weekend, I stayed away from that damned picture window.

The shipyard period was over soon, and we got underway again, this time again returning to the coast off of Florida, where we completed some specialized testing designed to establish the acoustic signature (underwater noise pattern) for our class of ships. Since this was one time when the pressure was not on the missile systems, I managed to get in a lot of studying. It also allowed Mark and I to make some finishing touches on the systems, touches that were nice to have, but were not the kind of things that we had found time for when we were bringing the systems on-line in the previous underway periods.

We returned to Norfolk in late November 1963, and we tied up to the piers for a break over the Christmas period. I was looking forward to some rest and relaxation and was debating whether to go home for Christmas. I liked being there for the holiday, but it would be a lot warmer and nicer if I waited until summer. Besides, Dad was usually away from home more during the summer months, and I didn't look forward to having another Christmas run-in with him.

Early that December, I was in the after computer room working on a perplexing equipment problem when I got a call from the ship's telephone switchboard operator. I picked up the handset and heard a deep, official-sounding voice say, "Is this FTM2 Noonan?"

"Yes."

The voice went on, "I'm Lieutenant Masterson from the Bureau of Naval Personnel. My job is to provide personnel for new-construction Navy ships and I've just received a request from the Missile Center in Port Hueneme, California, for a few specific enlisted people. They're picking a team for a new ship that's going to be the first of a new class of missile ships. You're one of the people that they're requesting. Are you interested?"

This came out of the blue. I had actually expected to stay aboard *Yarnell* and go to the Mediterranean the next year. Plus, I was not excited by the thought of going through the debugging of another new set of missile systems. I thought for a minute and then asked, "Can you tell me more about the ship and its schedule, Sir?"

"Sure. It'll be USS *Belknap* (DLG-26). It's under construction at Bath Iron Works up in Maine. If you take this offer, you'll get to Bath in May 1964. The ship is to be commissioned in November, and it's to be home-ported in Norfolk after that. The skipper is going to be Captain John Law. That's about everything that I know. Are you interested?"

I had missed most of his explanation because I was quickly calculating the time periods. I knew that Navy per diem had just risen to $24 per day, and Bath was still a per-diem assignment. He was offering me about six months of per diem in Bath, Maine! That was enough to overcome my reservations.

I said, "Count me in, Lieutenant. If the Missile Center wants me, I'd be honored to support them."

He signed off then, telling me that my orders would be coming within a week.

I just sat there looking at the phone in my hand and trying to sort out this latest development. This was definitely unplanned, and it would change my plans a good bit. I was still thinking about this when I heard the ship's speaker system come on and the announcement, "FTM1 Wilcoux, please call the switchboard."

I sat up straight as the obvious conclusion hit me: we had done well with the shakedown of the *Yarnell,* and now the Missile Center was hand-picking its crew for the next big ship program! I just knew that Wilcoux was having the same conversation that I had just had.

I got up and headed for the forward radar room, where I knew that Wilcoux was working that morning. I got there just in time to hear him say, "Yes Sir, I am always happy to return to New England."

I knew then that I was right.

He hung up the phone with a silly grin on his face and turned around to face me.

I stuck out my hand and said, "Welcome aboard, shipmate."

His smile widened, and he said, "*Belknap*? You too?"

"Yup."

He grabbed me in a huge bear hug, and we started laughing. Finally he drew away, saying "You know, for the first time since I joined this canoe club, I really do feel appreciated. It feels good!"

I agreed with him on that.

After that, we spent the day making plans. We both decided to go home for Christmas. Mark had planned to do that anyway, but I had been undecided. However, there wouldn't be much time later and now was probably my only chance, so I prepared a leave request and made plans to fly home for the holiday.

The next afternoon, Mark and I made some calls to the people we knew at the California Missile Center to ask for any documentation that they had on the *Belknap* and her new missile systems. It turned out that the *Belknap* was going to receive a whole new version of the type of missile systems that were aboard *Yarnell*.

It was going to be a challenge, but my engineer friends told me that they knew the new Commanding Officer and my new division officer, and they were very happy with their selection. I got the feeling that they had hand-selected the entire chain of command for this new ship.

When I was assured by two of them, in almost identical words, "This won't be another *Leahy*," I felt better.

I asked them who was going to be my first class in charge of the missile computer systems, and they surprised me with,

"There ain't going to be one, Jeff. The computers are going to be yours."

This floored me, but Mark was ecstatic about it, "You deserve it, Jeff. You've earned it, and you can handle it better than anyone I've known."

This was very flattering, but also very scary to me.

The documentation that we had requested came in a few days. It was classified, of course, so we locked it up and decided to study it in the after computer room where we had a lot of room to spread out prints. Since we were on the cusp of leaving for the Christmas holiday, we decided to leave it locked up until we returned.

CHAPTER TWENTY-EIGHT

No One Will Ever Find Your Body

I flew home on December 22, 1963, with two weeks of leave ahead of me. It had been two years since I had been home last, and there had been a lot of change since then. Patty was gone, and Kathy was married. Tim was seventeen years old and a senior in high school. Even little Danny, the baby of the family, was now five years old. Home was going to be a different place.

Mom and Kathy met the plane in Missoula with all of the normal hugs and compliments. It was really great to see them. I don't know what I had subconsciously been expecting, but I found myself quite surprised to see that both of them looked healthy and happy. I have to admit that my eyes did water a bit when I saw them, but they probably didn't notice much because Mom's waterworks far surpassed mine. It was good to be back.

On the way from Missoula to St. Regis, they talked nonstop about the changes in their lives since I had been home last. Mom was working at the school, cooking their noon lunches; a new Dairy Queen had opened, and she was working there also.

Kathy was married, of course, and seemed happy. She mentioned that she and her husband, Don, were living across town from where we were raised. She was also working, and was helping to baby sit our little brothers and sister when she could. But most importantly, she was able to give shelter when the family had to get out of the house because of Dad's tantrums. Her husband, although he was a friend of Dad's, had laid down some rules, and Dad was not allowed in Kathy's home when he was drunk. As a result, the old bunker was no longer in use.

Apparently Dad was still living at home, but it was obvious from the conversation that Mom was much more independent than she had been when I was there last. Neither Kathy nor Mom had much to say about him, so I was left with some questions in my mind, but I didn't bring them up because I didn't want to put a damper on the homecoming.

Once again, my eyes watered when we came over the mountain and the St. Regis Valley came into view. God, I missed this place!

Dad and all of the kids were home when we got there. Dad was obviously half-drunk, but he was in a good mood, so all went well. I was amazed at the growth of the kids. Tim was still stocky and jovial, but much more mature than I remembered. Lyle, at fifteen, was tall and well-built and was becoming a power on the school football team. The younger kids were all very shy around me, but that was normal. They had not seen me that often while they were growing up, and it would take some time for them to become reacquainted with this strange new big brother.

We had dinner at home and settled in to talk for the evening. Dad was soon bored and gave a lame excuse to get out of there. He left for downtown, and I didn't see him again for a couple of days.

The younger kids soon warmed up, and we had a nice evening. Mom was really excited when I told her about the people from the Missile Center selecting me for the new ship. That really seemed to mean a lot to her. The kids all wanted to hear about living on the ships, so I told them stories about the places I had been and the (G-rated) things that I had done. They were interested, and, in turn, I had them tell me about the excitement in their lives. Little Danny was absolutely adorable, telling me about things like a caterpillar he had caught the summer before and a fish that he had put back in the river "cause it was hurted." He looked like a perfect cherub with a round face, big ears, and a grin that lit up the world when it split his little round face.

It was an evening to remember. Life for the Noonan family looked a whole lot better than it had been only two short years ago. There was an obvious, but unmentioned, emptiness where Patty had been, but life was better for the family in spite of that.

Mom loaned me her car the next day, and I drove around town, looking up my old friends. Both Joe Thompson and another old friend, Dale, had been discharged and were home again. We talked for a while and agreed to meet the following day for a drink. I had some things to do with the family, so I reserved the day for them.

After scouting the town and renewing acquaintances, I went to the community cemetery to say hello and goodbye to Patty. Mom had been true to her word. There was a large stone at the head of Patty's grave and the one next to it. The stone had both Patty and Mom's names on it. It was under a big pine tree on the side of the cemetery. Patty's grave and the headstone made a huge impression on me. Somehow it was a symbol of everything that had been wrong with our childhood. Over that grave, I promised Patty that I would do everything in my power to make this world a better place whenever I could. I actually prayed over it, something I don't do often.

When I left there, I found Kathy's new home and went in to see her. I had brought presents from Norfolk for everyone. They were not big things; just an assortment of clothing, jewelry, and toys that I had bought at the Base Exchange. I brought them to Kathy's place, and we wrapped them before I took them home.

Later in the afternoon, I went with Tim and Lyle, and we cut a Christmas tree for the house. Then, in the evening, we decorated it and put out our presents. We had another really nice evening at home, laughing and joking as families do during the Christmas season.

The next day was Christmas Eve, and we were all lazy in the morning, just setting around gabbing. Mom went downtown to work in the morning, so I cooked some hot cakes for the kids and we spent the morning cleaning up so Mom would be surprised when she got home.

Then, late in the afternoon, Dad came home. Tim, Lyle, and I were in the kitchen talking to Mom, who had just come home from work. Dad stormed through the door, obviously mad as hell at something. He never explained himself; he just threw his coat on a sofa and came straight through the living room to where Mom was standing and hit her in the face. She went down hard, and he turned toward where I was standing across the kitchen. He charged at me, pulling back his big right fist, aiming to get me with another swing when he got close enough.

But he had forgotten that this time I could see him coming, and I was no longer the little boy that he had beaten so badly a few years ago. Instead of cowering back and waiting for him, I stepped into his charge and hit him with my absolute best shot; a hard right that came over my shoulder from way, way, back. It caught him right on the bridge of his nose and stopped him cold. Blood spattered everywhere.

He staggered back, and I got him in the gut with a hard left, then a right to the jaw. He went backward again and came within reach of Tim, who unloaded years of frustration in one huge right hand that caught him on the other side of his jaw. He went down—still conscious but totally incoherent, flopping around as if he had lost all control of his body! Then he just rolled over on his back and laid there with blood covering his face and pooling on the floor.

Tim and I could not believe what we had done. We just stood there, looking at each other and at Dad.

Mom surprised me then. Her reaction was, "Oh my God! Is he okay?" She was still on the floor where she had fallen, but she scuttled over to where he was and checked to see that he was breathing; which he was. She was bleeding from a cut on the side of her face, but she was honestly more concerned about her husband than she was about herself!

I could not understand this. Tim and I exchanged puzzled glances and then we went over and picked Mom up. She didn't want to leave Dad, even then.

I yelled at her, "Go get cleaned up! You don't want to be here when he gets up!"

She came out of her trance and left for the bathroom, just as Dad began moving again.

I can't describe the feelings that came over me as I stood there looking down on the man I had once loved and admired so much. They were more of sadness and pity rather than the fear and hatred that I had felt for so long. I looked at Tim and saw nothing but hate on his face. He had not known the father that I had known so many years ago. That fact hit me hard. What a horrible, horrible waste!

Tim grabbed a heavy piece of firewood and was ready to hit Dad with it, but I had him back up to where he was out of range. Tim was still in high school, and I didn't want Dad to blame him for this after I left.

Dad staggered to his feet and looked around dazedly. I didn't give him time to recover.

I told him, "Get out! Get out and don't come back here until you sober up." I kept repeating myself and I grabbed his shirt, pushing him toward the door.

He finally got a bit steadier and tried to turn toward me, but just then Tim stepped up beside me with his firewood held high. He said, very calmly, "Get out, you son-of-a-bitch, or I'll kill you!"

That was too much for Dad. The look on his face was absolute amazement. He turned toward the door, prepared to leave. I grabbed his jacket from the sofa where he had thrown it and followed him.

I said, "Wait a minute!" and he turned to look at me, his face blood-smeared and still looking dazed. But then he turned and went through the door onto the porch.

I followed him, with Tim and Lyle close behind me. Dad was going down the porch steps when yelled again, "I said *wait a minute,* God damn you."

He finally stopped and turned to face me. He was standing exactly where I had fallen from his sneak attack a couple of years earlier. Now that I had his attention, I threw his coat to him and said, "Do you remember how I used to live in the mountains when I was a kid?"

Confused, he replied, "Yeah."

My voice dropped an octave or two, still steady but somehow piercing through all of us in a way that I still can't explain, "Well, I still remember those mountains well. I know about a hundred places up there where no one will ever find your body. If I ever hear that you've hurt Mom or any of this family again, I'll be back and you'll disappear! Do you understand me? *You will disappear."* I was deadly serious.

265

Tim and Lyle moved forward to flank me.

Dad just stood there looking more and more stubborn. In his face, I could see that the rage was taking him over again.

I grabbed the firewood from Tim's hand and went toward Dad with it. We were about three feet apart, only separated by the porch steps, glaring at each other and I wasn't blinking when I repeated, in that same deadly tone, "*Do you understand me?*"

The boys moved forward again, putting the three of us shoulder to shoulder, facing him. The mindless rage on his face faded, and it looked like he was actually thinking about what I had said. Then he just nodded. He turned and left.

We stood there, watching him, until he had gone out of sight down the street. When we knew for sure that he was gone, I turned and hugged my brothers. I really didn't know what to say to them. As I drew them close, I realized that all three of us were shaking badly. This had been the hardest few minutes of any of our lives.

Tim was the first to speak, "Guys, we can never talk about this with anyone?"

Lyle pulled back and asked "Why?"

Tim replied, "Because if something *does* happen to that bastard, I don't want us to be blamed for it."

I followed up with, "Good thinking, Tim. We don't talk about this—ever."

We were all sitting in the living room when Mom came out of the bathroom with a bandage on her cheekbone. She looked around and asked where Dad was.

I said, "He just left," and the boys nodded. To the best of my knowledge, none of us ever spoke about that afternoon to anyone after that.

Dad came home while I was there several times after Christmas. Each time, he stayed just long enough to sleep, always leaving in the morning. I only saw him from a distance for the remainder of my stay. Tim later told me that he was far more subdued from then on whenever he was at home. Of course, he still drank and threw tantrums, but according to Tim, the all-out brutality was never again as bad as it had been before that Christmas Eve encounter.

We actually had a really nice Christmas that year. We opened presents in the morning, and Kathy had us to her home for Christmas dinner. It was almost as if we were a normal family. No one expressed any regrets about the missing family member.

I spent most of the next few days just hanging out with my friends. It was very cold, and we mostly just sat around in the Stag or St. Regis Bars and gabbed. Soon it was time to return to real life.

CHAPTER TWENTY-NINE

USS Belknap, Bath, Maine

Mark and I both returned to the *Yarnell* right after New Year's Day, 1964, and immediately threw ourselves into studying the paperwork and schematics that we had received describing the *Belknap's* new missile systems. It was January and we were due to leave for Bath in May. We both knew that we would be busy when we got there and we wanted to be as prepared for the new systems as possible.

For the first time ever, I thought about ignoring my studies for the upcoming promotion test. I figured that the *Belknap* studies were more important, since I was far too junior to be promoted anyway. I figured that I would have at least a couple of years to prepare for that promotion and the *Belknap* work was imminent, so *Belknap* was the priority. But this line of thought bothered the heck out of me and finally I gave in and studied for both the test and *Belknap*. The old "Please, Escape" concept just wouldn't let me slack off. For about two months, I studied every free moment, usually sleeping only four or five hours a night.

In February, I took the test for fire control technician first class. It seemed tough, but I didn't have any real hope of being promoted, so I mentally blew it off and kept working. I thought that, with the test over, at least now I could get a full night's sleep and maybe go to town once in a while.

The days dragged on, filled with the routine work on our equipment, normal duty days, heavy *Belknap* studying, and an occasional trip to Crawford Street. We got underway regularly and went to sea off Cape Hatteras for training purposes. *Yarnell* was preparing for its first trip to the Mediterranean, but that didn't hold any real interest for me. Both Mark and I were counting the days until we left for Bath.

One day in April, I was working in the forward computer room when Mark came down to where I was working. He said "C'mere Noonan. There's something on the mess decks that I want to show you." So I went along with him, thinking that he had uncovered some technical change in the *Belknap* schematics that he'd been studying, but he stopped in front of the ship's bulletin board and pointed at a name on a posted list.

I was being promoted to first class petty officer! I was going to be promoted to E-6 in a month. I could not believe it. Less than five years off the deck force and I was going to be a first class! I was absolutely astounded.

That night, the majority of the *Yarnell*'s Fire Control Crew went to Crawford Street and celebrated, even Mark who almost never went ashore.

In May 1964, two first class missile fire control technicians, Mark Wilcoux and Jeff Noonan, left USS *Harry E. Yarnell* in Norfolk enroute to Bath, Maine, and the new ship, *Belknap*.

Mark decided to take thirty days' leave on the way to spend some time with his family. I drove straight through to Brunswick and reported in within a couple of days of leaving the *Yarnell*. I had nothing better to do and I figured the sooner I got there, the more per diem I would get. Plus this time I planned on renting an apartment instead of living in the hotel, so the sooner I got there the better chance I would have of finding a decent apartment.

All went well and I received my per diem check as soon as I arrived. The same day I went to Bath and reported to the *Belknap* pre-commissioning detail, where I found that I was only about the sixth person to arrive. The Captain and my new division officer, Lieutenant Hurt, were there, but no one else in my chain of command had yet arrived.

The Captain's name was John Law and, because of his name, I was expecting a burly, by-the-book, tough-as-nails kind of guy. He was just the opposite; a slim, dignified man with an infectious smile and a totally relaxed manner. There was something about John Law that told you not to mess with him, but at the same time, you couldn't help but to like him.

John Hurt was about the same size as the Captain, and was equally easy-going, but the similarities ended there. Where the Captain was erect and dignified, John Hurt always walked in an easy slouch, usually with his hands in his pockets. Where the captain had a tanned complexion and closely-cropped dark hair, the Lieutenant was blond and looked like a mature surfer, with his long locks always down over his forehead.

They shared another common trait. They were both very intelligent, absolutely dedicated, Navy men who wanted *Belknap* to be the best ship in the Navy. I liked them both on sight and never had any reason to change my initial impression.

With the ship's permission, Mark and I had gathered copies of many of the *Yarnell*'s manuals and operating instructions before we left. As a result, the back seat of my car was filled with documents like "The Weapons Doctrine," *The* Yarnell *Operations Department Manual,* the Yarnell *Personnel Manual, Ship and Departmental Instructions,* and the like. These were documents that every ship had to have, and they were usually written by the crew in Bath. Mark and I had agreed that these were a huge pain in the butt and a distraction from the real work when we were in Bath before, so we decided to short-cut the process by bringing samples with us. These were well-received by the Captain. After he read them and made a few editorial changes, he turned the whole stack of documents over to the ship's yeoman with instructions to re-type them and change the ship name from *Yarnell* to *Belknap*. This freed up the whole crew, as they arrived, to concentrate on shipboard equipment work.

I made sure that the Captain and Lieutenant Hurt both knew that Mark had been my partner in getting the documents together. At this, Hurt remarked, "I knew that the pair of you would be an asset. I heard about you guys from the SQAT Teams in Port Hueneme." Apparently our reputations had preceded us.

When I checked in, the *Belknap's* yeoman gave me some mail that had been forwarded to me from the *Yarnell*. In this mail was a letter from my brother, Tim. This startled me because Tim had never written to me before. Looking at it, I immediately imagined the worst so I literally ripped it open. But the news inside was good, not bad. Tim had graduated from high school and had enlisted in the Navy. He wrote that he hoped that I didn't mind, but he had requested brother duty and schooling as a fire control technician. His Navy contract stated that he would go from Boot Camp to FT Class A School and then on to the *Belknap* for duty with his brother. I was ecstatic! Not only was Tim going to serve with me, but—and this was far more important to me—he had escaped. In my mind, this meant that Tim was going to survive.

The number of people moving beyond Dad's reach was growing. Kathy was married, Tim was in the Navy and, with Patty gone, Mom was able to work full time and earn a better living. But there were still four kids at home, and Dad was still Dad. Tim's letter was great news, but at the same time, that meant that one less stable head was there to protect the little ones. It was a time for rejoicing, but also a time for worry.

At lunch that first day with *Belknap*, I met another member of the new crew, a second class electronics technician named Pitt who was also looking for an apartment. We headed out and visited a few rentals before we settled on one that we liked. It was on the second floor of a big old New England farmhouse that had been converted to apartments. It had decent furniture and had a lot of old woodwork and hardwood floors, as well as two bedrooms and two baths. We both liked it, so we decided to go in together on it. We took it on the spot and then spent the rest of the evening at the exchange in Brunswick, buying blankets and household goodies that didn't come with the apartment. This was a real adventure, since neither of us had never really lived "on our own" before. We made sure that the refrigerator was well-stocked with beer, chips, soft drinks, and candy. I'm not sure that we bought anything that could be considered healthy.

We moved in that night, and since it was only two blocks away, we ate dinner at the same old bar-restaurant that I had frequented two years earlier with my shipyard friend, George LaCroix. As soon as I walked in, the owner recognized me and gave me a hearty welcome. George was there also, still sitting at the same barstool, looking a bit worse for the wear. So we had a few drinks with our cheeseburgers before we gave up for the night.

The next day, I was aboard the ship for almost ten hours. It was about the same size as the *Leahy* and *Yarnell*, but had some major differences. It only had two missile systems instead of four. They were on the forward end of the ship and there was a new gun fire control system with a five-inch gun aft. She also had a new type of 3-D search radar which I learned would be assigned to the fire-control gang for maintenance.

Belknap was impressive, and somehow I already liked this ship. I guess John Law and John Hurt had something to do with that. An old Navy adage says that a ship takes on the personality of its first Commanding Officer and never changes after that. In my experience, this is a fact.

I found that the construction discrepancies in my areas of responsibility were almost identical to those I had encountered aboard *Leahy*. Apparently the people who designed these ships never got the word that we had to have places to store our tools and technical manuals, especially lockable storage for classified manuals, so I put in change requests for those items, and soon the Captain had me going through all the other shipboard electronics spaces looking for similar problems. By the time Mark Wilcoux showed up, I had already submitted over a hundred change requests and was meeting daily with the Navy Supervisor's Office to get them approved. These meetings were my first real exposure to civilian business and business management, and I loved it.

The supervisor's representative in charge of the change request approval was another Navy lieutenant named Fox. He was a great guy who became good friends with John Hurt and, many years later, me. He had a full head of glistening grey-white hair, so he was known far and wide as the "Grey Fox." With him holding the purse strings, and with my boss being his good friend, we really got a lot done for the *Belknap*.

In the evening, Pitt and I had become accustomed to having dinner at the bar down the street from our apartment, having a drink or two, then going home to watch TV or read. It was becoming a quiet, slightly boring, existence. But all that soon changed.

I had been there a month or so when, one Saturday, I walked into our bar for a drink and met Debbie. She was a nice lady who was about two years older than me. She was tall and very fit, talking about her daily five-mile runs. She was a bit more refined than the average person who came to this bar, and it clearly showed in her every word. She and I started talking while I was ordering dinner, and we hit it off right away. I learned that her first name was Debbie and that she was from the state of Maine, but she wouldn't tell me more. When I tried to press for more details, she told me, "Back off, or you won't see me again." So I shut my mouth and we got along splendidly after that.

Pitt wasn't too sure how to take it when she was in the apartment the next morning, but after she cooked a great breakfast for us, he forgave me. For the next two weeks, she was a fixture in our apartment, and we had a great time going out and seeing the sights, eating at the better places and hitting different bars in the evening. I really got to know my way around that part of Maine.

Then, at the end of the two weeks, Debbie woke up and told me she was leaving for good and I shouldn't try to find her. She told me that, if I happened to see her, I was not to recognize her, and she would not know me. With that cryptic message, she left the apartment, and I never saw her again...in person.

I couldn't understand any of this. She had been mysterious from the start. I still didn't know her last name or where she actually lived. I had known this was strange, but I thought that time would break down the barriers, whatever they were, and she would tell me the truth about herself. I guess I was curious, but not really upset. We had enjoyed each other, but I really didn't have any strong feelings about her.

But my curiosity was up, so I quizzed the bartender where I had met her and other people who had seemed to know her. No one would tell me anything, if indeed they knew anything.

It was Pitt who finally solved the mystery. He was sitting in the apartment one morning reading the Sunday newspaper, when he suddenly said "Holy shit! Look at this!"

I leaned over and there, on the society page of the paper, was Debbie. But she was not called Debbie in the paper. She had a different and quite aristocratic-sounding name. She was dressed in a ball gown and was on the arm of a tall, distinguished-looking man who looked to be about ten years older than her. The write-up under the picture talked about how the man, her husband, had just returned from some time abroad and was once again taking over his duties as a corporate and municipal executive in a nearby town.

Debbie was always nice to me, so I will say no more. She was from Maine, but not from Bath. Pitt and I continued to live our bachelor life, but we seriously missed the good breakfasts we had enjoyed for a while.

CHAPTER THIRTY

Quebec City

The crew was starting to arrive in Bath and the Fire Control Division had already received three new chiefs; one was an E-7 and two were E-8 senior chiefs. The E-7 was a dedicated missile radar specialist who immediately hit it off with Mark and me. The two senior chiefs were both older and did not seem to be overly interested in anything beyond their administrative duties and the Bath bar scene. We all got along fine, and Mark, Chief Hall (the new E-7), and I had no problem covering all of the ship's pre-commissioning missile system responsibilities. Soon the engineers started arriving in Bath to get the missile systems on line, and we stayed busy, but not overly so.

Then, after we had been living there a while, I decided to get out of Bath on the weekend and see more of New England. So I took off on a Friday and went on a tour of Connecticut and Vermont. It was fun and I saw a lot of very interesting historical sites. When I got back, I told Pitt about it, and we decided to go someplace together the following weekend.

The following week, we received our per-diem checks for the next month, so we were temporarily wealthy. We decided to make a big weekend of it and go north into Canada, to either Montreal or Quebec City. We had heard about this French-speaking part of the world, but neither of us had ever visited it. We looked into it and discovered that Quebec City was about a five-hour drive, and we decided that was far enough. It sounded like an adventure and we were a bit bored with the Bath bar scene, so we were up for it.

The trip north was an adventure in itself. As soon as we crossed into Canada, the language changed everywhere, including on the road signs. Since neither of us spoke a word of French, it was an adventure just trying to find our way, but we managed, and we arrived in Quebec City on a beautiful Friday afternoon. We followed the signs for downtown and ended up at the Chateau Frontenac, a magnificent old hotel with a world of history surrounding it. I wanted to stay there, but a quick check proved that it was far too expensive for two young sailors.

We walked down the street a few blocks and went into a local café. Over lunch, we explained our hotel dilemma to a friendly waitress. She directed us to a small, quaint walk-up type of hotel that was more reasonably priced. She told us that it was where people from Quebec stayed when they came to the city. That sounded great, so we went there, and found a room at a reasonable price.

We checked in, unpacked, and cleaned up a bit. Then we set out to see the city. We left the room, walked down the hall, and when we hit the down button on the elevator, my life changed forever.

The elevator doors opened and we were facing two beautiful ladies who were about our age. We stepped into the elevator, and Pitt started talking immediately. He was much better at opening a conversation than I was, I must admit. By the time we got to the lobby, we were in a full-blown discussion about the city and its people. We sat in the lobby and talked with the two women for almost a half an hour. We learned that their names were Danielle and Yvonne and that they were from a city another hour-and-a-half further north in Quebec.

Yvonne was tall and redheaded, while Danielle was shorter, with dark-hair, brown eyes, and an infectious laugh. Since Pitt was tall and blond, he gravitated toward Yvonne and I was very happy to talk mostly with Danielle. Somehow, it just seemed like a natural fit. Both girls were French-speaking, with Yvonne speaking almost no English. But Danielle was more fluent. She explained that her father was an English professor who taught at a university up north where she lived.

After we talked for a while, the girls volunteered to show us the sights in downtown Quebec City. They were just here on a weekend vacation, much like Pitt and me, so it couldn't have worked out better. We set out afoot to see what we could see. First we went back to Chateau Frontenac, where they showed us some of the historical aspects of the place, and we picked up some brochures. Then we spent hours walking through the city's narrow alleyways where artists of every type showed their wares and let us watch them as they painted people and the beautiful sights for which the city is famous. I couldn't remember ever having a nicer, more relaxed time.

This was something really new for me. I was in a world that was entirely new to me; a world where people spoke in a new and exciting language and artistic people were everywhere. More importantly, I was talking with a sophisticated and obviously educated woman who seemed to be enjoying it as much as I did. I had seen half of the world and known some women, but all those experiences paled to nothing compared to what I was seeing and feeling now.

When the afternoon faded, we invited the ladies to dinner, and they accepted. They took us to a great little French restaurant and from there we again walked through the narrow alleyways and watched the artists at work. Then we moved to a night club in one of the larger hotels where we danced the night away to songs that sounded familiar, but which were sung in a language I didn't understand. It was definitely an enchanted evening; one that seemed, even to me, to be almost impossibly romantic.

When the night drew to a close, we escorted our new friends back to the hotel and split up in the lobby after shaking hands and agreeing to meet in the morning. I went to bed, alone, with a brand new set of dreams in my head. I don't think that I slept much that night.

Saturday was almost an instant replay of the day before. We met the ladies over breakfast and spent the day seeing the sights and enjoying one another. Pitt and Yvonne were having a hard time communicating since Yvonne didn't speak much English and Pitt knew absolutely no French. At first, this was a source of humor for us, but after a while, I could tell that it was working on the two of them.

But Danielle and I had no such problem. Her English wasn't perfect, but it was one hell of a lot better than my French and I appreciated it. I was trying hard to pick up a word here and there, so she helped me and we got on wonderfully. By the time the day was over, we had agreed that I would come to her home up north in a town called Kenogami two weeks in the future for a weekend. She talked about their little home town in the mountains of Quebec and it sounded a lot like a French-speaking version of St. Regis (except for a larger population), so I was anxious to visit there.

That night, when we said goodnight, I did get a chaste little kiss before we left one another. I noticed that Pitt was not so lucky.

Sunday morning, we met for breakfast again before we split up to go home. By this time, I had all the directions to her home in Kenogami and had every intention of going there as soon as I possibly could go. I was starting to have dreams of the little cottage with the white picket fence again. Maybe if I kept trying, I could someday have a normal life—the life that I dreamed of—after all.

The drive back to Bath was a fog for me. I remember that Pitt was far less excited than me, but that just didn't matter. Life had made a big turn for me and I wanted to think about it.

Monday morning, we went back to reality and our work aboard *Belknap*. I was a bit excited still, and I immediately told Mark about our weekend adventure. He had been raised in nearby Vermont and was of French-Canadian descent, so he was really enthused for me. He spoke French fluently, so he volunteered to help me a bit with that problem. I bought a self-teaching French course and did some work with it, but once again, my lack of any formal high school instruction jumped up and bit me. I didn't know an adverb from an adjective from a noun, so I was hopelessly confused by the course. I had to settle for some practical teachings by Mark, which did help me a lot. But fluent, I would never be.

We still had almost four months before the ship was due to leave Bath, so I worked out an agreement with Mark that gave us each a three or four-day weekend every other week. That way, Mark could go to Vermont and be with his family longer while I covered his work, and then I would be off the following week for a long weekend.

After studying the map to Danielle's home in Kenogami, I realized that it was an eight-hour trip each way, so I would need longer weekends. Mark liked the idea, so we talked to Chief Hall and Lieutenant Hurt and made it happen.

Mark and I went out of our way to make sure that all of our work was done to perfection so our new schedules wouldn't be jeopardized. I wasn't sure if I would need this new arrangement for more than the one weekend, but I was happy to make it happen for Mark even if it wasn't needed for me. As it happened, it worked out well for both of us.

The next weekend, Mark went home for a four-day weekend, and I covered the work on his radars as well as my computers. The system lite-off was still in its early stages, so there wasn't any real excitement. In fact, Chief Hall and I mostly just worked on paperwork that we would need later when the ship was operational.

Over the weekend, I had a long telephone conversation with Mom. She was really excited that I had gone to Canada and found a friend. After all, Mom was still a Canadian citizen, and she still had a lot of loyalty to her homeland. She also told me that things had gotten a lot better at home for her. She had finally asserted her independence with Dad, and he was not the threat that he had been. She also told me that Kathy was helping her a lot with the younger children, and that was allowing her to work more. She was particularly happy to tell me that she was actually current with all of her bills and hadn't been cut off from her favorite grocery store in over a year. That was, for both of us, a major accomplishment.

Mom's best friend, for the past twenty years or so, had been one of the St. Regis grocers that had been forced to cut off our family's credit time and time again. This had naturally placed a lot of strain on the relationship, but Mom was very proud to report that they were, once again, the best of friends. This was really good news for me because the grocer lady, Ida, had always been very good to me, and I liked her a lot.

CHAPTER THIRTY-ONE

Vive Quebec Libre'

It seemed like forever before my next trip to Quebec rolled around. I was supremely nervous. Had I misread the signs? Would I be welcome in this far northern French-Canadian stronghold? Wouldn't her father, the university professor, see right through the uneducated sailor and throw me out of their lives? What the hell was I getting into? I almost cancelled the trip because I was so nervous. Probably the only reason that I didn't cancel was the fact that I had talked so much about it with my friends that it would have been humiliating to not go through with it. So I got underway.

It was quite a trip. Danielle had warned me to fill up with gas before leaving Quebec City on the way through. She was right. Shortly after leaving Quebec City, I entered what the girls had called Laurentides Park.

The sign said "Reserve Faunique Des Laurentides," so I assumed I was in the right place and kept driving. Danielle had not been wrong about either the distance or the scenery. It was about 130 miles through this park and it was all mountainous. I passed by one of the most beautiful lakes that I had ever seen, Lac Jacques Cartier.

This country could easily tie Montana for beauty, I thought. It was stunning. In fact, it seemed much more pristine than even Montana. The rivers and waters were crystal clear and I saw no sign of the kind of clear-cut logging that had devastated much of Montana. Canada had obviously set this huge area aside for a reason, and I, for one, really appreciated the effort.

Finally I came out of the park and began seeing signs of life. Danielle had drawn me a rough map and I followed it from here. My road atlas didn't show the town of Kenogami, but she had told me that it lay between the larger town of Chicoutimi and Jonquire, so I headed for them. Soon I found roads and landmarks that showed up on her hand-drawn map and I zoomed in from there.

I really felt like a fool when I walked up to the door of her home that day. *What should I say?* I spoke no French, and that was obviously the only operative language within 200 miles of this place. I was out of my depth here. I almost turned around and headed for the safety of Maine.

But somehow I found myself knocking on a door that was attached to what looked like an older row home. An attractive middle-aged lady answered the door with a, "Oue?"

I managed to stammer out, "Does Danielle live here?"

Her face broke into a smile that lit up the whole area. She answered in rapid-fire French with about a billion words, the only ones of which I understood were "Oui" and "Jeff?"

I smiled and said, "Yes, Jeff," and pointed at my chest.

She then turned and shouted, in the manner of mothers everywhere, "Danielle, C'est ami, Jeff!"

Danielle came to the door, beaming at me. "You really did come!" Then mass confusion reigned. Danielle introduced me to her mother, the lady who had answered the door. By the time that was done, and I had been ushered into the living room, Danielle's father and three brothers were there. Apparently, an American sailor was quite a curiosity in this part of the world. Of course, I was wearing civilian clothes, but that didn't seem to make a difference. Her father, Georges, helped her interpret for the brothers, although the oldest one, Pierre, seemed to get along quite well in English. Her mother and the two younger boys spoke no English, so communicating with them soon became a source of hilarity for all of us. The family was warm and welcoming, and my fears soon faded.

It was getting late in the afternoon by now, and I was immediately invited to dinner with the family. The dinner was something that I had never heard of before—a French-Canadian specialty called pork pie. It sounded atrocious to me, so I tried to ease out of it by telling them that I had to go downtown and find a room. That didn't work at all. Nothing I said would dissuade them from not only dinner, but also the fact that I should stay at their home while I was in the area.

Since I couldn't get out of it, I decided to shut my mouth and try to get the pork pie down. I was pleasantly surprised. In fact, their pork pie, which was made with carefully spiced and baked ground pork, soon became one of my favorite meals. It was absolutely delicious!

The dinner conversation was very pleasant. Danielle's mother, Muriel, was a very interesting person who, using Danielle and Georges as translators, grilled me on my background, goals, and life in general. But she did it so pleasantly that I did not mind in the least. She was making sure that her daughter was safe, and I certainly didn't blame her for that.

When she was satisfied, she deftly turned the conversation to their family and other local relatives. By the time dinner was over, I knew a good bit about the family and felt that I had achieved a bit of a rapport with Muriel. Actually, I liked her, and I felt that the feeling was mutual.

The father, Georges, was a just as friendly, but was more interested in politics, quizzing me on my political views and wanting to hear about my father's political involvement. (Of course, I made no mention of Dad's alcohol problems, just his political life.) Georges was a short, stocky, man who was apparently solely focused on politics and the Free Quebec movement. His entire dinner conversation was on this topic.

Georges told me that, as a college professor, he had been one of the earliest members of the Alliance Laurentienne, the original movement founded in 1957 to free Quebec from Canada. By the time I arrived on the scene in 1964, the movement had evolved into two groups known as the RIN and the FLQ. The RIN was relatively moderate, trying to achieve independence by political means, but the FLQ was a much more extreme group that had no compunctions about violence and advocated armed insurrection if necessary to achieve independence. Georges claimed to be a member of the RIN, but he spoke very fondly of the FLQ people he knew and the things that they were doing.

I found out that the family had one relative who was not French; an Englishman who had married Georges's sister and who was adored by the family. I thought that was very interesting since Georges had made it very clear to me at dinner that he was, almost devoutly, opposed to all of what he called "English Canada." I remember being baffled by the fact that he was so radically opposed to their government, but was still tolerant of the English uncle and was so very hospitable to an American who spoke no French.

It was a dichotomy to me at the time, but I found out later that Americans and Englishmen (from Great Britain) were considered acceptable company, even allies, by the French-Canadian separatists. In their eyes, the enemy was any citizen of Canada who did not speak French.

After dinner, Danielle volunteered to show me the area so we climbed into my car and headed out. She didn't want to drive, so I did, following her directions to all of the area points of interest. As before, we had a wonderful conversation, complete with some laughs and a lot of personal information. I learned that she was from a large extended French-Canadian family, most of who were here in the Kenogami/Chicoutimi area.

Danielle and I stopped at a local night club for a drink and ran into Yvonne and some other friends. I was a bit of a celebrity with them since Americans were very uncommon in this lost little part of Canada. I enjoyed it tremendously.

By the time we got home, Danielle's parents had fixed a bed for me in their den (far, far away from their daughter's room), and I was soon asleep, exhausted from the trip and the events of the evening.

I was awakened the next morning by Danielle's brother, Pierre, who told me that they were getting ready for church. "Do you like to go with us?" he said.

I thought fast on that one. I knew that the French-Canadian people were overwhelmingly Catholic, and that was probably where they were planning to go. I had never been in a Catholic church before, but how bad could it be?

I knew that it would probably be important to the family, so I said, "Sure" and proceeded to get dressed. I had brought some slacks and a nice shirt, but nothing better, so I wasn't sure about the clothes. But Georges assured me that I would be fine, so I went with them.

On the way, I whispered to Danielle that I didn't know anything about a Catholic service, so she kept me from getting in any big trouble. Since the service was in Latin and French, I just did what I was told and pretended to understand it. I sat when I should have knelt and knelt when I should have stood, but overall, I passed the test and escaped alive.

When church was over, we all went to an aunt's home for a lunch in their garden. I remember thinking that it had to be considered the aunt's home, not the uncles, because this aunt was obviously in charge of anyone and everyone within her sphere of influence, which appeared to be continent-wide. The word "matriarch" fit her perfectly. She and her husband, a local banker, were obviously wealthy, and she was very much the boss. This was an interesting cultural phenomenon to me, particularly after being raised by the old boxer and his trained-to-be-submissive wife. Actually I didn't mind the arrangement except that the husband was too meek and looked almost afraid to be there or say anything. I remember thinking, *Why does there always have to be domination and submission? Why can't they be partners?*

I have to admit that I watched Danielle very carefully while I was around this aunt. But, although Danielle seemed to really adore her aunt, she didn't seem at all interested in emulating her. That was fine with me. I was looking for a partner, not a boss.

It was also very interesting that, whenever I was present, the family switched, as much as was possible, to English. They were very polite about this, and I appreciated it. Georges told me that it was out of respect for America and Americans. It also helped that I was awkwardly attempting to pick up some phrases in French. They really appreciated my efforts, small as they were, and they invariably stopped whatever they were doing to help me with this.

I didn't have to be back to Bath until Tuesday, so we spent the day lazily visiting with Danielle's family and relatives. It was a nice day, although I heard a tremendous amount of political discussion. It seemed that everyone in their circle of family and friends were seriously involved in the movement to free Quebec from Canada. In fact, the only two matters of discussion were the oppression of French Canadians and the fact that I was from a far-away, mythical, and magical land called "Montana." They were really interested in everything about my family and my home state. I kept the conversation light and concentrated mostly on Montana, only touching on the surface in the discussions about my family.

As the hours wore on, I noticed that Georges and his brother-in-law, the banker, were having some heated discussions. I had no idea what they were discussing until I happened to be standing close to them at one point.

Since I was in the vicinity, the banker courteously switched to English and said, "Come on, Georges, things aren't that bad here."

At that Georges exploded, "No, things are not bad if you are a rich banker who can buy his way out of their shit. But we are not all like you. What does it matter to you if our children have to work in crap jobs because we have to speak English to even be a salesman? Unless they read English, they cannot even take a driver's test! God damn it—we can't even get a mortgage contract that is written in French, and our people are forever being screwed because they can't even read the fine print, let alone understand it!" He went on, "Don't you see that our people are discriminated against as surely as if we were a bunch of darkies in Mississippi? But we aren't even as well off as they are. At least they have freedom riders trying to help them. In this country, if you speak French, you have no help and no rights. We're not as well off as black sharecroppers in Mississippi."

About this time, Matriarch Aunt intervened, telling him, "Georges, you know that I agree with you, but this isn't the time or place for our tempers to get loose." Then she turned to her husband and said something very quietly in French. The discussion stopped immediately.

Because my father had been so involved with the Democratic Party back in Montana, I had thought that I understood politics and political causes, but I had never experienced anything like this. These people were seriously and intensely committed to their cause. Some of them actually seemed ready to go to war. I was very careful not to offend anyone or make any comments that could be misconstrued. I wasn't uncomfortable, just careful.

The next morning, I left for Bath, but not without promising to return in two weeks when I got my next long weekend. Danielle's mother, Muriel, even fixed me a lunch to eat on the way home. It had been a magical weekend...one that gave me a lot to think about.

CHAPTER THIRTY-TWO

A Frenetic Engagement

It was July when I first met Danielle in Quebec City, and it was after the New Year when the *Belknap* left Boston heading south. My memory of this six month period is obscured by the haze that comes with doing too much too fast for too long. For me, these months can best be described as a frenetic maelstrom of events; events that came at me so continuously and rapidly that they have rolled together in my memory banks over the passing years. During this half-year, I think that I must have been living harder and faster than any time in my life. But it was all voluntary, and I know that I thoroughly enjoyed every bit of it.

The ship was in Bath until the last week of October, going through sea trials and pre-commissioning testing. I was working long, long hours in the shipyard, and whenever I could get two days free I was in Kenogami. Several times, I drove from Bath to Kenogami after work on a Friday just so I could go out with Danielle on Saturday and drive back on Sunday. It was an absolutely crazy schedule, but somehow I survived it.

Sometime that fall, I proposed to Danielle, and she accepted. We agreed on a long engagement because of my ship's schedule and all of the Catholic rituals we had to go through in order to be married in the church. I really wish I could remember details of this time period, but they are lost in my jumbled memory of the hectic schedule that I was living then. I just know that I was

291

happier than I could remember ever having been. My life was truly coming together. I was respected in my field of work, and I was engaged to a good woman. The memories of life with my father were fading fast, although I still had recurring nightmares.

I do remember telling the news to both of our parents. When we broke the news to Danielle's parents, her father and mother were both happy. Georges, in his typical fashion, did tell me that, "If you hurt my little girl, I will sic the FLQ on you, and they will do you great bodily harm!" But he was smiling when he said it. Muriel and I were good friends by now (in spite of our language barrier), and she was overjoyed.

After we told her parents, Danielle and I, together, called my mother and told her what we were planning. Mom was overjoyed that I had found someone, particularly since my fiancée was a Canadian. Mom pressed us to set a date because, in her words, "I am coming to that wedding even if I have to steal the money to get there." She was actually crying on the phone while she talked, and Danielle had some trouble understanding her, but we worked it out. That weekend, we took a lot of pictures and mailed some of them to Mom. Then, as usual, I headed for Bath.

Over the next weeks, as the ship's schedule firmed up, we picked a date for the planned wedding. We selected July 3, 1965, as the date. The ship would be back from Guantanamo and done with its first missile firings then. It would be in Norfolk Naval Shipyard then, and I shouldn't have a problem getting leave. I checked with Chief Hall and Lieutenant Hurt before I made plans, of course. It was too early for them to give a firm commitment, but they thought the timing would work, so we laid the plans.

The ship came together a lot faster than I wanted it to, and in late October, we took it to Boston. It was an interesting cruise from Bath to Boston because the ship's sonar dome, normally a huge, bulbous, underwater outcropping beneath the ship's bow, was tied down on the ship's foc'sle. The *Belknap* drew too much water to install it in Bath. If the dome had been installed, the ship would have gone aground attempting to transit down the Kennebec River from Bath to the Atlantic Ocean.

USS *Belknap* (DLG-26) was commissioned on November 7, 1964, at Pier Eleven in Boston Naval Shipyard. Then we went into dry dock to install the sonar dome, while my crew began installing all of the missile system changes that had been backlogged awaiting commissioning. The workload was tremendously demanding, but Mark and I made arrangements to get away for three-day weekends every other weekend while we were in Boston. That meant that we had to work at least twelve-hour days whenever we were on the ship, but neither of us minded as long as we could go "home" as often as possible. It really helped that both of us had been through this hectic post-commissioning period a few times before. We were able to get the job done with a minimum of rework and, in this complex work environment; our experience saved a lot of time and energy for both us and our crews.

The ship stood down for a liberal leave period over the Christmas and New Year Holidays. I took advantage of the stand-down to take leave and go to Kenogami. During this period, I met with the priest who was scheduled to marry us. Since I was going to be gone, he gave me a correspondence course to complete that was designed to teach infidels like myself about the intricacies of Catholic doctrine. I also had to swear that I would allow our children to be raised in the Catholic faith. Since I wasn't particularly religious, that didn't bother me, and we got over the "priest hurdles" rapidly enough. The wedding was firmly scheduled for July 3, and invitations went out.

When I got back to the ship after my leave, I had a surprise waiting for me. My brother, Tim, had reported aboard while I was gone. He really surprised me because I had expected him to stay in school longer. But he had passed the school he was in and had declined further school so he could come to *Belknap* with me. While I was gone, Lieutenant Hurt had assigned him to the missile radar crew, where he was working for Mark Wilcoux.

Having young Tim with me was something special for both of us. I remembered how raptly he had listened to my tales of far-away places. He had wanted a life like I had, and now he was living it. I couldn't cry while the troops were around, but I have to admit that my eyes did get damp later when I was alone. This was big for me. It meant that another of us had a chance to escape from the agonies that our Dad had created! First me, then Kathy, then (sadly) Patty, and now Tim had, in one way or another, escaped. Even Mom was getting out and working now.

Maybe there was hope after all. Only Lyle, Eleanor, Jimmy, and Danny were still at home, and according to Tim, the three youngest ones were spending a lot of time at Kathy's place. Only Lyle was staying independent. Tim said that Dad stayed pretty much clear of Lyle, since he was as big as Dad and often just as volatile.

Tim said, "Sometimes, I think that Dad's afraid of him."

Tim was soon settled in and was thoroughly enjoying the radar work. He, like me, was sending some money home to Mom, so he didn't go ashore much. I was focused solely on Kenogami, so we didn't get off ship much together in those early days. We did go see the historical sites in Boston a couple of times, but with Tim being only eighteen and both of us counting our pennies, we didn't do much else.

I was able to make another trip to Canada after my leave period and before the ship headed south. The time was mostly used in making arrangements for the wedding, which would be happening the next time I came back to Kenogami. I was going to be gone almost five months and was going to be married almost as soon as I returned! It was a tough schedule.

When I left Kenogami that time, it was both different and difficult. There were tears from both Danielle and her mother. Georges and I even had a little moisture showing, although neither of us would have admitted it. But the brothers, Pierre, Jean, and Gilles, were excited for a different reason. I was going to go on a ship to Cuba! That was exciting for them. I had to promise to bring souvenirs.

This was going to be a long separation

CHAPTER THIRTY-THREE

Brothers at Sea

The *Belknap* left Boston early in 1965, headed south for operations designed to test our systems and train the new crew. The first tests were tests of the engineering plant, tests that made sure that the 1200 PSI boilers and the machinery plant all operated correctly. Then we held training for all types of damage control evolutions. While all of this was going on, the captain and the bos'n mates were training the bridge crews. But, oblivious to all of this, Chief Hall, Mark, and I, and our crews worked long hours and never-ending days to get the missile system upgrades installed and the systems operational.

I will say that, of all the ships' crews that I had worked with to this point, the *Belknap* crew was the best that I had seen. I guess that a lot of that can be attributed to the leadership of Captain Law. He would regularly "drop by" our missile spaces, usually timing it to appear just as we were going through some unusually hard evolution. He would joke with us, volunteering a few words of encouragement, and showing a genuine interest in what we were doing. Never once did I ever hear of him saying anything discouraging or petty, even when our work areas were a disaster because of work messes. Both he and Lieutenant Hurt were true leaders and, as a result, they got far more out of the crew than would normally be expected. They made us proud of the work we were doing.

But the crew was exceptional also. Even the young kids that had never seen an actual missile system before were so dedicated that even I was impressed. I was very happy to see that Tim was fitting in with them well. He was a hard worker and was very smart. But more importantly, he was always cheerful, regardless of the difficulties encountered or the hours worked. He seemed to be truly happy to be there.

My relationship with Tim was a little difficult at first. I remembered him as a kid brother (that I had only seen occasionally since he was about nine years old). He was only six years younger than me, but at ages twenty-four and eighteen, that was a huge gap. In addition, I was a first class petty officer and he was a seaman, so there were leadership protocols that we had to follow. We were friends, but sometimes it was a bit strained. Thankfully, Tim seemed to just naturally understand the situation, and he never, ever, tried to take advantage of our relationship. After a few weeks, we both relaxed, and we were soon the best of friends as well as brothers. We stayed that way for many years, bonded in a unique way that I have never known with another person.

The ship went through some unusual times when we were on our shakedown cruise. Once, we lost power in the Norfolk harbor and were almost run over by a freighter before the engineers made repairs and we got underway.

On another occasion, we dropped anchor at sea and found out that we couldn't retrieve it with the winch because, when all of the anchor chain was fully deployed, it was just too heavy for the winch. So the crew formed a long line down the port side of the ship, heaving around on a long rope, pulling the anchor up bit by bit while the Bos'n on watch chanted "Heave, Heave, Heave" over the ship's loudspeakers.

But the unique event that stays in my mind most vividly took place when we were in the Port of Miami. We had been in the area testing the ship's sonar systems, and we visited Miami for a weekend. We were hosting local civilians on a tour of the ship when Miami had a total power failure, and the entire city went dark. Captain Law, being Captain Law, did the unexpected and volunteered the ship's power to the city. The ship's Engineering Department fired up the ship's 1200 PSI plant and brought all four of our 1,500-kilowatt generators on line at once. The ship fed all of Miami's emergency services for almost a full day before they restored local power.

The ship received a commendation from the City of Miami for that one, and we made the local papers. But even more importantly, the Miami Playboy Club waived their membership requirements and gave the whole ship's crew an open invitation to visit the club. Tim and I went to town and checked out the Playboy Club for an hour or so, but Tim wasn't old enough to drink and I was an engaged man who was feeling guilty for being there, so we came back to the ship very early.

After we returned to the ship that evening, Tim and I got a cup of coffee and went up to set on the deck above the bridge (called the flying bridge). It was quiet there, and we were alone, just watching the skyline and the sights of Miami from our vantage point. It was a beautiful evening and we were both quietly melancholy. We didn't say much at first.

Then Tim opened with, "Jeff, do you ever think about home?" The question startled me, and then I realized that I hadn't talked about home to him at all since he arrived.

I said, "Yes, of course. Why do you ask?"

"Because, since the first day I was here, you haven't talked about anything except the ship, work, and your girlfriend. I just wondered. I guess I kind of wanted to know your thoughts on Dad and all that crap that we left behind in St. Regis."

I thought about the question for a while before answering him, "Sorry, I never thought about it. I mean I just never thought about talking about it. I guess that I've spent too many years training myself not to think about it. When I'm home, everything there is so impossible. I try, but I can't make a difference. So when I'm on a ship, it just seems like another world, except at night when it's dark and I lie there, trying to make sense out of it all. Do you know what I mean?"

It was his turn to hesitate before answering, "I guess so, but I guess that I haven't been away long enough yet. It's still all that I think about. When you do think about it, do you have any thoughts or ideas that could change things?"

My answer was easy this time, "No, I don't have any answers. Dad is a drunk and a bully, and there isn't a damned thing that any of us can do about it. The only one that can do anything is Mom. She needs to kick his ass out, but she won't because still loves him in spite of everything. I've tried to talk to her, but she refuses to see how bad things are and she keeps hoping for some kind of turnaround; a turnaround that will never come. My biggest fear is that he'll kill Mom or one of the kids before Mom realizes how bad things really are."

Tim was quiet for a while before he answered, "Maybe he's already killing us from the inside out, if you know what I mean."

That stopped me cold. I said, "No. What do you mean?"

Tim replied, "Look at us. You're only twenty-four years old, and you have already been out in the world for over ten years. The story around St. Regis is that you were one of the smartest kids in grade school. You even skipped a grade. But you never got through high school. Then there is Kathy. She married a guy who's eons older than her just to get out of the house. Now she's devoting her life to keeping the little kids away from Dad. As for me, I'm here, just escaping from life." He paused, as if he was thinking about what he had just said. Then he went on, "Lyle seems all right on the outside, but he admires Dad and doesn't seem to understand right from wrong. I've seen him punch out girls at school and think that there was nothing wrong with it. As for the younger kids, it's probably too soon to know about them, but what can they expect from life?"

Tim paused again and then quietly said, "Maybe he's already killed us. Maybe he's killed any chance that we might ever have of living a normal life!"

His voice was quavering. I looked at him and saw the tears quietly running down his cheeks. I choked up and couldn't say anything. I just took my little brother in my arms and held him while he broke loose; crying in a horrible, deep, choking way that tore at my very soul. All the awful feelings that I had held back for years finally caught up with me and we just stood there for a long, long, time, just crying and holding on to one another.

Finally I composed myself enough to gently push us apart. I looked at him and tried a weak joke, "If anybody sees us, they'll think we're queer, and then we won't even have a job."

He grinned through the tears and we sheepishly began wiping the evidence of our feelings off of our faces.

We sat back down and I turned serious. I said, "Tim, I've never thought of it the way you just described it; I guess I've never really thought about why I do what I do. I've just thought that I had to fight to get away and find myself in the world. Mom told me a long time ago that I needed to escape and give the rest of you an example to follow. That's what I've tried to do."

He interrupted me with, "You've done a good job of that."

I said, "Please shut up and listen to me. You have to understand something. We are *not* victims! Maybe we're survivors, but we're not victims. If we start thinking that we're just victims, we've lost everything we fought for, and we *will* become victims! Not only that, but you need to realize that *you* are an example now. The little ones don't even know me, but they look up at you. You need to give them something to hope for. They need an example. I'm passing that torch on to you!"

He sat back with a stunned look on his face. He thought for a minute before saying, "Well at least it isn't as bad as it was before you came home the last time. After we ran him out of the house that time, he hasn't been the same. He still gets mad and tries to bully the family, but he really hasn't gone off like he used to for a long time now. He's been tougher on Jimmy than on any of the others. But now-a-days he's more of an embarrassment than a threat, if you know what I mean."

He paused then continued, "Remember, you told him that you'd kill him. I think he remembers that, but I'm not sure. Maybe he's just running out of steam. By the way, I've been wondering for a long time; what would you do if he started beating Mom again?"

I had honestly thought a lot about this. My reply summed up my thoughts on that question, "I dunno, Tim. I honestly don't know. But I do know that I'd have to do something. I couldn't live with myself if he ended up killing Mom or one of the kids and I hadn't done anything to stop it."

We sat there for a long time, staring at the Miami skyline and thinking our thoughts; then we went below and went to bed. I kept thinking about the concepts raised by Tim's questions, and I didn't sleep much that night, but thanks to the comforting hum of the ship's systems, at least I didn't have any bad dreams when I finally did drift off.

The following Monday we got underway again and we were far too busy to worry about home. The ship's first missile firings were coming soon, right after the eight-week training period at Guantanamo Bay, and we had a lot of work to do to be ready in time. The rest of the ship' crew was getting ready for Gitmo, conducting drills and training the crew. But we were continuously working on the missile systems. It seemed like the *Belknap's* modernized systems were a lot harder to bring online than the previous versions had been. I was convinced that the *Belknap* crew was the best I had seen, and we were making headway, but it was a long, hard struggle.

A few weeks after we left Miami, we pulled into San Juan, Puerto Rico. Tim and I, along with a group of friends, decided to go see the sights. We picked up some brochures, made a plan and headed out. Our first stop was the old military fortifications that we had seen from the ship when we passed them on the way into port. The old fort, known as Moro Castle, was spectacular, and we all thoroughly enjoyed it.

I still remember laughing as Tim and a friend named Don fought a mock swordfight on the battlements using sticks they had found somewhere. They fought up stairs and across the walkways, with tourists all around taking pictures and cheering their favorites on. When they had been at it a while, and the heat was getting to them, they both faked mortal wounds and fell down howling with laughter.

I envied Tim his ability to put everything aside and just have fun. It seemed like I always had to preserve my dignity, so I couldn't just let go, be silly, and enjoy life—I don't know why—I was just never able to do that. I could laugh at his grandiose mock swordfight, but I couldn't imagine doing the same thing myself.

We spent the afternoon at Moro Castle, exploring it and loving the history and adventure that the place brought out in our minds. But it was a hot, hot day and by the end of the visit, we were ready for dinner and a drink, so we headed for the Hilton, where we had been told the dinners were excellent.

The hotel was far superior anything that we had experienced recently—a huge place with multiple restaurants, bars, and casinos. We found a restaurant and settled in for a well-deserved dinner, the first that I had eaten off the ship since I returned from Kenogami.

We downed a few drinks with dinner and were ready for more when we finished. One of the guys decided that he wanted to try a casino, so we paid up and went in.

As soon as we hit the casino, the free drinks started flowing, and we took full advantage of that fact. We split up in the casino since the guys wanted to play different games. I stayed with Tim, watching as he headed for a blackjack table. I wasn't playing, but I could drink and watch, so that's what I did.

Tim was a good player—a fact that surprised me. I hadn't seen this kind of gambling much before, and I was startled that he knew what he was doing. But he did, and as the night went on, he started winning. The table wasn't a high-stakes table, but for us it was big. Slowly the other guys that were with us lost their limits and came to join us, but Tim played on. We made quite a scene; a group of mildly intoxicated sailors, in full uniform, noisily rooting for our lone player. The tourists were all around, amusedly tolerating us.

Finally, the dealer pushed a stack of chips at Tim for about the fourth or fifth time, and Tim swiveled to look at me. He said, "That's enough, I think."

I was surprised. Not being a gambler, I would have ridden his winning streak to riches (or oblivion) if it had been me. But it was his call.

I said, "Okay, let's head on out then."

Tim grinned at me, a bit tipsily, and told the dealer to cash him out. He had won a little over $1,200. That was a fortune to us! He pocketed the money, and we all headed for the door, noisily congratulating him on the winnings.

We got to the hotel lobby and stopped to confer on the next destination.

I said that I was going back to the ship from there, but most of the guys wanted to go downtown to some of the rougher bars where, as one guy put it, "The drinks are cheap and the girls are cheaper."

After a discussion, Don (Tim's sword-fighting companion), and I decided to go back to the ship, and the rest of the guys were headed downtown.

Tim took me aside and handed me a wad of cash and asked me "Will you take this to the ship for me? I don't want to carry it downtown."

I readily agreed and we separated. Don and I got back to the ship just before taps and settled in for the night. I locked the money in my locker after counting it to see what was there. Tim had given me $1,000.

The guys returned to the ship in the wee hours of the morning. They were very cheerfully drunker than skunks, and they woke the whole compartment up before they finally calmed down. Judging from the sea stories they babbled out to anyone that would listen, they had thoroughly enjoyed themselves.

The next morning was a Sunday and the ship was having a Sunday brunch instead of the standard breakfast. I was setting on the mess decks talking to friends when Tim came up and sat down. He looked like he had been through a huge wringer, with eyes that looked ready to fall out on his cheeks. We all laughed at him and gave him a hard time, of course. But he was very serious, looking very upset in addition to being hung over.

Finally, I asked him, "What's wrong, Tim?"

He said, "Jeff, you won't believe this. I lost all of that money that I won last night. I know that I must have had at least a thousand dollars when I left the casino. But I've got less than fifty dollars left. I don't know where it all went! I must have been robbed by one of those hookers last night!"

I couldn't help myself. I started laughing. The other two guys at our table looked at me as if I was crazy.

Tim turned red and looked mad as hell before he blurted out, "God damn it! It ain't funny! I lost it all! You wouldn't laugh if it was you!"

I was choking and sputtering as I tried to answer. Finally I got it out, "You gave it to me, you shithead! Don't you remember?"

I cannot even begin to describe the look that slowly, oh so slowly, came over his face. The red subsided, the pissed-off look faded, the grin started, and slowly his whole face lit up as only Tim's face could. It looked like he had even forgotten that he had a hangover. He couldn't even talk right. He just sat there and stared, "No shit? Did I really give it to you?" Then, "How much did I give you?"

"A thousand dollars."

Tim jumped up, yelling and slapping his thighs. The whole mess decks turned to watch the spectacle, but he didn't care. He was one happy sailor at that moment.

Finally he settled down. The other guys at the table finished their brunch and left, but I stayed to talk to Tim. We talked for a while about the night before. Then he turned the conversation to the money. "It is going home to Mom" he said.

I nodded, "I thought that some of it probably would. She can use it to catch up on the grocery bills as long as Dad doesn't get his hands on it."

At the mention of Dad and money, Tim looked at me quizzically, saying, "You know, I never thought to tell you, but things have changed at home when it comes to money since you were there."

I asked, "How so?"

"Man, every since the Old Man calmed down some, Mom is doing a lot better. She's never late with a bill, and she runs her own money. She got her own bank account, and she doesn't let Dad touch it. Now she works two jobs and saves every penny she can. She gets what she can from Dad on paydays, but no one is counting on much there. She puts the money that we send home in a separate bank account, and she won't touch it unless there is an emergency with one of the kids."

I must have looked as surprised as I felt, because Tim went on, "I'm not sending this money home for any of that. When I was home before I came to the *Belknap*, Mom was saving every dime she made, trying to put together enough to go to your wedding. This is free money, and I can't think of a better use for it. That's why I was so torn up when I thought I had lost it!"

I couldn't look at him. I knew that I would lose it if I did. I sat there for a few minutes and then said, "Let's go down to the compartment, and I'll give you the money." My voice was a little shaky, and he just grinned at me. He knew how I felt.

The ship went through the Guantanamo Bay training period as if it were nothing unusual. As with my other new construction ships, the missile crew and its embarked engineers worked through most of the drills and training exercises. Lieutenant Hurt and Chief Hall, with the discreet support of Captain Law, kept us clear of most of the training drills, and we were able to get the systems ready for anything. I had real confidence in our systems, and I was absolutely certain that the computers were head and shoulders above any that I had worked before. When we headed from Guantanamo to the missile range at Roosevelt Roads, we knew we were ready.

The missile firings went off smoothly, and we did very well. I don't think that I have ever seen Tim as excited as he was when he saw his first Terrier Missile leave the launcher, heading for a drone aircraft target somewhere over the horizon. He had been allowed to go, with a couple of other young sailors, up to the flying bridge to watch the launch. I swear that, if I had re-enlistment papers with me when they came down to the computer room after that, they all would have signed on the spot. They were really a proud bunch of kids, and Tim had that beamingly unforgettable look on his face that he got whenever something wonderful happened.

Shortly after the missile firings, I received a Letter of Commendation from Captain Law for the work that I had done on the *Belknap* missile systems. Of all the letters and commendations that I've received, both before and after that date, this is the one that meant the most to me, because of who it came from.

We left Puerto Rico and sailed north; justly proud of the welded steel and untrained crew that we had turned into a fighting machine.

CHAPTER THIRTY-FOUR

The End of Alone

I had requested thirty days' leave that was to start the day after we reached the states. Of course, the first thing that I did when we reached port was to call Danielle. All was well there, and we talked for over an hour about the wedding arrangements and our plans. The priest had approved our plans to be married in the Catholic Church after receiving the correspondence course that I had mailed to him. The reception was going to be in a big hotel in Chicoutimi. All was well there.

Danielle had received a call from Mom, and she told me that Mom was definitely coming to the wedding. Not only was Mom coming, but a friend of hers was also coming. Danielle couldn't remember the friend's name, but it was a lady. So, when we finished talking, I called Mom. She was very excited by the planned trip. Tim's gambling gift had helped a lot. She was coming with her best friend, Ida. The two of them had made some big plans and, for them, this was going to be the trip of a lifetime.

I was both surprised and happy to hear that Ida was coming with Mom. I had always really liked Ida, who was also one of the grocers who had carried the family's grocery bills for so many years during the bad times. But, even before the bad times, I remembered Mom and Ida telling me that they had made plans when I was about five years old that eventually I would grow up and marry Ida's oldest daughter, Linda. *Wow,*

I'm going to hear about that when they get to Kenogami, I thought.

Mom and Ida had gone even further with their trip. They had decided to go all out, and they had each borrowed some money from the local bank to make the trip into a real, once-in-a-lifetime, event. They were scheduled to fly to Quebec City, where they expected me to meet them. Then they were going to the wedding, after which they were flying to New York, where the World's Fair was in full swing. After visiting the Fair, they were going to Washington, DC, where Mom had arranged for them to stay with Senator Mansfield for a few days while they toured the city. It would be a trip to remember, and I was proud of Mom as well as being astounded that she was actually doing it.

Mom was both excited and scared on the telephone. But to me, the whole conversation was magical. The woman talking to me on the telephone, describing all of this, was not the same beaten housewife that I had known for too long. This was much more the mother that I remembered from our homebuilding days. Both of us were happy and proud of her for what she was doing.

I had to jokingly tell her to "Stop blubbering," several times, mainly so that I wouldn't start up myself.

The next morning, bright and early, I left *Belknap*, driving north on the last trip to Kenogami that I would make as a single man. I don't think that I even saw the road between Virginia and northern Quebec. My mind was full, and dreams, good dreams, were everywhere.

The next thing I knew, I was standing in the doorway in Kenogami that Pierre had just opened. Danielle flew down the stairs into my arms. She never looked more beautiful to me than she did that day. We had just come through the first of our many long military separations, and we were still in love!

We were soon caught up in the myriad of things that still had to be done before the big day. I had to get fitted for a tux, we had to make sure the reception was on track, and we had a series of meetings with the priest. A thousand details awaited our attention.

Tim had not come for the wedding. He didn't have a lot of leave on the books, and he wanted to save it for his next trip home. He begged off, and I didn't blame him. Weddings are just not something to waste leave on when you're a teenaged sailor.

My best man was going to be my old friend from USS *Leahy*, George Kaplan. The two of us had stayed in touch over the years, and he was due to arrive in Kenogami from his home in New Jersey any day. Another old friend, a man named Clete from Pittsburgh who had been on the *Yarnell* with me, was also coming to the wedding. We made arrangements for the two of them, along with Mom and Ida, to stay in the hotel where the reception was planned.

When the guys showed up, a few days before the wedding, Yvonne volunteered to show them the sights. She and George were soon good friends. That freed up Danielle and I to get the work done that needed doing.

Finally, several days before the wedding, Mom and Ida arrived in Quebec City. Danielle and I went to meet them, and Mom and Danielle hit it off immediately. I had not known it, but Mom actually spoke some French. It was very rusty, not having been used since she was a teacher about thirty years earlier, but she could make herself understood, and she was trying to communicate with it. That was very important to both Danielle and all the other the French Canadians.

More importantly to me, Mom was her old, confident, self. I was tremendously proud of her. She was the center of attention wherever she went for the next few days. She and Ida made friends everywhere and were obviously having the time of their lives. In fact, I swear that, a couple of times I caught them feeling no pain as they went from home to home and party to party. It seemed that all of Kenogami was partying in celebration of the wedding. Maybe that's because Danielle had so many relatives in the area, but whatever the reason, it was fun for all of us.

Finally, the night before the wedding came. Danielle was closeted with her friends and family. As appropriate to the occasion, I had reserved a room at the same hotel where my friends and Mom were staying. Early in the evening, George, Clete, and I had gone out for dinner and a few drinks. But we didn't even stay out late. Somehow the thought of a bachelor party or anything like that just wasn't there. We just had a few drinks and went back to the hotel to get a good night's sleep before the big day.

When I got to the hotel, I looked for Mom and Ida and found them sitting in the hotel lounge having a nightcap. I joined them and Ida instantly asked me, "Well, Jeff, are you ready for your big day?

I answered with a big smile and, "Sure. I've been looking forward to this for a long time now."

Mom responded with, "Is there anything that you are afraid of? Or worried about?"

I had to think about that for a minute before I answered, "I have some bad nightmares sometimes. My only worry is that I might have one right away and scare Danielle. I haven't told her about them."

Ida popped in with, "For God's sake, Jeff, tell her. You don't want to surprise her with that."

I just grimaced at that. It was too late now. I wasn't going to cloud the wedding day with this, even if I had to stay awake all of the first night.

Mom had listened to us talk about nightmares with a thoughtful look on her face. She asked me, "What are the dreams about?"

I replied, "I'm always in a hole with something bad hunting for me above the hole. It has a lot of different details, but that is always the main idea."

Mom looked at Ida and said, "Those God-damned bunkers! They probably saved our lives, but they left some horrible memories for all of us." Then she looked at me and softened, "It was a rough time, Jeff. Maybe it will go away now that you're settling down and starting a normal life."

I said, "I hope so, Mom, for all of us. Did you know that Tim has nightmares, too? His are a little different, but still pretty rough for him."

Mom's eyes watered as she held back the tears. She said, softly, "No. I didn't know that."

Ida came to the rescue then with, "Okay you two, this is supposed to be a happy time. Let's forget the horror stories and enjoy our time together." She was absolutely right, so we changed the subject to talk about the people they had met in Kenogami and how wonderful they had been to us all.

Then Mom changed the subject again. She said, "I had a long talk with your friends George and Clete this morning. They really got me thinking. Until I talked to them, I hadn't realized what you'd really done in the Navy. They told me all about the things they know about you, and let me tell you, those guys didn't have a bad word about anything. You've really come a long way, Jeff."

I started to say something but she held up her hand to stop me.

Then she continued, "That really got me thinking. If you can do what you've done, why am I not doing more? I have the education and the ability, but I'm just cooking food for people when I should be really doing something with my life. When I get back, I'm going to get my American citizenship, and when I get it, I'm going to use my education and find a job that I can be proud of. I've been down too long. I'm fifty-three years old, and I've made up my mind that I'm finally going to do what I should have been doing for years. I was given an education, and I haven't used it for almost thirty years. But that's going to change, starting now. To hell with the people that say it can't be done!"

I had been quiet through all of this. Now I said, "Mom, if you can come through what you've come through and still be sitting here talking like you're talking, you can do anything. Go for it!"

We talked a bit about jobs that she might aspire to in St. Regis, and that led to a general conversation about our hometown and people we all knew that lived there. I learned that Ida had recently separated from her husband, who had been one of Dad's drinking buddies. She was now on her own. Mom, on the other hand, still lived in the same home with Dad, but both had their own rooms, and there was no longer much interaction.

Mom explained, "Since about the Christmas before last, when you were home, Dad's been pretty quiet. He still blows up sometimes, but nothing like before. But he's drunk all of the time. I hardly ever see him, and when I do, he doesn't have a lot to say."

Since Kathy was babysitting the kids while Mom was on her trip, I asked Mom how all of them were doing.

She said, "Well, I'm a bit worried about Kathy. She is spending a lot of time taking care of the kids. Between that and working, she always seems tired to me. But she does seem to be handling everything all right." She looked a little worried then, and went on, "She seems to think that she has to keep the little ones close to her for fear that they will be attacked by Dad or something like that."

I didn't want to open the subject of the bad stuff again, but now I didn't feel that I had any choice. I said, "Mom, Tim and I had a long talk a few weeks ago. He said that he was worried about the kids." I went on to tell her about the conversation that Tim and I had on the flying bridge that night. I finished it with, "I've learned to have a lot of respect for Tim. He's smart, and he seems to have a sense of people that's remarkable. When he says that maybe we have already been ruined by Dad, I have to wonder if he's right. He seems to think that our futures are already written, and they don't look good because of what we've been through. I don't know if he's right on this, but the thought has had me scared ever since we had that talk."

Mom was obviously taken aback by this. "I didn't know that Tim thought this way. But then I didn't know that the two of you have nightmares either. I hope I'm not missing something big, but..." her voice trailed off, and the silence enveloped us for a moment.

She was obviously in deep thought as she sipped on her drink and leaned back in her chair. Then she went on, "Tim's wrong, Jeff. If I thought that he was right, I'd probably go shoot myself." Another pause, then, "In my opinion, life is what you make of it. Everybody's dealt a hand to start out with. Some hands are better than others, but regardless, we all have to live with the hand we're dealt. It's up to each of us to take the cards we're handed and turn them into winners. Some people do this, and some people don't. But we can't start blaming our lives on the way the cards were dealt. In my experience, if people start out planning for failure, they end up failing. There don't seem to be any exceptions."

Ida chimed in about this time with, "Jeff, you listen to your mother. She knows what she's talking about. This talk about being ruined for life is crazy talk. Look at you, for God's sake. You are already more of a success than most of the people I know and you are just getting started. If your dad were going to ruin anyone's chances, it would have been yours. You and your mother were the two that always got beat the worst!"

I guess there really were no secrets in our little hometown.

I looked at Ida and laughed, "Ida, all of my life, you've been telling me, 'Listen to your mother, Jeff,' and that's the truth!" We all got a laugh out of that, because it really was true and we all knew it.

Then the conversation turned serious again. Mom said, "Jeff, These ideas of Tim's are really bothering me. I'll have a long talk with him when I see him next time. If he keeps thinking that he has no chance, he is going to have a rough time in life."

I replied, "Certainly, Mom, I'll try. But I have to admit that I'm still scared as hell that he could somehow be at least partly right. I'm not so scared for me, because I don't really want a lot out of life, and tomorrow, I'll be almost where I want to be. The only thing missing is a little house with a white picket fence— and that's going to come. I'm far more scared for the others than I am for myself."

"He isn't right, Jeff. He just isn't right. I don't know how to say it any stronger. He just isn't right. Life is a journey that starts somewhere and ends somewhere. But the starting point doesn't dictate where it ends. The ending depends on what you put into it along the way."

Then, with the wisdom of mothers everywhere, her next words were, "Let's give it up for the night. We have a big day tomorrow."

We got up and headed for the elevators.

As she was getting off the elevator, Mom put her hand over the door's edge, holding the door open. As Ida walked down the hall, Mom turned to me and said, "Jeff, I remember telling you to escape and give the kids an example to follow. Do you remember?"

I said, "Yeah, I do. We were all in a bunker when you said that. I never forgot it."

She went on, "Well, you have done that job better than anyone could ever expect, Jeff. You've been an example to all of us." She smiled at me and then said, "But I might have been wrong about one thing. Maybe none of us can ever really escape. Maybe it's too deep in here." She tapped her finger on her temple as she went on, "But maybe it doesn't matter. After all, it's the hand that we were dealt."

She was still holding the elevator door. She reached over and pulled me into a bear hug with her free hand. Then she pulled back and looked me in the eyes, saying something that, while simple, was so profound that it guided me through all of the years that followed.

"Jeff, life always goes on. With you or without you, life does go on!"

It did.

EPILOGUE

Danielle and I were married on schedule the next day. We had two beautiful daughters together before the long separations and strain of a military career caused us to drift apart. A few years later, I remarried and, with my new wife, raised a son and another daughter. All four of the children are doing well, and they have given me, at last count, six wonderful grandchildren.

I retired from the Navy as a commissioned warrant officer. After retiring, I worked in engineering firms, managing the design and installation of military electronic systems. Eventually I started my own engineering firm.

Shortly after my sixtieth birthday, I sold my part of the company and retired to St. Regis, where I served for four years as the chairman of the Town Council. I'm now completely retired and still living in western Montana. I still have nightmares, but that's the hand that I was dealt.

Dad never did improve significantly. But as he became more and more incapacitated, the family learned to work around him. He died of a stroke in the spring of 1974. He was sixty-five. I cried when we buried him, remembering the man that I so admired twenty-five years earlier.

Mom got her American citizenship and ran for political office. She was first elected as a county treasurer and later as a county commissioner. She never remarried and she didn't retire until she was almost eighty years old. She died of natural causes in 2008 at the age of ninety-six.

Kathy had one daughter, then was divorced and worked her way through college. She is now a retired schoolteacher who dotes on her two grandchildren.

Tim got out of the Navy after four years and went to college to study electrical engineering. He later married and had a son. When I started my first company, he joined me and we worked together for several years. He was semi-crippled in an automobile accident and subsequently battled demon rum for a few years before dying in 1990 at the age of forty-four.

Lyle was drafted into the Army and served in Vietnam. Later he married and had two children, a girl and a boy, before divorcing and living alone. He never got over his war experiences and he fought his demons to the end. He died in 2005 at the age of fifty-seven.

Eleanor graduated from college with a degree in Law Enforcement, married, and had three children. She and her husband have had successful careers in the state of Alaska. They now have three grandchildren.

Jim is married and has five children and six grandchildren. He went to college with Tim for a couple of years and is now a computer specialist working in western Montana.

Dan, the youngest of us, is the successful owner of a home-construction business in western Montana. He is married, with three children and two grandchildren.

At the time of this writing, Mom and Dad have thirty-seven living descendents, all doing well and making the most out of the hands that they were dealt. Life does go on.

ABOUT THE AUTHOR

Jeff Noonan is a Montana native who retired in 2001 as the president of a nationwide corporation. He is married with four children and six grandchildren.

As a young man, Jeff worked as a laborer for farms, ranches, lumber mills, and a railroad. He then served in both the Army and the Navy, retiring from the Navy as a commissioned warrant officer. While in the Navy, he commissioned five ships at Bath Iron Works, worked in guided missile research at White Sands Missile Range, and served two and a half years in Viet Nam operations. When he retired, he was a combat systems officer in Philadelphia Naval Shipyard.

After leaving the military, Jeff worked his way up from an entry-level technical position to become the executive-vice president of a 900-person corporation with offices worldwide. During this era, he moved two companies into the impoverished city of Camden, New Jersey, in order to provide jobs where none existed. Then he took over a troubled seven-person North Carolina company and turned it into a solvent corporation with over 250 employees. In recognition of these efforts, a U.S. Congressional Committee officially awarded him their 1999 North Carolina Businessman of the Year plaque during a Washington, DC, ceremony.

Jeff sold his business interests in 2001 and retired to his hometown where he was soon elected president of the St. Regis Community Council, a position he held for four years. He was also the president of the Mineral County Chamber of Commerce for two years. He still lives in western Montana.

26532621R00176

Made in the USA
Lexington, KY
05 October 2013